MAMORIBITO

The One Who Protects

MAMORIBITO

The One Who Protects

Kevin A. Reynolds

The characters and events portrayed in this book are fictitious. Any similarity to real persons, living or dead, is coincidental and not intended by the author.

No part of this book may be reproduced, or stored in a retrieval system, or transmitted in any form or by any means, electronic, mechanical, photocopying, recording, or otherwise, without express written permission of the publisher.

Copyright © 2020 Kevin A. Reynolds
All Rights Reserved
ISBN: 979-8-636-40558-0

For Bob & Jonathan

See you on the ice

I am dead.

Any moment now the sluice gates will open and this cold, unforgiving concrete tomb will fill with a million gallons of water cascading down from the lake three hundred feet above.

I have failed. Failed myself, failed my brother, failed my wife and daughter, failed everyone who believed in me.

If only the Kunoichi were here, but she doesn't even know where I am.

What was I thinking? All my training, my experience, every ounce of my being was screaming at me to stop, to find another way — but I walked into it, willingly, blindly, idiotically.

I will die here, in this uncaring, unsympathetic place, alone with my tears and the useless thoughts of what could have happened if I had chosen a different path.

How many more will die because of me?
I am not who they think I am.
I am not the Mamoribito.

One

ENGLAND

I was driving quickly.

It was a beautiful late September morning, and the twisty little 'B' road with its short straights and low hedgerows was the stuff armchair racing drivers dream of. Not that I thought of myself as an armchair racer – I'd once spent a long, hot summer racing a pretty quick Mini Cooper on the club circuits in southern England – but that was twenty years ago, and since then I'd moved to Japan, started a family, become sensible and slowed down forever.

Perhaps not forever, I reminded myself as I took a satisfying line through a long left-hander. Still there, as if in a glass case with 'Only to be used in case of emergency' stamped on it. Except that today there was no emergency. Today I was driving quickly because I was back in England for a week and wanted to, because that unfulfilled racer inside me wanted to.

Ahead, the Sun peered over the Sussex South Downs and cast its morning light directly through the front windscreen of the Mini Cooper S I'd hired the day before. Nice car it was too, although the current model wasn't as much fun as the one I used to race. This had more power and was far more comfortable for longer journeys, but it didn't set my pulse racing. The suspension was a shade too soft and the car a touch too heavy. Or maybe Peter Walker-san was just getting too old and sensible for his own good. Probably not quite sensible yet, considering the supposedly original Raybans I'd picked up in Soho that were now proving themselves barely dark enough to stop me screwing up my pale blue eyes. Cheaper than they should have been, but they looked like the real thing.

"Poser," I told myself as I raced past an overloaded tractor.

Still there.

A long straight gave me another opportunity to try the radio, but what with the customary energetic DJs and their morning melodies there still wasn't much worth listening to. It had been that way the whole trip down. I called myself all sorts of helpful names for not having the sense to bring the boxset of Led Zeppelin CDs I'd bought at Virgin records in Oxford Street. Instead I'd packed them in my suitcase and sent the whole lot off to the All Nippon Airlines customer service center at Heathrow. With any luck my luggage would be waiting for me the following afternoon ready for check-in. Great service, provided you hadn't packed something you shouldn't have.

The road began to snake into a series of S-bends. With the view uncluttered by hedgerows and perfect for reliving past memories, I drove the racing line, all the while heel-toe-downshifting and keeping the revs high, which on this Mini required switching off the stability control – much more my kind of thing. I hadn't done this for a long time, just driving for the sheer fun of it. Of course, it wasn't quite the same as blasting around Brands Hatch, but where I lived near Nagano City there were no roads like this. Besides, Yuko would have a fit if she saw me driving this way. I had once secretly gone down to Tsukuba circuit near Tokyo and borrowed a friend's Honda S2000 for a 'fun-fast blast' of twenty laps, as she'd put it. Yuko had found the photos on my phone. I had told her that I was visiting friends, but with the evidence piled against me I didn't have a lot to say in my defence. Yuko had made me promise to never do that again. I hadn't wanted to promise anything, as I knew what I was doing, but I had been deceitful and that was the thing that had made her so upset. Plus, she was scared that I would hurt myself. So, I had said 'Yes darling,' and on my next secret visit to Tsukuba circuit I had left the damn phone switched off. And that, I told myself, was the only time I had ever been unfaithful.

We roared under a railway bridge and past the aging forecourt of the even more aging Dawson & Loughbridge Cars, which meant I was at last entering Wynbeck. The dashboard clock read eight-fifteen. Bang on time – Mike might even be up.

I slowed down to a responsible speed and drove through the center of the small, sleepy town, taking a right after the Blue Lamb. I hadn't had a drink there in years and was looking forward to making up for lost time later. The pub was less than fifty yards from Mike's place. I pictured him there on a Friday evening, Guinness in hand, entertaining the other regulars with tales of divorce cases and housing contracts – such was the heady life of an English country solicitor.

I drove up to the house. Mike's Jag wasn't to be seen, which was a bit unusual but probably meant it was in the garage undergoing some form of invasive surgery. I parked and gave the horn a quick toot, only to be met by silence. I wasn't surprised. It wouldn't have been the first time Mike had overslept the morning after the night before. He would have been late for his own wedding if I hadn't kicked the dickhead out of bed and thrown him into an ice-cold shower. As it was, Mike had said his vows with a raging hangover and had to promise Julie never to be even mildly inebriated again as long as they both shall live. Mike had kept that promise for ten years. But that was a lifetime ago, and today we were playing eighteen holes before drinking way too much until the early hours of the night.

At least that was the plan.

I grabbed my reproduction leather fighter pilot jacket and got out of the car. I considered ringing the doorbell but instead went over to the birdbath and retrieved the spare front door key from under a loose stone at the base, where it had likely remained undisturbed since my previous visit. I put the key onto my keyring as I was pretty sure I would need it when we staggered back later. I was about to unlock the front door and creep upstairs to shake Mike awake when my mobile phone buzzed in my jacket pocket. It was Mike.

"Where are you?" he said.

"Outside your front door." I searched the upstairs windows – there was no sign of anyone. "Where are you?"

"In Welton Hall."

That was a surprise. "Welton Hall? What are you doing there?"

"Waiting for you."

"Well, I'm here waiting for you," I said, stating the obvious.

"Well, I've been trying to call you for the last hour, but I kept getting this funny Japanese voice that I assume was telling me to leave a message. So I did. Four to be precise. Fat lot of good that was."

"I had it on vibration mode."

"Sitting on it, were you?"

"Actually, it was in my jacket pocket." I looked through the garage window. The Jag wasn't there, which meant Mike may well have been where he said he was. "I thought we were supposed to be playing golf, not visiting the landed gentry."

"Golf's cancelled."

Another surprise. "What?" I wasn't much of an actor, but I was impressed by the incredulity in my voice. Come to think of it, I wasn't acting.

"It's going to rain," Mike said.

"Doesn't look much like rain to me." I scanned the grey clouds in the far distance. "At least not yet. Sun's shining. It's going to be a lovely day."

It had snowed the last time we had played, but that hadn't

stopped us. It was the first time I had ever beaten Mike, and he must have out for revenge. Except, he didn't seem particularly concerned about that, at least not today

"Just get over here as fast as you can," he said. "There's something I want to show you."

"And what would that be?"

"I'll show you when you get here, which I would like you to do as soon as inhumanly possible. You remember the way, don't you?"

"I think so." This time the irony in my voice deserved an Oscar. I knew the way to Welton Hall, all right. When Mike and I were boys we had liberated so many apples we'd carved a trench under the orchard fence. Lord Welton was a bit of a recluse and if he had ever seen the two of us, he had never done anything about it. I hadn't been there for twenty-five years. Or was that thirty?

Shit, Walker, you really are getting old.

"Is Welton one of your clients?" I asked, suddenly making the connection.

"Was. But the old bugger buggered off last month and I'm handling the estate, which is why I want you to come and have a look at something."

"I see. Sounds interesting. And what about golf?"

"We'll try after lunch. If it's not raining."

"This had better be good Mike," I replied, although I knew it had to be more than 'good' for Mike to contemplate postponing our annual game, which considering I hadn't been in England for five years no longer qualified as annual.

"You'll love it, I promise you," he said. "Now are you coming or what?"

"Coming. But I'm busting for a widdle. Can I use your loo first?"

"The key's under the bird bath."

"Already found it," I said, letting myself in.

"The thermos is under the sink. Be a good chap and make the coffee. And there's bacon in the fridge and Branston in the cupboard so make a bunch of sarnies too.

And hurry up, I didn't have time for breakfast and I'm bloody starving."

"Yes sir. Mr. Branding, sir. I'll see you in thirty minutes."

"And Pete."

"Yep?"

"Remember, more than three shakes is masturbation."

"You should know, wanker."

#

After proving Mike wrong, I set the ancient percolator going, threw as many bacon rashers as I could into the microwave, then searched around until I found a Harrods bag under the stairs. The bacon was ready before the coffee and I made six rounds of sandwiches, each overflowing with Branston Pickle. I wrapped them in clingfilm and put them into the bag.

The coffee was going to be a couple more minutes, so I went into the study to say hello to Julie. Her portrait was where it always was, hanging quietly in the corner, overlooking the garden she had loved.

"Hey Jules." I said, touching the frame and looking into her sparkling eyes. The portrait painter, an old friend, had captured her spirit and vivacity in a way no photograph of her ever had. We all preferred to remember her that way; beautiful and with a smile that could charm the coolest heart. Julie had fallen for Mike the second she saw him, according to Mike. The two of them had made for an interesting sight. Mike was six foot-three and built like a brick-shit house. Jules was a four-foot eight statue of Venus. If Mike hadn't been my half-brother I would have been after her like a Russell Terrier on heat. But now subject and artist we both gone. Julie from cancer and Simon Rogers from a helicopter crash patrolling southern Afghanistan.

Two good friends lost far too young.

I turned around. There was a selection of cups and plaques in Mike's trophy cupboard. Most were from The

Royal Arundel Golf Club and had "Michael Branding, 1st Place" engraved on them. How such a giant had the finesse to be so good at the game was something I could never figure out. A silver cup on the top shelf was smaller than the others but had pride of place. I picked it up and read the inscription I knew so well. *"Peter Walker, 1st in Class. Brands Hatch Motor Racing Circuit. June 2nd, 2009."* I had given the cup to Mike as a keepsake before I went backpacking in Asia, two months after we had lost Julie.

Behind the cup was a photograph of Mike and Julie sitting on the bonnet of Octavius, our racing Mini Cooper, the two of them wet with cheap Champagne but happy as anything. All I could see of myself were teeth smiling broadly in the shadows as I sat at the wheel. It had been a good day. Our first and last victory, won against the odds against teams with better drivers and actual budgets. Not bad for three amateurs with a box of spanners and a half-decent engine. If I hadn't over-revved it the following weekend at Goodwood, I might have had another cup instead of a broken camshaft and a finished racing career – if it could ever have been called that.

"The best of times," I said quietly.

From the kitchen came the asthmatic cough of the percolator gasping its last. "See you later, Jules," I said. "I'm off to find out what that bonehead husband of yours is up to."

Five minutes later I was back in the Mini and heading off to Welton Hall.

Two

I drove in through the rusting iron gates and up the long drive towards the familiar house. From a distance it hadn't changed, looking as it had the last time I had been there, although I knew it must have been different from the building of my youth. Things had a habit of changing, despite how solid and recognizable they appeared on the outside. People too.

A small fleet of trucks were parked in a line, with Mike's Jag nearest the front door, meaning he had arrived first. I stopped the Mini behind the last truck and got out. Men in blue overalls were carrying various cloth-wrapped packages and loading them gently into the trucks. One of the packages was picture-shaped, another a chair. The sides of each vehicle all said the same thing; 'Washburn Fine Antiques and Auctioneers.' This must have been what Mike meant by handling Welton's estate.

The house was big enough, but now that I was standing there it looked smaller than I remembered, as childhood haunts often did when you revisited them. '1846' was carved in stone above the doorway, which sounded about right. From the drive Welton Hall had been impressive, the house of generations of wealth, but from eight yards away I could see the signs of neglect. I counted four cracks snaking their way up the off-white walls and supposed there were more at the rear of the house. Paint was peeling off the window frames and each of the five front steps was crumbling at the leading edge. To my right, several tiles were missing from the roof of a long, low building which I took to be a stable converted into a garage. Tall rose bushes that needed pruning populated two of the flowerbeds that ran along the front of the house. The others were full of weeds. The expansive front lawn was on the way to becoming a meadow and could have done with some expert care and attention. Even inexpert care would have helped. This wasn't how I remembered the place.

I asked a workman where Mike was.

"I think Mr. Branding's upstairs, sir," was the well-educated reply. "Are you Mr. Walker, by any chance?"

"Yes."

"He said he was expecting you. Just go straight up."

"Thanks," I replied, adding, "Are you chaps selling off the whole house?"

"Not yet. Everything is going into storage for auction later, once it's all settled. And it's good stuff too. Well, some of it is. Some of it is old junk, frankly, but you do get a lot of that in our line of work. The trick is in knowing how to sort it all out, which is of course where we come in. I'm not sure about the house, though."

"Someone will buy it."

"I expect they'll sell it to an ignorant philistine who'll turn it into a housing estate, as if we don't already have enough of those."

"Yes," I said, thinking the place would fetch a couple of million, despite its rundown state. "Well, I'll go upstairs and look. Thank you."

Before I could put a foot on the first step a voice boomed from above, "Pete! Up here!" Mike was waving from what looked like an attic window.

"Hello mush! Where's here?"

"West attic. Up the stairs, turn left, along the corridor, past a couple of bedrooms and a bathroom, then up another set of stairs. Watch out, the second stairs are a bit old and creaky."

"Like you."

Mike ignored the comment. "I'll wait here for you."

"OK, fat boy," I said, knowing Mike hated being called that.

"Don't call me that," Mike said as his head disappeared inside.

"OK!" I waited a second before adding quietly, "Fat boy."

"I heard that!"

I couldn't help smiling. "Bollocks you did." I said, this time loud enough to be heard. I gave a cursory wave to the antiques man and went inside.

#

Welton Hall smelled of damp wood and old carpet.

I stood in the main entrance hall while my eyes adjusted to the relative darkness, an old habit that I had no intention of breaking. When I could fully see I nudged a half-open door and sneaked a look into a small room, probably a study. Empty. I checked two more rooms, also empty. Back in the main hall a naked light bulb hung above my head where there should have been a chandelier. The whole place was being stripped to the bone.

What a waste.

I made my way up the stairs to the first floor and from there along the corridor, where I found the second flight of stairs.

"Hello laddie!" Mike said, bear-hugging the breath out of me the moment I stepped into the attic.

"Hello Mike," I managed to reply. At fifteen stone going on twenty, Mike was as big and strong as an ox. He was the kind of man-mountain pub rugby teams loved. He was so big he could have taken on a whole scrum, could have *been* a whole scrum. How the hell he managed to fit into his Jaguar, or any other car for that matter, was one of life's little mysteries, as was how we could be related and not look like each at all. That came from having the same father but different mothers, but even then we were the most unbrotherly looking half-brothers you could imagine.

"It's good to see you, Pete, it really is."

"And you Mike. Can I breathe now, please?"

Mike let go. "Sorry." He stepped back. "Good to see you Pete."

"You just said that."

Mike smiled. "Well it is. So, you found it all right then?"

"No problem. I remembered the way perfectly, despite the senility."

"Good trip down? Break any records?"

"No.'

'Unlikely.'

I smiled. "I drove very carefully, Michael." The only time I ever drove 'very carefully' was when my wife and daughter were with me.

Mike knew better. "Like hell you did," he said, then immediately got down to more serious matters. "Sandwiches?"

I held up the Harrods bag. "Bacon and Branston, as ordered." I opened the bag and handed over Mike's unfair share.

"Perfect."

Mike took a huge bite that reduced his first sandwich to the size of a potato crisp. I stared in amazement as he started on his second.

"And you wonder why I call you fat boy."

Mike grinned happily – his mouth too full to reply.

I took a far more reasonable bite, then opened the thermos flask, handed over a cup and poured. "Here you go. So, what are we doing here? Or have you finally laid your hands on Welton's family jewels?"

Mike nodded, then shook his head and said something camouflaged by an excess of sliced wholemeal.

"Was that 'not yet'?" I asked. Mike nodded, but an intelligible reply would require more chewing. "OK," I said.

"I'll take that as yes, which sounds sort of interesting."

Mike grunted and continued chomping.

"We'll get to that later," he said, the sandwich finally gone. "But first, I want to know, how was the, er, 'meeting'?"

Mike did his best to empathise the word meeting by doing the quotation mark gesture people do with their fingers, but it looked out of place coming from him.

"The 'meeting' was fine," I replied, copying the gesture.

"Was it at HQ, at Vauxhall?" He was referring to the headquarters of the SIS, the UK's Secret Intelligence Service, at Vauxhall Cross. From the way he asked I could see he thought of it as a something from a Bond movie. From my viewpoint it had been interesting but rather mundane, the one worthwhile thing having been a free round trip to London.

"I can't tell you," I said, although in reality I could tell him without breaking the Official Secrets Act. Bending it a touch, but nothing that would get me into any trouble.

"Oh, do tell, Pete."

"Later." I was going to tell him pretty much everything anyway, such as it was. But you never knew who would be listening, so here wasn't the place, not with the Washburn Antiques crew walking around.

"Ok," he said, taking a more reasonable bite from sandwich number three. "I'll hold you to that. And I want to know all, the whole thing."

"Yes sir," I said. "But it's not half as interesting as you think it is." It was time to get back to why we were there. "So, come on then. What's this thing you've got that's so good it's worth cancelling golf?"

"Told you, it's going to rain. Anyway, the auctioneers are here," Mike said, as if that explained everything.

"I can see that."

"I mean I have to be here because they're here."

"But you've found something. Right?"

"First things first. Come and have a look at this."

The attic was spacious and had four windows, two each

that overlooked the front and back gardens. It was big enough to be converted into a bunch of servant bedrooms. Maybe that had been part of the plan sometime, but those plans were undoubtedly shelved long ago. I followed Mike to the garden window.

"Remember Welton's vegetable patch?" he said, pointing to the orchard.

"How could I forget."

"Twenty-five years ago, you and I were stealing apples and running like hell every time we thought Sam the one-eyed gardener spotted us. Which, of course he never did, being mono-visionistic. And now I'm the solicitor handling the estate and you're here looking out the window with me. Funny how things work out, don't you think?"

"It's one of those circle of life things," I said, not particularly in the mood to get philosophical. "Was Welton your dad's client, our dad's client, before yours, I mean?"

"For thirty years." Mike said. "I took over last year and now I'm tidying things up. Welton had no heirs so we're basically getting ready to sell everything off. But the National Trust are interested, it's in his will so it could go to them for free, and then they'll to want open it up for the public, so we're putting the best of the furniture into storage, just in case. Which will be a tad ironic, because as you well know the old sod was a recluse and never had any visitors except for his nurse, and myself, of course, every Sunday morning for the past six months. The things I do for my clients. I wasn't planning to be here this morning because not only were we supposed to be playing golf, but I'm also fed up with the place. Not to mention that the people from Washburn antiques can look after themselves anyway."

"But we are here, Mike. And you did say you had to be here because the auctioneers are here."

"I did?"

I nodded.

"Well, in that case, the main reason I'm here, we're here, is because something rather interesting came up last night."

"And what was that?" I said, glad that we had finally gotten there.

Mike gave one of his naughty schoolboy grins. "Well, I was going through some of Welton's papers when I found this." He took a sheet of paper from an inside jacket pocket and passed it across. It was a plan of a house and grounds, drawn by a shaky hand. The detail was sparse – the driveway, the house itself, and shaded areas that I took to be trees.

"Welton Hall?"

Mike nodded. "Look at the back."

I flipped the sheet over and read out loud the single line of quivering, barely legible handwriting. *'To he who seeks, he shall find.'*

"Well. What do you think?" Mike asked.

"Sounds like a tattoo on a monk's arse."

"That's what I thought," Mike pointed upwards. "Hold it up to the light."

I held the paper up and saw a feint mark, revealed by sixty watts of Osram power. "Is that supposed to be an X?"

"X marks the spot, and I'm pretty certain the spot is here, in this loft. And the seeker's reward is, well, that's what we're here to find out."

I smiled and shook my head. "Come on Mike, you're making this up. And it's not even April first."

"No, I am not. I found it at half one this morning amongst a bunch of old receipts Welton had. At first I thought it was nothing, you know, just something that fell into the file, but then I thought, mmm, maybe. So I did the old 'I-Spy' thing and held it against my desk lamp, et voila, on est arrive a la magnifique conclusion da la jour. So I thought I'd cancel the golf, seeing it was going to rain, and ask if you wanted to come along and give me a hand."

I stared at the paper in my hand, not at all convinced. "Why do I get the feeling you're having me on?"

"Would I do that to you?"

"Yes."

"What if it's the family fortune? It has to be somewhere.

It's certainly not in his bloody bank account. Accounts."

"Unless there isn't one," I replied. "So you're saying this is map of hidden treasure?" Mike was the last person to be taken in by something this daft. "It could have been drawn by anybody. Plus, there's no such thing as hidden treasure outside Disney, and even that's fake, same as this."

"I think not, Holmes. It was in his private files, for Christ's sake. Oh, come on. Pete, it'll be fun. I'm dying to find out what Welton's got stashed away. I've been here since half-six this morning, and apart from mouse shit I haven't find a bloody thing."

I studied the paper again, more to give myself thinking time than to look for anything. Nobody leaves treasure maps, and if they did, I would never find one. To be accurate, though, Mike was the one who had found it, but it wasn't like him to be so gullible. There was something in Mike's eyes, though, that little boy look he had kept despite all the tough times he had lived through. It wasn't for me to spoil things. And who could say, maybe he was right.

Sod it, why not?

"In that case, my dear Watson," I said, "you need to look harder."

#

We searched for half-an-hour, prodding at loose floorboards and crumbling plaster, all the time giggling at stupid schoolboy jokes. After knocking on every brick and floorboard I climbed on Mike's broad shoulders and banged on the rafters above our heads. We found nothing, not even mouse shit.

"There's nought here, laddie," I said in a bad northern accent. "I think old Welton was having us on."

Mike's disappointment was palpable. He scratched his chin. "Are we looking in the wrong place, Pete? What do you think?"

I shrugged. "I think we're wasting our time. A waste of golf time, that is."

A shout came from outside. "Mr. Branding!"

Mike stuck his head through the open window and shouted back. "Up here!"

"We need you to move the cars, sir, if that's OK."

"Coming." Mike pulled his head back in. "Give me your keys. I won't be long. And here, you have the Long John Silver map thing and keep looking. I'll be back in a jiffy."

"OK."

I handed over the car keys and watched as Mike edged his way down the narrow staircase. When he was gone, I searched again in all the places we had already tried, just to be sure, but all I found were our own fingerprints in the dust. I held the map up to the light again. Maybe there was something we had missed, or maybe there was nothing and we really were wasting our time. I began to feel I was being wound up. Somewhere up above Lord Welton was having a good old chuckle. On the other hand, nowhere did it concretely say we had to look in the attic. That X could be on any floor in the building – and you could say the X was outside the line of the wall. Well, not fully outside, but the hand that drew the map was frail and parts of the X were technically in the garden.

Now I was starting to get interested. This gold-rush-fever thing was catching. I poked my head out of the back window and spotted a pair of cellar doors directly below. I smiled; it was so obvious I had to ask myself why we hadn't thought of it before. Too stupid for this job, apparently. I went to the other window and tried to signal Mike. He had moved the cars but was engaged in what looked a serious conversation with two of the auctioneers – he could be a while.

Deciding not to wait, I went down the old staircase and quickly found a way out through the kitchen and into the garden.

#

The doors were thick and heavy, but the old hinges were rust-free and offered minimal resistance. I went down the short flight of concrete steps into the darkness and searched for a light switch, which I found on a thick wooden pillar. The fluorescent tube flashed into life and tried its best to illuminate the cellar, which was large, murky and empty. I went around tapping on the walls. Everything was solid and I assumed nothing was hidden behind the brickwork – the masonry was too thick for that. Or if there was something, I'd never find it like this. What I needed was a metal detector.

I stood there for a while. Out of options, it was time to leave. I switched off the light but immediately switched it back on again. In the corner by the steps a drainpipe ran from ceiling to floor. It hadn't registered when I had been tapping the walls, but a drainpipe *inside* the cellar? Since when did it start to rain inside the house – or underneath it?

I moved over for a closer look. The top and bottom of the piping were flush with the ceiling and floor, and there was plastic taping where there should have been all-weather sealant. Why would you need sealant where it didn't rain? I tugged at the drainpipe, not too hard in case I was wrong and got covered in rotting leaves, but after several firm-enough heaves it came away to reveal bricks and concrete, but no drainage system.

I was right, the drainpipe was false – which should have been obvious from the outset if you weren't as thick-headed as me. It was also too heavy for an empty plastic tube. The piping was narrow, but wide enough for me to squeeze a hand down. I felt something soft, took hold and pulled. Out came a cloth wrapped around a long, slender object. I knew what it was – I could feel its shape under the fibers. I climbed the steps, laid the bundle on the soft lawn, and unwrapped the cloth.

"Bloody hell," I gasped.

It was a Japanese *Tachi*, the sword of a mounted Samurai. I rolled down my shirtsleeves, carefully picked up the sword by the hilt and held it up to the light of the Sun, resting the blade on the cotton of my left sleeve.

I had an idea what to look for. I studied the sword, trying

to do it the right way. It was perfect – not a scratch, no rust, not the faintest nick on the blade, which meant either the polisher was a genius or the sword had never been used in anger. The hilt was encrusted with jewels and gold foil, making this the weapon of a rich and powerful man. Either that or it was made recently by one of the few remaining Japanese swordsmiths. I hoped it wasn't the latter. I had two swords at home in Japan, both gifts from my father-in-law and both made within the last twenty years, but they were nothing like this. Compared to my motley collection this was a Rembrandt in a paint-by-numbers exhibition.

I sensed someone behind me. It was Michael. "Bloody hell," he whispered.

"Exactly."

"Where did you find that?"

"In the cellar. We were looking in the wrong place."

"Oh, yes, of course. Why didn't I think of that? Is it Japanese?"

"Yes."

"How can you tell? It might be Chinese."

"It's Japanese, Mike. Trust me."

"Where's the sheath?" Mike asked.

"It's a scabbard, not a sheath. You don't need a condom for one of these things."

"Where's the scabbard?"

"No idea. Got a tissue?" I wanted to touch the blade without greasing it with sweat from my fingers.

"No. Why?"

"Never mind."

"Are those real?" Mike said, pointing at the jewels visible beneath the grip of my right hand.

"I've no idea, Mike. I wouldn't know an emerald from a topaz. But if they are, and this is real gold inlay, then –"

"Then it could be worth something."

I glanced to my right. "Typical lawyer. Yes, Watson, this could well be something rather special."

I stood up and held the sword in front of me with my

right leg forward, in the *Sega no Kamae* posture. "This kind of sword is called a *Tachi*," I said, entering lecture mode. "Which means a mounted Samurai used it. You can tell that from the curved blade, which makes it easier to use from horseback. If it were straight it would be a *Katana*, which was a foot soldier's weapon. Foot soldier Samurai, that is. I'd say it's a ceremonial sword made for a Daimyo."

"What's a Daimyo?"

"A kind of Lord of the county, but with a bigger army and less money. Lots of rice, though. Shit, this might even be a lost sword. We'd have to check it out."

"Now I see what Welton meant."

"Any idea where it came from, how he got it?"

Mike shrugged. "Not a clue. God, I can't believe it. For years the old bugger was pleading poverty but all the time he had this thing stick in his cellar. The crafty old sod. The partners have been complaining for months that Welton deserved a dose of euthanasia to put us all out of our misery, and all the time he had his wealth locked up in this thing. Incredible."

"Yes, but we don't know that, do we Mike," I said. "This 'thing' could be a movie prop for all we know." I hoped not, though. I really, really hoped not.

"What, hidden away in the cellar like that? No way, Pete. This is the real thing, I bet you anything you like."

"Then all your problems are solved, aren't they? You can sell it and donate everything to charity." I was still holding the sword in front of me and could sense that Mike wanted to hold it too. I wasn't going to let him though, not yet.

"We can't sell a thing like this without proof of ownership. You know that, Pete." Mike said, sounding like the solicitor he was instead of the happy treasure hunter he had become.

"You can find out," I said. "There's someone in Tokyo who knows everything there is to know about swords. And, wait a minute, we just found it, and you want to sell it already!"

"It was your idea."

That was true. Maybe I'd said it because I'd be the one wanting to buy it – all I'd need was a winning Euro lottery ticket.

"Except technically speaking," I said, "I found it, so I guess I get to make the call, don't I? About selling it, I mean."

Or keeping it.

Mike rubbed his chin, a sign of mental cogwheels grinding out an idea. Whatever it was, he didn't get a chance to say. The same voice as before came from inside the house, "Mr. Branding, sir!"

"You are popular today," I quipped.

"Coming!" Mike bellowed, before adding in low whisper, "We'd better not let anybody see that."

"Good point."

I put the sword back in its protective cloth and watched Mike as he went back into the house, wondering how he could be so blasé, as if finding a Japanese Samurai sword hidden in a drainpipe in the cellar was an everyday occurrence.

I made sure nobody was looking and unwrapped the cloth once more. This time I didn't pick up the sword – instead I gazed at it as an art critique who'd discovered a Monet. I shook my head in disbelief. Was this real? And if so, how did Welton get his hands on it? Had his Lordship had ever been to Japan? He was wealthy enough and could have travelled in his youth. He could have been stationed with the allied occupying forces after the war, too, or he could have found it in a pawn shop in the Brighton lanes, in which case we were in for a big disappointment. Could this be a missing Japanese national treasure? As far as I knew all the famous swords were accounted for somewhere. But I was hardly an expert. All I knew for certain was that in front of my, lying on a woollen cloth, was one of the most beautiful, most entrancing things I had ever seen.

So, what the fuck was it doing in a fake drainpipe in the cellar?

I had a feeling that somebody was watching, most likely

one of the porters carrying something far less intriguing past an upstairs window. I covered the sword and stared at the bundle, waiting for the sense of agitation to pass, at the same time wondering if *finders-keepers* was a legal expression.

Mike's voice boomed from inside the house – someone was doing something wrong. I looked over my shoulder. The feeling I had of being watched was gone now, but it was replaced by another type of unease. Something wasn't adding up, not making sense. I picked up the sword in its bundle and walked back down the cellar steps. The plastic drainpipe was lying in the floor where I had left it. I carefully put the sword down and examined the tubing. I wasn't sure what I was looking for – I just felt the need to look.

After a minute or two I realized that both ends of the drainpipe were smoothly cut, as if by a practised hand. The all-weather tape used to secure it to the ceiling and the floor had been neatly wound and the exposed surfaces were still sticky. I knelt and ran my fingers over the cloth covering the sword. It was soft, as if it had recently been washed. I couldn't say for certain, but was that the tang of detergent?

Heavy footsteps thundered above my head. Mike was in the kitchen, on his way to the garden.

"Down here, Mike!" I shouted.

"They've gone, at last," Mike said, bending low as he descended into the cellar. "Is this where you found it?"

"Yep." I pointed out the objects at my feet. "It was wrapped in that cloth, shoved down the middle of that tubing and then the whole thing wedged in the corner and taped up with a yard of all-weather, obviously to make it look part of the drainage system. Except that cellars don't have drainage systems, so what was the point of doing that, we should ask ourselves."

"I see," said Mike, staring at the corner.

"If you ask me, mate, whoever did this must have had access to the house, and to the cellar. Which, is fairly obvious I suppose, otherwise it wouldn't be here in the first place."

"Welton would have."

"How old was he, Mike?"

"Hundred and three."

"You're joking."

Mike shook his head.

"Watch this." I repositioned the plastic tubing in the corner. It fit snugly but needed a good shove. "Not the kind of thing a frail old man could do," I said. "He'd have needed help."

Mike tugged at the plastic. "You're right. Someone must have put it here on Welton's behalf."

I pulled the tubing out from its place and pointed an end towards Mike. "And the tape is still sticky, which means it hasn't had enough time to dry out, which to my simple brain means it was put there recently."

Mike fingered the tape, quietly contemplating the evidence.

"And that cloth smells like it's just been washed," I said. "As if whoever put it here wanted to keep the sword clean. You know what I think?"

"Never have, never will."

"Insurance fraud," I said. "Someone, with or without Welton's knowledge, faked that treasure map, stuck it in Welton's files and planted the sword here so that Lord Welton's solicitor would find it. Which means you. And me too, now."

"And exactly which of his non-existent heirs would be claiming this insurance?"

As ideas went, it wasn't one of my best. "Good point."

"Look, Pete, apart from Welton, the only person who had access to his files was me. It's his house, his sword, it must have been Welton."

"Then what for?"

"Stolen national treasure, like you said. He wanted to return it to its rightful owner."

As ideas went, it wasn't one of Mike's best. "Then why all this?" I said. "Why not just give it straight to you? You are his lawyer; you could handle the return. Something's a bit fishy here, mate. I think we should go and tell the police before we find ourselves charged with possession."

Mike folded his arms. "Yes, yes, of course you're right, Pete. If you put it like that, indeed, stolen goods. Could be tricky. We should do that, tell the police, I mean."

He didn't sound convinced. "But you don't really think so, do you?" I said.

Mike unfolded his arms and placed hands on his hips. "What I think is," he said, with a touch of the dramatic, "that we should go home, where I'll have a good look through Welton's files and you have a good Google, and when we've found out what the hell we're actually bloody dealing with, then we can go to the police. Or at least I can after you've gone back to Japan. How's that sound?"

"Sounds like a plan. Almost."

I picked up the sword, and together we headed up the steps. Mike led the way into the house, but I stopped at the kitchen door. That nagging feeling was there again – we were being watched. It was a feeling I'd had before, not only here but in the hills of Afghanistan too, where it had saved my life. I trusted it, though I could never explain it. I turned to face the trees by the road at the far edge of the gardens. Someone was there, I was sure of it, and even though I couldn't see him, I knew he was observing us.

I stared hard to let him know I was aware, then followed Mike through the house.

Three

Mike had a smart new Lenovo in his study with an Intel i7 4-Core and enough storage to conquer the universe, but his internet connection was based on British Telecom's slowest offering and was making this particular user wanting his money back. Except it wasn't my money and the whole package wasn't that slow, but it was a snail compared to the set-up I had in Japan.

At least my Guinness was cold.

It was five thirty and pouring with rain, so spending the best part of the day not playing golf and searching for information on a newly discovered sword was not a bad combination. The trouble was, I was getting nowhere, and it wasn't all BT's fault. I'd tried the Japanese sword museum in Tokyo, but there was nothing there that I could find. There were several English sites from various locations around the world, but none had anything on our sword. The way things were going, I'd have been surprised if they had.

I wasn't sure what I was looking for, other than a direct photograph or a copy of the pattern on the blade. I knew some designs, the Emperor's cherry blossom being amongst the rarest but also the most well-known, but the one on this sword was new to me. If I took it to Yamaguchi-san he would undoubtedly tell all about it in a flash and quote its history all afternoon. Yamaguchi-san was one of the leading experts in Japan, but in comparison I was just some bloke sitting on a chair – nowhere remotely near the same league. I had taken a series of photos with my phone, but my old friend was from a different generation and didn't have a computer let alone email, so I couldn't send him anything. That still left the little riddle of what the hell was going on anyway.

"Penny for your thoughts, Pete."

Mike was sitting on the floor with Welton's files scattered around and scraps of paper everywhere, while four empty cans of Guinness were neatly stacked to his left. It was obvious what his priorities were in life.

"I'm still wondering why Welton didn't just tell you where the sword was – if he meant it to be found that is," I said. "And how come you can drink so much and still stand."

"I'm sitting. Did you find anything?"

I shook my head. "Nothing much. How about you?"

"Oh, lots of stuff I'd missed before. But as far as mysterious Samurai swords go, no receipts, no records, no nothing."

"So definitely not an insurance scam, then."

"Obviously not." Mike rubbed the small of his back. "Look, Pete, I'm getting fed up sitting here. Shall we shoot off down the Blue Lamb and grab some dinner? I'm starving."

"Yeah. Me too."

Mike stood up, one hand firmly on his kidneys. "I can have another look tomorrow." He began to tidy up, which for him meant throwing everything back onto the table. If Mike were my secretary, I'd have fired him years ago.

"We could try the Japanese Embassy," I said. "Or rather you could, since I'm flying home tomorrow. They might have somebody who can tell you what it is. After that you can try the police, but I doubt they'll know anything. Well, I don't know, maybe they would. Maybe there's a registry of lost swords at Interpol HQ. There might be a reward going. You might even get your picture in the paper."

"No thanks, though I'll take the reward. But, as you said,

you're the one who found it, so it's your call."

I smiled in reply. The prospect of this masterpiece hanging over my mantelpiece had been at the back of my mind for several hours. Correction – at the front of my mind.

Mike gestured towards the sword. "Do you think we should put it in something a bit more solid before we go?"

"Such as?"

"I've an idea."

Mike left the study and went upstairs. As his dainty feet pounded the floorboards I was struck once again by the feeling of knowing something about the sword. I'd had the feeling driving back from Welton Hall but couldn't place it. The pattern on the Hamon, perhaps – the shape that resulted from the insulating clay the swordsmith used to cover the hardened edge before heating and then quenching in water. The pattern on the steel followed the pattern of the clay and was often unique to the swordsmith. But modern smiths could reproduce these patterns and I didn't know enough about them to be sure. But there was definitely something familiar about it. Then there was that feeling I had of being watched. I hadn't seen anyone, but someone had been there, I was sure of that. Were they aware? Or was it merely a kid stealing apples from the orchard, as Mike and I had done? It troubled me, not having answers.

Mike announced his return with, "Wad'ya think of this?"

He placed a long, black rectangular box on the table. It was old and beaten up, with rusted catches and a handle that was in danger of falling off despite the plastic tape strapped around it. On the front was a fading sticker of Jimi Hendrix playing The Star-Spangled Banner at Woodstock. I recognized it instantly.

"That's your Stratocaster," I said, as if Mike didn't already know.

Mike opened the case, took out the Fender and placed it on the sofa. It had been a wedding present from Julie's father, who had bought it new and kept it in a cupboard for reasons best known to himself. Mike hadn't played it since Julie died.

I carefully positioned the sword in the guitar-shaped gap in the foam. It fit quite well, as if they were made for each other.

"Good thinking, Batman."

Mike shut the case and slotted it in the gap between the bookcase and the wall. He pulled the curtain as far to the left as it would go so that the case was hidden. "Perfect," he said.

"You expecting visitors?"

"You never know who might drop in unexpectedly. The Jensens were burgled a couple of months back. No point in advertising, is there?"

"What about that?" I pointed to the guitar. "It's a sixty-three, isn't it? Worth more than the house."

"It's a sixty-two. And it's insured."

"For more than the house?"

"Of course not. But, just to be sure." Mike picked up the Fender, went upstairs, blundered around a bit and was down again in no time. "I put her under the bed, in case I can't remember anything in the morning. Now, shall we go? You're buying."

"I am?"

#

The Blue Lamb was as it had been since time immemorial; dark but in a comfortable way – and quiet. Mike bought the first round together with dinner, even though I was supposed to be paying. I knew he'd carry on all night like that. I wasn't exactly broke, but Mike was a lot better off than me. He knew that, I knew that he knew, he knew that I knew he knew – so he always paid, and I never complained.

Shit, it was only six fifteen and my mind was already getting fuddled. I'd have to watch my alcohol intake or the flight home the next day would be one long headache. Mike, typically, was impervious, unalterable, unaffected – and unable to stop himself.

"So, Petey Wetey," he began, knowing I liked being called that about as much as he loved being called fat boy. "Tell me all about this secret squirrel stuff."

We were seated at a corner table, in semi-darkness, in a less than half-full pub, so I supposed Mike felt it was a good enough setting to finally ask me. He'd probably been waiting all day, too, despite our discovering the sword and spending that day in the privacy of his house trying to understand what we had found. Mike was good at compartmentalizing things, handling them when and, as he was doing right now, where he felt it was best to do so.

It wasn't as if I was about to give away state secrets, but I leant forward and kept my voice low. "OK," I said, "but it's confidential, not official secrets act level confidential, but keep it under wraps."

Mike feigned offense by the suggestion. "Of course! Who do you think I am?"

"My big-mouthed big brother, that's who."

"My sips are lealed, Peter."

"I'm sure they are. Anyway, remember Doggy Barnes?"

Mike nodded. "Tall bloke, one of your Territorial pals, wasn't he?"

"Yeah, that's him. In fact, it was Doggy who got me to join up in the first place. Anyway, after we came back from Afghanistan, he moved up to the regulars full time and then after that the SIS, the Secret Intelligence Service."

"I do know what it means, Pete. MI6, right?"

"Amongst other things," I said, "Well, he's now top dog for defence of the nuclear industry. Anti-terrorism secret-squirreling, that kind of thing."

"I see," Mike said, his sight of me ironically blocked by the pint of Guinness he was downing.

"Well, it seems the Japanese want to up-level their QRF capabilities for a small-scale attack on a nuclear facility by a fast-raiding party, and they wanted our help, Doggy's help, especially on the anti-terror part." The look on Mike's face told me that he was pretending to understand. "QFR, quick reaction force." I explained.

Mike corrected me. "QRF."

"That's what I said."

"No you didn't."

"Whatever." I wasn't going to argue. "So, they've got a team coming over here in a few months to do some joint exercises, anti-terror training, fast response envelopes, whatever. The thing is, the Japanese are saying they have things in place here, there, in Japan I mean, and only want the training, not facilities evaluation."

Mike leaned closer, pushing the table away with the broad girth of his stomach. He pulled things back to their proper positions. "Things in place meaning, what, exactly?" he asked, enjoying himself being M's understudy.

"Security fences around plants, motion detection cameras, infrared, fast call buttons in the control rooms, documented emergency procedures, radiation suits, back-up generators, remote reactor control systems, the works."

"I see," said Mike. "And do they?"

"Well, that's the point. Doggy wanted to know how it is there, how well set up they are, what kind of measures they have in place already. Not that he didn't trust them, but The Japan Times has plenty of stories on how plant reactivation has been delayed because they weren't ready."

"Anti-terror ready, you mean?"

"And earthquake measures, tsunami defences, all that, too. Don't forget the whole nuclear industry has been shut down since Fukushima. So, anyway, Doggy contacted me and asked me to do a walk around of some key installations, do a first level observation, and report back."

Mike chomped at his chips. "And walk around means, what, exactly?" he asked, his mouth full of potato and ketchup.

"Exactly that. Walk around some of the bigger plants, assess how good their defences were and how I would overcome them. And don't tell anyone what I was doing."

"And the Japs didn't mind?"

It was a slip of the tongue, but Mike should have known better. "The *Japanese*, Mike, didn't know. Doggy got me credentialed as a reporter for the Times, the London one, so I could say I was writing an article on Japan's nuclear industry. It's amazing how many doors will open if you have a piece of plastic with 'member of the press' written on it."

"I see," Mike said, impressed. "And Doggy paid for your flight here to do the report, verbally, face to face, I suppose."

"Super-economy, no less. And he owed me a favour or two, anyway." Doggy did, too, not least of which was me introducing him to the now Mrs. Barnes.

"And what did you find? Or is that a state secret?"

"They're not ready, Mike," I said. "Hopelessly open, in fact. Even you could break into half the facilities in broad bloody daylight."

"That bad?"

"Yep. That bad."

"So that's your entire report? Doggy must have wanted his money back."

"There was a bit more to it," I replied. "And I had to meet a real reporter at The Times so they could write a real article."

"Ah, maintaining the cover story. Good plan, good plan. Which also implies The Times is in league with MI6, just as I had always expected." Mike downed the last of his Guinness. "So, you know about that kind of thing, then, attacking nuclear power plants?"

I did. Quite a bit, in fact. "Doggy and I were on the UK QRF, as back-up to the regulars. We did a bunch of red on blue, that's attackers against defenders, and vice versa. So, yeah, I know where to put the charges. And how to defeat them, too."

"You never told me that before."

"We weren't allowed to."

"In that case," Mike said, "you can buy the next bloody round."

#

I ended up buying a few more bloody rounds than that. We

began playing bar billiards, at which Mike won comfortably, downing two pints of Guinness for each half that I managed. The man was a menace. It didn't affect his aim, though. If anything, he got better as the evening wore on. How he did that was anybody's guess. Fed-up being thrashed I suggested darts and won three five-oh-ones in a row. Things were looking up.

Towards eight the regulars shuffled in, greeting Michael Branding like the good friend he was and pulling his leg endlessly about his inability to hit a double – his one weakness in life. I recognized several faces and spent an hour or so remembering times past. Mike was at his best, entertaining the crowd with his usual lewd jokes and witty comebacks. I was worried that he would start telling everyone about the sword, but he didn't. In all the years I had known him, my big, big hearted half-brother had never lost his mental faculties no matter he much he drank. Except for his stag night, that was, when we had poured so much Vodka into his Guinness it was a wonder he could stand for his big day. But he managed, somehow.

Somebody I didn't recognize said the bar billiards table was available again and invited Mike to play. Being on my fourth pint of the evening I stayed where I was and entered listening and observation mode. I hadn't had this much to drink since I was twenty-nine and an English teacher in Tokyo. I had tried to teach the next morning but had hardly been able to lift my eyes and had left half-way through the lesson to throw-up. 'Never again,' I had told myself. It was as an English teacher that I had fallen for one of my students, a small, beautiful and cultured Japanese lady, Yuko. Nine years and one child later we had been through the usual ups and downs of marriage, and although we hadn't passed those tests with flying colours, they were behind us. Whatever tomorrow would bring we would cope, I was sure of that. A few more years of developing the hotel and maybe, just maybe, we'd have enough to buy the little cottage with a garden in West Sussex we had always dreamed of. I pictured the place; built when houses were built to last, walls thick and solid, with central heating and no need for air conditioning, the garden thirty yards long with tall evergreens lining the fences on both sides, and no pool. I didn't want a pool, too much work, too much algae, too much chlorine. No thanks, not for me.

One day, but not today.

"Hello Peter, fancy seeing you here. Is Michael around, by chance?"

I looked over my shoulder. It was Bob Smith, the handyman who could fix anything, except his Yorkshire accent — which I'd always assumed was him putting it on more than he needed to. Still, I liked him, although he tended to talk more than most.

"Oh, hi Smithy. Playing billiards, I think," I answered, pointing across the room, hoping not to get embroiled in the latest story of his life.

"Oh, I see. Looks busy, he does. Well, I'm on me way out now so could you tell him I'll be needing me Black and Decker back. I'll collect off him in t'morning. Only I've got a bit of work needs doing over the weekend, and that garden table he was doing come out quite nicely, so the missus says. She can see it from her window, see. Anyways, I'll be round in the morning if you could tell him that for me."

"Will do Smithy."

"Nice seeing you again, Peter. But I can't stop and chat, her indoors will kill me if I'm not back in five minutes." He held up his cellular phone. "Biggest bloody mistake of my life, buying this thing."

I smiled, secretly glad that he wasn't going to hang around. We shook hands. "See you on the ice, Smithy," I said, as he left.

Mike came and sat down. "You all right, Pete?"

"I could use a bit of fresh air."

"Hashtag me too. Let's go," Mike said, sounding a lot more sober than he had a right to be. "I feel the strange desire to eat something dreadfully fattening."

"We just ate."

"That, my son, was a lifetime ago."

#

We said our goodbyes and headed through a light drizzle back to Mike's via the fish 'n chip shop. We each bought a cod special loaded with chips, vinegar and salt, with an additional leg of chicken for Mike. Real good stuff for the arteries. We kept the wrappings unwrapped and left the shop.

"How's the family, by the way?" Mike asked, for the first time.

"Good, good. Miki passed some ballet exam, and Yuko's still doing her flower arranging thing. Ikebana, as they say, but she doesn't have much time for it. So, not doing it much, come to think of it."

"And are you still not doing that Ninja thing of yours?"

That 'Ninja thing' was hardly what I would have preferred to call it, but I let it go. "Yep, not doing that. Too busy with the hotel. No time," I said. "Plus, I live a four-hour drive from the dojo, so doubly no time."

"And how is Octavius?"

Octavius the second, to be precise. A forty-year-old Mini Cooper that I had bought to celebrate our seventh wedding anniversary. It had been tough convincing Yuko that it wasn't a waste of money, that I needed a hobby, that I wouldn't drive it fast, that other women wouldn't be interested in riding with me, that I didn't want to be a racing driver again, that it wasn't a better idea to buy a new Toyota. A year later she still wasn't convinced, but we did get that new Toyota.

"He's good," I said. "Starter motor's a bit wonky. Goes click and does nothing every now and then."

"You need to strip it down and do a complete rewire," Mike said. "Make sure you change the brushes and everything. You know how to do that, right?"

"Yeah, but I don't have the tools for it." A slight fib, but I didn't want to admit that I didn't know how to rebuild something as simple as a starter motor.

"Buy some! You know, Pete, that's the story of your pathetic little life."

"I have no tools?"

"Not quite getting there."

"Not quite getting where?" I said, although I knew what was coming. There were times when my big brother overplayed his role.

"You wanted to be a formula one driver but gave up."

"We were broke. So was the car." I thought it was a passably good joke, but Mike missed it.

"Yes, but you could have found a way," he said. "And you left the special army whatnot. You could have had a career there."

"You know why I left."

"I'm still trying to figure out why you joined up in the first place. But you could have stayed and made a difference. And then you piddled off to Japan, met a nice Japanese girl, did that Ninja thing, then stopped, it seems, sort of. Not sure on that. But at least it proves you can take the warrior out of the war, but you can't –"

"Take the war out of the warrior," I said it for him. "As you often say."

"Well, it's bloody true."

Mike led the way across the road. He was eating the leg of chicken, another one of his uniquely ironic moments. "Then you started that English school training company, thing, whatever, and you'll probably stop that soon. Correction, have stopped, right?"

"I didn't have any choice."

"And you can't even fix a wonky solenoid by yourself. I rest my case. Which begs the question, what does all that raging success hold in store for this hotelier fad?"

The family hotel. It had felt like a good idea at the time, taking it over from Yuko's parents as they retired to Hokkaido, refurbishing it, upgrading the systems, the rooms, the restaurant, the food, getting it modernised and ready to be sold after a few years of operation so that we could then decide where we wanted to go next. Of course, it hadn't turned out that way, at least not yet. It never failed to amaze me how long it was going to take, how much it would cost, and how dumb I was for agreeing to it in the first place. The fact that it was half-way up a mountain in Nagano was both a wonder and, frankly, a worry. I should have insisted we stayed put in Tokyo and try to make a success of my one-man-band English conversation school. I was constantly bombarded by self-doubt. What if we ran out of money? What if no-one wanted to buy it? What if the location was too remote for some, or not remote enough for others? What if, what if, what if. It was one of the reasons I had readily agreed to Doggy's request – to give me some thinking space.

"It's not a fad," I said, not appreciating Mike lecturing me this way. "We inherited it from Yuko's parents. It's her bloody family home. And besides, it's all going to plan." It wasn't exactly a lie, but it wasn't exactly the honest truth either.

Michael stopped and faced me. I couldn't tell if this was him being serious or not. "All I'm saying is you have a history of starting, then stopping," he said. "I'm worried that when the chips are down, you might not be up to it."

"Up to what?"

"Whatever it is you need to be up to."

"Well, thanks, bro, for the inspiring pep talk," I said, realizing he was being serious. "The hotel will be fine, thank you. And so will I."

"I just don't want to see you get hurt, that's all."

Considering all I'd been through in my thirty-eight years on planet Earth, it was a bit late for him to start worrying about that. "Are you all right, Mike? What's gotten into you all of a sudden?"

"Call it brotherly love."

"Oh yeah, I'm really feeling the love here, mate."

"And so you should." Mike threw his now-empty wrappings into the rubbish bin he was standing next to. So, he had stopped for that — made sense. I was barely half finished but did the same.

"Come on, Walker," he said. "Man of action and bonehead stupidity, let's head on home."

We walked on. The drizzle had stopped drizzling and the night air was cool and refreshing — and quiet, the perfect evening for a stroll.

"So, the question still remains, who placed the sword in the drainpipe?" I said, wanting to move on to things less serious.

"Indeed, Caruthers!"

"The butler did it," I replied, happy that Mike was back to his normal, frivolous self.

"No butler."

"Ah, then the gardener did it. In the study, with the hosepipe."

"Unlikely. No gardener for the past six months."

"Well, can't be him then, can it," I said. "Which leaves nursy. You know, bugger the old bugger, then bugger off with his dosh. Or his sword."

"Except for that she would have to actually take the sword." Mike pulled his phone from his pocket. "And besides, she's far too cute."

He showed me a photo of nursy standing next to Lord Welton, who was lying on his bed looking old, surrounded by expensive medical equipment — which explained where all the money had gone. But I ignored that, which was easy, because with her long hair and classic Asian features, nursy was one of the most stunningly beautiful women I had never met.

"Ye gods," I said softly.

"Ye goddesses I think," Mike countered. "Japanese, at his particular request. Naomi Yamaguchi."

"What a way to go. And did you and Naomi, by any chance?"

"There will only ever be one for me, Pete, you know that."

I did indeed know that. "And far too beautiful to be our

culprit here, of course," I said.

"Indeed. And besides, she's buggered off to New Zealand, so we are none the wiser there."

I stared at the photograph, mainly as a cover while I contemplated telling Mike about the feeling I had of being watched at Welton Hall. No, that wasn't the reason I was staring, but it was a good enough excuse.

"You know, Mike, back at the house…"

"Yeah?" he said.

I let it go. "Nothing. I mean. Just, I thought, well, thanks, for letting me find the sword like that."

"I didn't *let* you, Peter."

"I know, but, you know, thanks anyway."

We were standing in the middle of the road. A car came towards us, the driver tapped his horn to encourage us to use the pavement.

"We'd better move before we get our arses run over," I said.

#

By the time we got back to the house we concluded that we had no idea who put Lord Donald Walton's sword in the cellar, or why, and probably never would.

"Brandy?" Mike suggested as he opened the front door.

I shook my head. "Nah, I'll stick to water. You go ahead and ruin your liver."

"Too late."

Mike headed for the drinks cabinet and I headed for the kitchen, where I grabbed a bottle of Evian from the fridge, then went into the lounge. Mike had retrieved his guitar case and was staring at the contents, sipping at his brandy.

"You know, Petey-Wetey, if this thing turns out to belong to nobody, I'm going to send it out to you in Japan-land. You're the one who found it, you deserve it."

"Thank you, sir. You're a gentleman. And a drunkard."

"My pleasure. What a day, hey? I certainly wasn't

expecting it to turn out this way."

"Me neither"

Mike switched on the TV. "You want to watch the forty-niners? There's a game on tonight."

"Yeah, all right," I said. Well, I wasn't going anywhere.

We sat and watched the game for thirty minutes before I finally ran out of steam and headed upstairs. As I slid under the covers, I realised I had forgotten to tell Mike about Bob Smith needing his Black and Decker back.

Never mind. I would tell him in the morning.

Four

I screamed.

I could hear myself through the fog of a dream within a dream, beneath the shroud of a sleep so deep you can't get out, but not deep enough to stop you from trying. It was loud enough to wake myself, as I sometimes did, with Yuko thumping me on the shoulder. She'd have been scared and wouldn't have been able to get back to sleep for hours. I'd have told her it was aliens, or running from monsters, or some other plausible explanation that sounded like a real nightmare – anything to hide the real story. I never told her the truth of that dream, that haunting of my soul, the one that kept coming back, the one that wouldn't leave me alone. Although I thought, deep down, Yuko knew and was waiting for me to tell her.

But tonight I woke up alone.

I sat up sweating, breathing hard. Had Mike heard? If he had, he would have let me be. He was the only one who knew about those dreams, even though I hadn't told him the whole story. I picked up my phone. It was two-seventeen in the morning. It shook in my hand, as if vibration mode was on. But it was me doing the shaking, not the phone. I took a long drink from the Evian bottle – more to calm my nerves than to prevent the onset of a hangover.

I lay back down but couldn't settle. Names, faces, friends, enemies wouldn't leave me alone – all gone, lost in time, never to return. One squeeze on a trigger, then everything changes for someone. More than just some-one, many. Their friends, their family, their names – all extinguished with a few pounds of finger pressure. And what for? So the selfish adventurer Peter Walker could prove himself to be better than them? Is that why I joined up? Surely not for Queen and country – it was never for that. I had no right to call myself a saviour, a releaser, a liberator. Who the hell did I think I was? Who the hell did we think we were? If I could go back in time, I'd-

A sound.

I sat up. It was quiet for a while, but there it was again; voices, coming from outside, near the house, very near, around the front doorstep. I got out of bed and looked out of the window, but the porch was blocking my view of the front door. I saw a car parked across the end of the driveway, doors open, waiting. I couldn't see the driver; it was too dark. He was talking to someone – I could hear them whispering. I quickly slipped on my jeans and t-shirt. I figured they were either debating whether to ring the doorbell and then run, or else they were a couple of incompetent burglars. Either way I would deal with it – somehow.

I quietly left the bedroom.

From the top of the stairs I heard the faint but unmistakable creak of a lounge window. Mike had been meaning to replace the hinges for years but had never gotten around to it. Had he been so drunk he'd left them open? For a brief second I considered waking him but that would have been impossible – Mike would be imitating a concrete slab after that amount of alcohol. I started downstairs. My intention was simple; sneak up on the sneak thieves and do something before they knew what was happening. I hoped I'd figure out what 'something' would be when I got there.

I went as stealthily as I could. I knew a thing or two about that – being quiet, hiding in the shadows. I stopped halfway, crouching low to keep myself from silhouetting against the wall. The lounge door was open and I caught a glimpse of someone gliding silently across the floor, but whoever it was disappeared from view. A silhouette was at the window – someone was standing outside, backlit by the streetlamps, not bothering to hide.

Were they armed? I knew how difficult and dangerous it could be dealing with knives. Even a penknife could do serious damage. It's hard to defend yourself against someone wielding a blade – very hard. I had trained against wooden knives for years and knew what to do. I'd also had more than my fair share of dealing with the steel variety. Some people may have described me as being good at it. I was, but that didn't make it any less risky.

My heart was thumping very, very loudly. I tried to control my breathing, but I was sure it must have been audible. It seemed I was no longer quite the brave-heart I was upstairs. I hadn't been that for years, but at least I could still breathe; there had been times when that had been nearly impossible. Fuck, I should have woken Mike. One look at that massive frame of his and they would've fled screaming. On the other hand, simply crouching and observing wasn't going to get me anywhere. But this was Mike and Julie's house, and nobody had a right to come in without a formal invitation. I stood up. It was time to do something other than think. I could startle them and wake Mike at the same time. All I needed to do was bellow something loud enough to wake the neighbours.

I was too late. The silhouette slipped away, and a dark shape suddenly bolted across the lounge and jumped through the open window, under his arm the unmistakable dark rectangle of Mike's guitar case.

"HEY YOU!" I shouted, having finally figured out what to say. "Come back here you bastard!" I followed that up with, "Mike, there's someone in the house!

For all my stealthy preparations, I had come up with three brainless sentences and done nothing apart from raising my voice. The thieves were getting away. So much for sorting things out.

Then action-man took over.

I ran into the lounge, dived through the open window, rolled on to the lawn and sprinted after the two dark figures, adrenalin pouring through me. They were fast, faster than me. The drive was a good twenty-five yards long and they got to their car in a matter of seconds. The first of the two thieves hurtled into the driver seat, immediately followed by the second one, guitar case in hand, into the rear seat. I heard a resounding thud and a curse as something human smacked into the case. Good. I hoped it bloody hurt.

The doors slammed shut. I arrived two seconds later and grabbed the driver side doorhandle, but the front wheels were already spinning furiously, spewing out grey smoke as they squealed in protest at the excessive amounts of power surging through the rubber. I let go just as the car roared off into the night. I tried to get the license number, but the illumination bulb wasn't working, and the streetlights were too dim to compensate. Then from behind I heard Mike's Jaguar starting up. He must have heard the commotion.

'Mike, they've got the bloody sword!" I shouted as I ran.

Mike accelerated, forcing me to jump out of the way.

"Jesus Mike!"

Mike poked his head through the open driver's window. "I'm going after them, you call the police."

"I'll come with you." I ran around to the passenger side.

"No time!" Mike shouted, and floored the throttle, nearly running me over for the second time. I ran after the Jag but Mike was gone, charging up the road with a tremendous twelve-cylinder roar that left me standing there, gawping in amazement.

What the hell?

I bolted indoors, tore up the stairs, grabbed the keys for the Mini together with my phone, jammed my trainers on and hurtled back outside. The car started quickly, and I said a silent thank you to whoever wasn't listening for making me irresponsible enough to rent the Cooper S instead of the cheaper and more sensible standard offering.

I sped off into the darkness, driving through the deserted streets of Wynbeck as fast as I dared. Some way ahead I could see twin pairs of brake lights heading north towards the A27. I knew a short cut through country lanes that could get me there before either of them. I braked sharply and took a screaming right past the local police station. If anyone was on night duty the chances of them not having heard were remote. With any luck an alert sergeant would send out an APB, or whatever it was called. Good – I had a pretty bad feeling about all of this.

I focused my attention on the road ahead and pushed the Mini hard. I had all the lights on, including the flashing hazard warning lights. I wanted anybody who might be unwise enough to be out in the small hours to know I was coming, and to get the hell out of the way. I opened the windows so I could hear the tyres as I took the bends and drove in Formula Ford mode – hard on the accelerator, hard on the brakes and very little in-between.

I hoped I was right. If they weren't heading for the London road, I'd have set a new speed record for nothing. But if I was quick enough, I was sure I could get to the Mad-Mile first. The Mini was as fast as the other car, which I now realized was a Ford Escort, the old 2000 turbo, and faster in capable hands: my hands. My phone was securely in a cupholder, the idea in my head was to call the police and sit on the Escort's tail until either one of us ran out of petrol or the police caught up with us – and I had a three-quarter full tank.

I swung the Mini through a charging handbrake turn into a narrow lane that would link-up with the Mad-Mile a hundred yards ahead. I raced up the short incline and slammed the brake pedal hard at the top, skidding dangerously into the middle of the carriage way, which was thankfully empty. That wasn't clever – but at least I was there first, and there were two sets of lights heading my way.

Straight and fast, the Mad-Mile got its name from idiots like me who raced down it in the dead of night. At the east end was a sharp right-hander that had caught out many unsuspecting motorists on foggy evenings, which was where I now sat waiting, the four cylinders of the Mini beating softly in the darkness. I switched off the hazard warning lights and took the headlights off main beam. I could smell the rubber from the tyres and the distinctive odour of brake pads that had been working too hard. I was lucky I hadn't cooked them. After the furious pace of the last few minutes the quiet was intense. My body was shaking with the thump, thump, thump of my heart.

The lights were getting nearer now, heading straight for me. I suddenly realized I was on the wrong side of the road; I was facing west, but the two cars were heading east. Charging east, in fact. I would have to find a way across the grass and bushes of the central reservation. I spotted a right turn a short distance ahead, drove towards it and waited in the gap in the reservation for the two cars to pass – and at the speed they were going it wouldn't take long.

The Escort flashed by; the driver already hard on the brakes for the sharp right-hander fifty yards ahead. I caught sight of two people in the car, but not enough to pick them out on an identity parade. No problem – if my plan worked they would soon be in Her Majesty's custody, forgoing the need for formal identification. I looked back up the road. Mike was about a hundred yards behind, the Jaguar bouncing precariously as its soft suspension cushioned the uneven road surface. Designed for smooth, luxurious cruising, the Jag wasn't built for a chase. It was frighteningly fast on a long straight though, as Mike was now proving.

Too fast.

"Slow down, Mike!" I shouted as the Jaguar hurtled past.

There was no way he could have heard me, but the brake lights came on, except at that speed Mike couldn't possibly reduce speed in time to take the corner. I watched helplessly as smoke poured from the front tyres and the back end, lightened by the intense braking that had shifted the weight forward, began to turn sideways. Mike frantically turned the steering wheel, trying desperately to regain control, but there was none to be had. The Jaguar, heavy with its own tremendous momentum, gracefully slid off the road and burst through a low stone wall, sending fragments of metal, glass and gravel spiralling into the night air. The car flipped over sideways and slammed into the trees, hitting roof first with a terrible sound before crashing to the ground in a shower of bark and leaves.

For five seconds I did nothing. I was rooted to the spot, staring, incapable of moving, Then I snapped out of it.

"Christ, no!"

I hurriedly drove the short distance to the end of the Mad-Mile. Switching the lights to full beam I left the engine running, jumped out of the car, and clambered over an untouched part of the wall. Glass and metal littered the edge of the forest, much of it barely visible in the shadows at my feet and forcing me to take a wide berth to avoid the debris.

The Jaguar looked hideous in the Mini's headlights. The rear section of roof had crushed the back seats, and the entire length of the passenger's side had caved-in from hitting the wall.

"Mike!" I called out. He was lying across what was left of the passenger seat, red with blood. I put a hand through the broken driver side window and unlocked the door. I tugged hard. The door opened a little then jammed solid, caught on the latch and other bits of twisted metal. I couldn't open it.

"Jesus!" I cried.

I crawled over the bonnet and reached in through the smashed windshield to feel Mike's throat. He had a pulse. Thank God. I carefully checked the back of his neck, but I couldn't tell if it was broken or not.

"Mike," I said, urgency in my voice. "It's Pete. Listen to me. You've had a crash. If you can, open your eyes, move a finger, open your mouth, anything." I trembled as I spoke. Mike didn't reply.

"Michael, I'm going to call for help. Hang on. Focus on being conscious, on being alive. I'll be straight back."

I sprinted to the Mini, found my phone and made an emergency call as I hurried back to Mike. The woman who answered was smart and efficient and knew where the Mad Mile was. She promised that the emergency services would arrive quickly.

That gave me some comfort, but I couldn't simply stand and wait – petrol fumes were everywhere, and I was terrified that the whole thing would burst into flames. I had to get Mike out. I tried the door again, but muscle power alone was hopeless. I hunted around and found a two-foot metal bar lying behind the Jaguar. I wasn't sure where it had come from and didn't care, though I guessed that the stone wall had been reinforced with similar metal bars. Probably this wasn't the first time someone had driven through it.

Funny what goes through your mind at a time like this.

I slowed and caught my breath. I needed to step back, to think, to reason my way through this. If I did the wrong thing, I could hurt Mike even more than he was hurt now. What about the petrol? I mustn't do anything to cause a spark, but with the engine still hot it could all go up in flames at any moment. The fact that it hadn't already was a good sign. Still, I had to act, and act fast.

I jammed one end of the bar into the door latch and heaved. When that didn't work, I rocked the bar backwards and forwards, levering my body weight against the metal, bending the bar. I pushed and pulled with one hand and hauled on the door with the other, all the while cursing and swearing into the darkness. When the bar was too bent I found another and heaved again, praying the fire brigade would arrive soon with their hydraulic pincers that could cut through the roof in seconds. This time I made progress. Soon there was enough of an opening for me to jam my back against the car body and thrust the door all the way open with my legs. I crouched low and felt Mike's pulse again – he was still alive, but with his legs trapped under the steering column it would be impossible for me to drag him out. My improvised crowbar wouldn't be enough – it needed specialized equipment.

For God's sake hurry.

Mike's head looked bad, but I was hesitant to feel for a cracked skull in case I made it worse. God, I hoped I hadn't done anything to his neck when I checked earlier. Mike's face was covered with small pieces of glass from the shattered windscreen. I moved those nearest his eyes. I leant over to check for injuries, but I wasn't worried about external cuts; it was what had happened to the soft brain tissue inside Mike's head that worried me. He must have hit something solid and hard, if not the tree then at minimum the ceiling of the Jag, and the shock of the impact would have caused serious damage. There was a gash on Mike's back, under his shirt, just above his belt. Blood was oozing out, but not in dangerous amounts. His right leg was bent at an impossible angle and there was ivory white bone protruding from his calf – a clean break. There were a whole series of other surface injuries, but none of them life-threatening. It was internal injuries that I was concerned about.

"Mike," I said. "It's me, Pete. Help is on its way. They'll be here soon, hang on in there. You're unconscious but you're not badly injured. You're going to be okay. You're going to get out of here and you're going to be fine."

I was rambling, saying things in the hope that Mike could hear. Then I sensed movement. "Mike!" I squeezed his hand: if his arm was broken it would hurt like hell and snap him awake. Nothing. I squeezed again. "Mike, wake up, for Christ's sake!"

Michael Branding's eyes opened. I moved so he could see my face.

"Pete," he whispered. "I'm so sorry."

"Don't worry Mike, we'll have you out of here in no time."

"I should have told you."

"Told me what?" I said.

"Everything."

"We can save the sinful life confessions for later, Mike. Don't say anything else. Conserve your strength." Multiple sirens wailed in the distance. "Listen, they're on their way. They'll be here any second. You are going to be fine. They'll get you out of here and you're going to be fine."

"Julie's here, Pete. She says hello."

This was serious. "No, Mike. Listen. Julie is not here. It's just you and me."

Mike wasn't listening. "No, she's here, behind you."

I didn't know why but I turned to look. There was nothing. "Mike. Julie wants you to stay here with me, not go with her. Do you hear me, Mike? You have to stay here. Do you understand?"

"Pete, Julie says, where there is light, there is hope."

Mike closed his eyes.

"Mike!" I urged. "Don't do this to me Michael Branding. Wake up fat boy. Mike!"

A muffled crack was followed by a shaft of flame that leapt from under the bonnet. I had seen vehicles burn before and knew how quickly they could go from a small fire to a smouldering wreck. I had to do something fast. There wasn't time to worry about trying to wake Mike up, or if moving him would damage his neck or back. I had to get him out, immediately. I knew instinctively there was no way I could move the steering column, but I tried anyway. Not a chance, it was stuck solid. There was only one thing for it – I pulled Mike up into a seated position, put my hands under his armpits and linked them across his chest. With one foot against the doorsill I tugged as hard as I dared, but Mike's legs were trapped – I couldn't move him.

The fire was growing stronger; any second now flames would burst through what was left of the dashboard and engulf us both. I was becoming frantic. Beyond caring about causing further injury, I grabbed at Mike's legs and tried to wrench them out from under the steering column. A tongue of yellow fire licked at Mike's Nike training shoes. I thought, stupidly, that if Mike had actually run in them then he'd be thinner, and I could get him out. I tried again to force the steering wheel upwards but couldn't move it at all.

Flames burst into the passenger compartment, forcing me back. I shielded my face with a forearm and tried to get closer, but it was impossible. Fire was everywhere now. An intense, terrifying inferno engulfed the car, reaching up to the upper branches and lighting up the surrounding area like a village bonfire on fireworks night. Except there was no joy here for me. In all my life I had never felt so helpless. Light bulbs popped in quick succession, followed by a tyre exploding with a tremendous crack. The whole world filled with the awful, terrible shrieks of twisted, tortured metal. The sounds of death.

This was hell on earth, and inside it all was my brother.
Dear God, let him feel no pain.
People ran past. Someone was pulling at my arm and shouting. I turned to look. The man's mouth was moving and I could hear the words, but they didn't make sense. I went with the pull and was led past a fire-engine, away from Mike. I didn't resist. How could I? I had nothing left.

"Are you hurt sir?" somebody asked. I shook my head. I wasn't sure if I heard what was said, or if I had lip-read it, or even if I had thought it. Another face came into view. The two of them started to say something to each other. I watched as fire-fighters sprayed Mike's Jag with mountains of foam, everything in slow motion.

"Are you all right, sir?" It was the second face, a female paramedic. The fire-officer had gone without me noticing.

"I'm okay," I said, feeling myself returning to the real world.

"What's your name sir?"

"Peter."

"And I'm Wendy." She started to examine me. "Are you hurt Peter? Cut anywhere?"

"I don't think so."

"You're covered in blood, Peter."

My T-shirt and trousers were dark and sticky. "It's not mine."

"Let's check and see shall we." Wendy lifted my T-shirt. I

watched, as if it were happening to somebody else.

"I'm fine, really," I said.

"Just making sure. Will you sit down for me, please?"

An ambulance was right behind me. I hadn't noticed. I sat on the open back shelf and let her check me over. There were voices, some nearby, others from the radio, none of which had registered before. Wendy had a nice smile with friendly eyes and gentle hands, and I could feel her soft breath on my face as she examined my head for signs of impact.

The realization of what had happened sank in.

"Mike's dead," I said, fighting the tears.

"I know," she replied softly. "But you seem to be all right, Peter. No bones broken, no open wounds. I expect you're a bit shocked by it all."

I nodded. No reply necessary.

"I'll be back in a sec," she said. "Just need to check on something." She walked away to speak to someone.

I sat and watched as the last of the flames died down, and against them the silhouettes of the fire crews as they did their brave and unselfish work. From the top of the fire-trucks strong floodlights illuminated the scene. I turned my gaze. I knew the car would still be too hot to handle right now, but I didn't want to see the fire crews cutting away at the roof to get to Mike's charred body. Jesus, would I be asked to identify the remains? I recoiled at the thought. There wouldn't be anything left to identify. I'd have to tell the police, though. They would want to know what had happened. They could catch the Escort if they were quick enough. I closed my eyes and tried to recall the licence plate, but I hadn't got a good look in the first place. Nor had I seen anyone's face. All I had was that they had stolen the sword, we had given chase and now Mike was dead.

My head in my hands, I prepared myself for the inevitable questions. *Had I been drinking?* Yes officer, but I sobered up quickly, always do. *And what about Mr. Branding?* More than me, but then he could handle it. *Apparently not, Sir.* He made a driving error, going too fast, too late on the brakes. *Did you get a look at anyone?* No, it was too dark. *Why two cars? Were you racing, sir?* No, we gave chase separately because there was more chance of catching them. We weren't racing, if that's what you are thinking, officer –.

Suddenly it hit me.

How the hell did Mike get to his car so quickly?

I stared at the road surface beneath my feet, my mind racing. It was impossible, Mike couldn't have moved that fast, couldn't have woken and rushed downstairs in a matter of seconds, then put on his trainers and got in the car. He must have already been dressed. No, wait a minute, he had crashed out on the sofa watching the football. But then he would have done something when the thieves opened the window, or I would have seen him.

And what did Mike mean, *'I should have told you'?* Told me what?

As I sat there as the pieces of the puzzle began to slot together. Mike wasn't asleep in his room, he was already awake, possibly downstairs, waiting. That's how he managed to get to his car so quickly. The voices I had heard, from outside, whose were they? I replayed them in my head. Was one of them was Mike's? It hadn't struck me before, but now I could hear him as clear as anything.

Or could I?

No, the puzzle wasn't slotting together. Mike, in league with the thieves? My mind was starting to play tricks on me. I was trembling. It must have been the shock, or worse, the beginnings of a post-traumatic stress episode. I knew how that felt. My breathing came faster, heavier. If I wasn't careful I'd hyperventilate, and then God knows what would happen.

Be calm, center yourself.

I steadied my breath, breathing deeply, purposefully. Two police officers were walking towards me, one with a small box in his left hand, both with writing pads in their right. I knew what coming, but I had to think fast. Until I knew for sure what Mike had been up to, or what was even going on in my wild imagination, I'd have to bullshit my way through. I had to protect Mike, protect his memory – and protect myself, too. I stood up as they drew near. Whatever I was about to tell them had to sound plausible.

"God rest, Mike," I said, softly, while they were still out of earshot. "But would you mind telling me just what the fuck is going on?"

Five

"Please don't touch anything, sir," Officer Patterson said as we stood on the lawn outside the open lounge window. "They'll be wanting to dust for prints, I expect, when the team get here."

"Of course, officer," I obediently replied, like the good boy my grandmother had brought me up to be. Nanna was a regular Miss Marple and had always been able to see through my little lies. Officers Patterson and Newhawk were mere traffic cops and so couldn't have been as sharp as her, nobody was, and they had bought my story – no doubt helped by the incredible fact that I had passed the breathalyzer.

Mike's classic 1962 Fender Stratocaster had been stolen from right under his nose, I had told them. I clearly saw the guitar case, officers, as the thief carried it with him out of the window. Yes, I was certain of that. No, I didn't know how much it was worth exactly, but it was his pride and joy, a wedding present from his late wife's late father, and could have gone for fifty thousand at auction, as Mike had once said. Or more. That's why he had chased so them so hard. It wasn't the money, though, the guitar had such special meaning for him. Mike must have switched off the TV and crashed out on the sofa, unseen in the shadows, and the thieves would have thought the coast was clear. I was awake – I couldn't sleep for some reason – and heard a window opening, went to investigate, shouted as loud as I could and bolted through the window after them, waking Mike up in the process. We both gave chase in separate cars, more chance of catching them that way.

The story wasn't entirely a fabrication, and it made sense to me. It would work until I could figure out what was going on. And if someone searched under Mike's bed and found his guitar, well, I'd have to handle it there and then. In which case my plan was to say that I had no idea why it was there and not in its case – which was vaguely true.

For the sake of my story the only way I could get Mike into his car so quickly was to have him already asleep on the sofa. Was that what had happened? It was better than the alternative of Mike sitting there and waiting for the thieves to turn up, in which case they wouldn't have been thieves. Did he invite them in? Was it planned? If he knew they were coming, why didn't he ask me to wait with him? Not much else made sense. Mike must have known; he must have been awake.

But that was ridiculous.

Correction. I was ridiculous. Nevertheless, my getting away with drinking half a gallon of Guinness yet still being under the limit was either an act of God or the more mundane result of excessive adrenaline. Either way it was a minor miracle, and I was thankful for that. Would there be a Police charge for dangerous driving? I was half-sure they believed me when I said that we weren't racing, but I had been speeding and that was technically an offence. With half of me trying to weave a story, and the other half trying to figure out what Mike had been doing, I could get things muddled up pretty quickly. I would have to tread carefully.

There were two clear footprints in the soft earth of the flowerbed, both from different shoes. I took off my right trainer and checked the pattern on the sole. "That's mine," I said, pointing down, trying to be helpful but also looking for ways to further convince them of my tale. "The other must be the burglar's."

Patterson compared the two designs. "Could be, could be. Well sir, that should help them quite a lot, I'd say."

I put the trainer back on and pointed as I retold my story. "They were parked over there. That's where I ran, that's where I almost caught him. Mike was parked there and then he went off that way and I followed. The Mini was where it was now. As I said, I turned right on Blackwater road, and went after them that way."

"And they gained entry through this window, is that what you were saying before, sir?"

"Well, yes. That's what I'm assuming. Entry and exit through here.'

Patterson appeared pensive. I had the impression he was rather enjoying playing detective rather than the traffic policeman that was his proper job. "No sign of a forced entry," he said. "But I suppose the window could have been left open. Do you mind if we go inside and have a look?"

"Sure. And I think it was open. Last night, I mean. The window." I learned a long time ago that a good way to deceive was to sound a little stupid, but I was close to overdoing it. If they checked up on me they'd realize I knew more about the art of deception than the average Joe, and that wouldn't be helpful. If it came to that I'd have to call up Doggy Barnes and get him to tug hard on a few strings. Hopefully, it wouldn't come to that.

I opened the front door using the spare key I had put on my key ring twenty-four hours earlier. I paused for a moment; it wasn't easy walking into that empty house.

"All right, Sir?"

"Yes, sorry." I stepped back. "After you, officer."

"Why don't you go in first, sir, and we'll follow."

I went in and stood at the entrance to the lounge. "Is it OK to go in there?" I asked. "We won't be disturbing any evidence, will we?"

"Perhaps we could take a quick look, sir. We'll be careful, of course."

I moved as Patterson eased passed. He walked to the

lounge window and stood there, observing, thinking. Were the open window and the footprints outside enough to convince the man? I told myself I was being paranoid; the evidence was right in front of us. Still, I had no great desire to spend the next few hours in a police interrogation cell.

Patterson turned and said, "I expect the local CID team will get here pretty soon. I'm just a traffic cop, if you see what I mean, not my area but I wanted to see for myself. I'm afraid you'll have to go over your story again with them, but they'll be the ones who'll carry on from here. They'll also be the ones taking a full statement, but they'll explain how that's done. There'll be an investigation, so you'll need to be here a while for that, sir. Plus some formalities regarding the deceased. The CID boys will tell you about that. As for the burglars, we've already put in a call to find the Escort. I'd say if the license number shows clearly on the speed cameras then we have a good chance of catching them."

"I hope so, too," I replied. I was wrong about these two officers – both were plenty smart, and their playing slightly dumb was a ruse to get me to say something that could be used in evidence against me later. I wasn't the only one who knew how to play that game. Nanna would have been impressed.

Patterson went on, "Well, sir, there's not a lot more that we can do right now. I suggest you go and get yourself cleaned up. You don't want to be looking like that when CID arrive. I'll wait here, if you don't mind, until they turn up."

"No problem," I said, although I guessed he was making sure I didn't try to tamper with any evidence, or disappear either. "Should I wash my clothes? Would they want them for the investigation?"

"I shouldn't think they'd need them, sir. But maybe you could put them to one side, just in case. And as a reminder, sir, please don't touch anything when you come back downstairs. In fact, best to keep out of the lounge altogether.

"Understood."

"And I am sorry about your brother sir."

"Thank you," I said.

"They shouldn't take long."

I went upstairs feeling like an intruder in Mike and Julie's house. I heard Patterson make a radio call on his handset and from the bedroom window I could see Officer Newhawk answering from the car. Poor Newhawk, he hadn't been able to conceal his disappointment when I passed the breathalyzer. I'd almost felt sorry for him. But now the only person I was feeling sorry for was myself.

I sighed. A deep, heavy sigh. God, I was tired. I undressed and showered, the water briefly running red as the last of Mike's blood washed off my hands. There was a change of clothes in my rucksack. I slowly dressed, then sat on the edge of the bed. It was a familiar posture, I had sat the same way on the back of the ambulance, but now things were quiet and I had space to think. It was time to focus on practicalities. Someone would have to contact Mike's friends and arrange the funeral, and that someone would be me. I'd also have to call Yuko and tell her that I wouldn't be flying back today. I was best man at Mike's wedding, so did that make me best pallbearer? I didn't even know what they had done with his remains. Hang on, someone had said, hadn't they? Wasn't it one of the firemen? No, it was Officer Patterson back at the accident. What the hell had he said?

Fuck, I couldn't remember. Yes I could. Patterson had said the local CID would tell me what to do when they got here. He also said I was going to have to stay a while for the investigation. But how long was a while? Could they take my passport away? No, not for something such as this, surely not.

So much for sorting out the practicalities. I could hardly think straight.

The sound of a car coming up the drive brought me back to reality. Three men got out, one tall and thin, the second short and powerfully built. The third looked like he had just graduated from the local comprehensive. Officer Patterson stepped outside and spoke to them briefly, before driving away with Officer Newhawk.

So, this was it. The CID were here, and the official part of the investigation was about to start. As I left the bedroom, I asked myself why I didn't tell them the truth and be done with it. These guys weren't stupid and would soon see through the gaps in my story. It could be that all this bullshit I was feeding them was holding them back from finding the thieves. But, then again, those bastards hadn't directly caused Mike to crash. A little more driving skill and care on his part, if I had gotten there quicker, if I'd never found that damn sword…

No, I told myself. I would stick to what I had already said. I still had to protect Mike, still had to figure out was going on, to find out what he was up to. I owed him that. Maybe I was also protecting myself, for all I knew. Either way, I was good at deception, provided I kept my wits about me.

I went downstairs to the front door, where the short one said, "Mr. Walker?"

"Yes." We shook hands.

"Detective Sergeant Harry Masters. This here is Constables Hawkins and Davis. We understand you've had a bit of a break-in, sir."

"That's right."

"And then an incident as you gave chase to the departing thieves, where the owner of this house was deceased in a car accident. We're here to talk to you about that."

"Yes, of course." I stood there with what must have been an empty look on my face.

"Would you mind, sir? The scene of the burglary, we'd like to start there, if we can."

I apologised. "Yes, Sorry, it's been a long night."

I led Sergeant Harry Masters and Constables Hawkins and Davis into the house and showed them the lounge window. I went over my story for the second time. Masters asked the questions and Hawkins took notes while Davis dusted the window for fingerprints and took enough shots to prove he loved his work – though it made me wonder if police budget cuts hadn't left the force a bit shorthanded.

"We'll have to be asking you to make a formal statement sir," said Masters. "We'll need you to go over things once again, putting it in writing, and then your signature. I know you've already told your story a couple of times, but this will be the official one."

I wanted them out of the house so I could get some thinking space. "Do I have to do that right now? I mean, I have a lot of phone calls to make and I also need to change my flight."

Masters thought about it for all of two seconds. "You can come down to the station after lunch. How about two thirty, if that works for you, sir?"

That didn't sound too bad. No pressure, no aggression, no 'would you mind accompanying me to the station, sir.' They weren't going to take me to one of those interview cells and grill the shit out of me. Well, I would stick to my ninety-five-percent true version of events if they did. And, besides, I'd been grilled before, with the wrong end of a rather nasty looking metal tube pointing at my head. I could handle a couple of British bobbies with their tea and biscuits.

"Two thirty is fine," I said.

"Thank you, sir.' Masters said. "Well, we'll be moving on now. I think we've got everything, Davis?" Davis nodded as he tidied up his gear. "We'll see you later then, Mr. Walker." We shook hands again, and they left.

Suddenly I felt more alone than I had felt in years.

Six

I made myself a pot of coffee, then sat at the desk in Mike's study and stared at the picture of Julie on the wall. If there was a Heaven, they'd be together. And if there wasn't, well, what the hell.

I knew I had to start making a series of phone calls, but I lacked the mental fortitude. With so many people to tell I'd have to find the will from somewhere. I had been going through the list: there were at least thirty people scattered around the world who I had to contact. Some would be asleep, some in the middle of their day. Lack of fortitude or not, I had no choice. I had to start making those calls.

I picked up the phone and hit the "Pete & Yuko" key. The number auto dialled, as it had done for Mike so often before.

Yuko answered. *"Mushi mushi."*

"Hello darling, it's me."

"Doshita no?"

What's wrong? Good question. It must have been something in my voice. When you have been married eight years, you can sense these things.

"It's Mike," I said. "He's had a car crash this morning. He died. I'm sorry." I should have said it more softly than that.

"Mike? You mean Michael, your brother?"

"Yes, Michael."

"In a car crash?"

"He was driving, and then he hit a wall, and the car burst into flames. I tried to pull him out, but I couldn't. And he just burned up. And, now, well, now I'm –"

I sobbed. Yuko let the tears fall. "Are you OK?" she asked softly.

I wiped my eyes. "Yeah, I'll be OK."

"Were you in the car, too?"

"No. I was following him, going another route. Taking a short cut."

"What happened?"

I told her the whole story. The whole story, that was, except for the sword – she didn't need to know about that, not yet.

"I'll have to stay here and sort out the funeral and all that sort of thing," I said, feeling a little better. "It'll only be for a few days. I'll have to change my flight and come back later in the week. I'll let you know when I know, but I promise not to be too long, Wednesday or Thursday at the latest."

Yuko wanted me to come back sooner than that, but she understood.

"I'll call again later when I know which flight I'm on," I said. "Maybe you should set the answering machine to the sleep thing, so I won't wake you up."

"I don't mind, you can wake me up."

"It might be three in the morning. You should set it, darling."

"OK. I love you," Yuko said.

"Love you too."

The next phone calls were equally as hard. I sat at Mike's desk, using Mike's phone, called our mutual friends, all the time saying the same thing: Mike was dead – not a thing you'd ever get used to. I found Mike's business diary and rang Mark Deane, one of Mike's partners from his firm. Mark knew what to do. He would arrange the funeral and take care of all the necessary legal procedures, which I gratefully accepted, and would meet me at the police station to be on the safe side. I didn't know Mark that well, but already I could see that he was the type who could keep a level head in a crisis.

Then I called ANA and managed, after convincing a reluctant customer service representative that I really did have a family bereavement, to change my flight to Thursday afternoon. I hoped the funeral would be before then, but as it was the one available slot for the coming week I'd have to ask Mark to do what he could. Finally, I called Yuko again and told her that I'd be back late Friday evening. She was happy with that. I put the phone down, missing my wife and daughter very much.

The clock on the wall showed twelve-thirty. I went into the kitchen and made more coffee, but I was overdosed from caffeine and couldn't drink it. I sat at the kitchen table and stared at the wall, too tired to think.

The doorbell chimed. Shit, were the police back? I left the kitchen and opened the front door to find Bob Smith standing there.

"Hello Bob," I said, without warmth, empty.

"Morning Peter. Sorry to come round so early, like, but did you tell Michael about me power saw? Only like I said I need it this morning. Sorry to ask, but you know, me needing it and all."

I had forgotten. I stared at Bob's chest, saying nothing, having run out of words.

"Gone out, has he? Only his car's not there so I suppose he has. It'll be in the garage, most likely. That's where he does most of his work. Only I need it now 'cos the missus wants her cabinet done and I'll never get it finished without me saw." Bob ducked his head and looked up at me. "You all right, Peter? Bit of a hangover, have we?"

Bob Smith, just about the nicest man you could ever hope to meet despite his continual rambling. Why was it me who had to be the bringer of bad news? Because I was at hand, that's why.

"Bob, Mike's dead. He died in a car crash early this morning." Better that way, be direct, no beating around the bush. But that didn't make it any easier to say.

It wasn't easy to hear, either. "Dead? He can't be. Oh no, that's, oh, that's terrible, Peter. Michael, dead in a car crash? That's, well, that's a hell of a shock. I can't, well I just can't believe it. Just can't. How'd it happen?"

"We had burglars. Mike chased them in his car, but he was going too quick and went off the Mad Mile. The police are investigating, and they'll... I mean I'm sure they'll find out who the burglars were." Brief and to the point; I didn't have the energy to tell the whole story.

Bob sighed, a deep heavy outflow of breath. He dug his hands in his pockets and turned his head up the road. We were both quiet for a while.

"Ah, Peter," Bob said, breaking the awkward silence. "I am sorry. Sorry for you, you being his brother and all. Look, if you need anything, any help, anyone to look after things for you, or whatever, you've only to ask. You know that don't you."

I nodded. "Thanks Bob. I'll let you know about the funeral. I expect quite a few people around here would like to come."

"You're right there, son, you're right there."

Then with us both having run out of words, I said, "I'll get your power saw for you."

"In the garage, I expect." Bob said, gently placing his hand on my shoulder.

I retrieved the garage key from the study, went outside and opened the big double doors to the garage. Bob spotted his power saw and left, reminding me that all he had to do was ask. I thanked him, but I wasn't listening – my mind was caught by the three-foot length of plastic tubing held in the vice on Mike's workbench and the familiar cloth in a bundle on the floor. I unwound the vice and picked up the tubing to take a closer look. It had been cleanly cut through, most likely by Bob Smith's power saw, with the other end now discarded in the cellar at Welton Hall along with the remainder of the cloth, which I was sure was the same.

"All right Michael." I said softly. "For the second time today, would you mind telling me just what the fuck you were doing?"

Seven

The drive to Welton Hall should have given me the opportunity to get my thoughts straight, but as I drove through those old iron gates I had more questions than answers – hundreds more.

I parked in the same spot as the day before, then picked up the tubing and cloth from the passenger seat and found my way around the side of the house to the cellar. The doors were still open. I deposited the items from Mike's garage on the grass, went down the steps and reached for the light switch. The neon flickered into life. At my feet were the cloth and plastic drainpipe, still where I had left them. I gathered everything up, switched off the light and emerged into the sunlight. As I had thought, they were the same as the ones I had brought with me – the cuts even matched-up on the tubing.

Now what the fuck was I going to do? Take it all back to Mike's of course. Then what? I still had my appointment with the police in the afternoon. My choice was simple, either I was I going to keep to the story I had told them in the morning or show them the evidence in front of me and admit I'd been lying. I could probably get away with that, but I didn't want to, not until I'd figured out what Mike was up to. Even the dead had reputations, and I didn't want to sully his. Even so, I had a responsibility here, I couldn't just-

I stopped in mid-thought. I was being watched again. I

could feel it, as I had the day before. I stood up and approached the cluster of trees at the edge of the garden. Someone was there. I couldn't see him, but I could feel his eyes on me. I stopped five yards from the nearest trunk.

"I know you're there," I said. "So why don't you – fuck!"

A shape darted out, from behind which tree I had no idea, and bolted away. I ran after him. Why I was chasing him, I didn't know. Instinct, perhaps. But it wasn't much of an instinct as it took me several long seconds to realize I was chasing a she, not a he. Her long hair was a bit of a giveaway, but so was the way she ran; elegant, yet strong and powerful.

"Hey!" I called out. "Come here!"

But she didn't. She was faster than me, and I wasn't going to catch her. We ran down a slope between tall oak trees, then she took a sharp left and went back up the same slope. She shot right and I followed her, trying to cut her off before she got to the orchard, but she was too quick. I was duly impressed – it's not everyone who can outpace me. I shouted after her again, but it continued to have no effect. There was a narrow road the other side of the orchard, and that's where she was likely heading.

I was wrong about that, because instead of jumping over the garden wall she turned left and headed back to the house. I followed her back down the slope, the same one we had run up and down moments before. This wasn't what I was expecting. By now I was tiring more than she and was ready to stop the pointless pursuit. In fact, she didn't seem tired in the slightest. She had been no more than ten yards ahead of me throughout, but that ten yards was a sprint too far, and now she was leading me around on a literal wild goose chase.

I stopped dead in my tracks. Yeah gods, I was so, so slow, and so, so dumb. Why hadn't I realised it before? That run, that canter, that movement – I had seen it before. She was the one I had chased out of Mike's house, the one who was carrying the sword, and although the only speed record I was going to break tonight was for the slowest realization of the obvious, I was aware that I knew her name.

"Naomi!" I called out. "Stop, stop. For God's sake stop."

She stopped and turned to face me. I was right – it was Naomi Yamaguchi, Lord Welton's nurse, who was supposed to be in New Zealand, not here in Welton Hall. We stared at each other for what can't have been more than seconds, but it was enough time for another hundred questions to hit me.

"Naomi?" I said. "It is you, right?" Considering everything else I could have asked it wasn't very inspired. It would have to do.

She gave the slightest of nods. There was something about the look in her eyes, an intensity, a potency, an unseen reservoir of strength that said there was more to nurse Naomi Yamaguchi than whatever was written on her CV.

"Naomi. What the hell is going on?"

"I'm sorry, Peter," she said. "It wasn't meant to be this way."

She knew my name, which implied she was part of this charade of Mike's. Of course she was, Walker, that was the whole point.

"How was it meant to be, Naomi?" I stepped forward, she stepped backwards. I stood still. There was no way I would catch up with her if she ran again.

"It will come to you again, if it is truly yours. But you must search for it." She sounded like the treasure map Mike had found in Welton's files.

"Look for what?" I knew what she was talking about, but I wanted to hear it from her.

"You already know."

"No I don't."

"You know, because of who you are."

She was beginning to talk in riddles. "I'm Peter Walker, that's who I am." I was good at stating the obvious.

"That is only your name."

"You have the sword, Naomi. You took it. I was there, I saw you. I chased after you. You have it, why this?"

"What was taken must be found." As Naomi turned away, she said, "Sayonara, Peter Walker."

"Wait!" I shouted.

She stopped, still facing away from me.

"Naomi, please, tell me, please." I was begging. "Mike was my brother."

She turned around and came closer. I stood my ground until Naomi was right in front of me. The photo that Mike had of her was nothing compared to the real thing – at this distance she was stunning. She put a hand on my cheek, looked into my eyes, and gently kissed me on the lips.

"When you find me again, I will tell you everything."

And with that she sprinted away, Gazelle quick.

I didn't bother trying to follow her. Instead I watched as she vaulted the garden wall, put on a motorcycle helmet and drove away loud and fast on the bike that had evidently been concealed on the other side, with only her head and shoulders visible above the brickwork.

"Oh, I'll find you again, Naomi Yamaguchi. You can count on that," I said.

I walked over to the cellar, picked up the cloth and plastic tubing, and headed back to Mike's house.

Eight

I usually loved airports, even Heathrow, but today was different. Terminal Two was the same, the throng of travellers was the same, the duty-free was the same, the announcements were the same, the aircraft at the gate still had ANA painted in big, bold letters on its sides. It was the same one I flew over on, too – I recognized the name; "Spirit of The Skies." No, no change there. But Peter Walker-san wasn't sure if he was still Peter Walker-san anymore.

It had been a long week. One hundred and twenty-seven people had attended Mike's funeral; their sad faces filling the pews, their voices, as their hearts, subdued. Mike would have preferred laughter, wine and expensive but pointless going away presents. He was always that way, except at Julie's funeral. I had done my best to make a meaningful speech, but I only managed to say it was heart-breaking to lose my two best friends so young. *'They were together now,'* was how I had finished. It wasn't much of a eulogy. I should have known better than to stand there and simply say what was on my mind. I should have prepared better, but there were too many other things to think about.

At least the police had been understanding, bordering on helpful. They'd taken my statement, showed me stills from the speed cameras on the mad mile, absolved me from blame and promised they'd do their best to find the thieves. I'd said that I hoped they did, for Mike's sake, and mine, but I doubted they'd find anything or anyone, and my guess was that whatever and whoever they were looking for were long gone. It might have helped if I had told the truth, especially about Naomi, but I had lied, deceived and generally perjured my way through the interview; and I still wasn't sure why. I blamed myself, constantly. If only I hadn't found that sword none of this would have happened. If only I had stopped Mike from driving off in his car. If only I had the strength to pull him out of the wreck. Survivor's guilt.

And every time I had those thoughts, I saw Naomi right there in front of me, telling me that I was someone I wasn't, that I knew something I didn't.

And that kiss.

I should have been able to forget about it, to put it out of my mind, to treat it as a tactic, a deliberate strategy to get me to do something – such as following her back to Japan and finding her again.

The trouble was it was working.

I had a family, a life, some sort of future. Was that about to change? Is that what Mike had meant when he was asking me if I would be up to it? I was beginning to doubt who I was. I knew this feeling. I'd had it before, coming home from Afghanistan, fighting PTSD and the self-destructive guilt that came with that. But I'd gotten through it. Julie had done that for me, more than anyone. A psychiatrist specialising in sad-luck cases such as me, Julie never told Mike about our sessions together, and neither did I. He might not have understood that we were only talking, nothing more. I fell in love with her a little bit, too. Maybe a lot. Transference, it's called. Nothing happened between us, apart from the fact that she had saved me. When I needed someone, Julie was there. But the funeral was over, Mike and Julie were gone, today was another day, and life would go on: for some.

And then there were the two documents that Mark Deane, Mike's partner-in-law, had given to me after the funeral. The first was a copy of Mike's will, which Mark was the executer of. I knew what was in it, Mike had told me years ago. The house, Mike's money, his possessions; everything was now mine and Yuko's. It wasn't the kind of gift I wanted to have, at least not like this, and I'd have to figure out what to do about it all. Mark would manage everything until I sorted myself out, and from there he'd handle whatever I'd ask him to do. All for no fee. Mike was his friend, too.

But it was the other document that had affected me the most. It came in a white, unopened, non-descript A4 envelope addressed, 'Peter – In the event of my untimely demise' in Mike's handwriting. I had it my hand and looked at it again, for the hundredth time. It was a laser-printed photograph of a Japanese parchment, with a drawing of the sword, our sword, surrounded by Japanese writing, stylized and bordering on undecipherable. Undecipherable to me, that was. My reading skills were passable enough to scan a newspaper and grasp the meaning – but not enough for this. I knew people in Tokyo that could read it, people that I trusted, Yamaguchi-san being at the top of that list. I wished Mike had added some kind of explanation – anything would have helped. Why all this secrecy, this charade?

And that kiss.

I'd lost count of how many times I'd searched for Naomi Yamaguchi, but I tried my phone again anyway. There were hundreds of them all over Facebook, LinkedIn, Instagram. Thousands, even. All I needed was a picture – and not everyone had one, and of the ones that did, none of them were of her.

The call went out to board the plane. Good. I needed to get going, to leave this all behind. I put the paper from Mike in my jacket pocket and joined the business class queue, one of the perks of flying super-economy. I took off my rucksack and accidentally nudged the man in front of me when I dropped it to the floor. It was nothing, no more than the slightest of touches on the back of his calf, but he turned and glared at me with a cold intensity his eyes. I didn't recognize him, but I had the feeling that he had recognized me. He had the kind of face that was hard to forget, so I put it down to my natural reaction to his aggressive rudeness.

"Sumimasen," I said politely.

He grunted and turned away as the line moved ahead.

We were on board in no time. Mr. Angry headed into business class and I went in the opposite direction. I found my seat, jammed my rucksack in the overhead locker and looked around to track the emergency exits. I was above the wing and counted the rows ahead and behind. If there was an incident and the cabin was full of smoke, I'd know how far I had to crawl to get out. You're supposed to do it even if you were a backpacker on your way to Tokyo, never mind being a special forces reject. Old habits die hard.

The flight wasn't crowded and I had the row to myself, all two seats of it. I waited until boarding was complete and the doors were shut before moving to the window side. The cabin crew conducted their pre-flight checks, and the captain went through the usual routine of welcoming us on board. Fifteen minutes later we were airborne and heading out over the North Sea.

Going home, at last.

The cabin crew came round with the drinks trolleys shortly after we reached thirty thousand feet. I asked for a can of Asahi Super Dry, then sat back and re-lived every detail of the past seven days. So much for leaving everything behind. By my third can I'd come up with a plan. I already knew I was going to see Yamaguchi-san. Small, wiry and tough, he was an ex-Imperial Army translator and had fought and interrogated his way across Asia and back again. He was also kind and gentle – a true martial artist. But, more importantly, he came from a family of expert swordsmiths, and if he didn't know about the sword then nobody knew.

Would he also know Naomi? Yamaguchi is as common a surname in Japan as Smith is in the West. But the sword might be the connection. I'd ask him, and if he didn't know Naomi then I'd keep searching the nursing agencies, the English teacher network, the British Embassy, or anywhere that might have a record of her. Maybe I'd try calling up

Doggy Barnes and get him to hack into a year's worth of airline passenger lists. I'd find her, somehow. And then what? I'd figure that out later.

Shit, that wasn't much of a plan.

Dinner was served and I had the choice of steak or something Japanese. I had the steak and followed it up with coffee. Trying to take my mind off everything I decided to watch one of the videos on the in-flight channels. I chose an old black and white Samurai film, but I must have nodded off halfway through because I woke with a start to find the lights dimmed and everyone asleep.

I took off my headphones and fumbled with the blanket. I tried to recline the seat but for some reason the button on the armrest wasn't working. Was I was pressing the wrong one? I pushed another button that was supposed to turn on my reading light. Nothing. I tried the 'call' button, but no stewardess came. I guessed a wire or two somewhere had become disconnected. I decided to get up, but I couldn't undo my seatbelt. Shit, the place was falling apart.

I heard footsteps approaching. I looked up to be confronted with the most extraordinary sight I had ever seen – a Samurai warrior in full battle dress, glowing softly in the pale of the night-lights. He walked towards me, dark searching eyes fixed on mine, spearing me to the seat, and stopped right in front of me.

I couldn't move.

"*Tatte*," he commanded.

I stood up. Slowly the Samurai reached out his hand. He was holding a sword.

"*Hai*," he said, offering it to me.

"*Onegaishimasu*." I answered, and took the sword from him in the proper manner, as if this was the kind of thing I did every day. The Samurai turned and walked away.

Then I really woke up.

"Jesus Christ." I said, but I doubt he was listening.

#

It was only a dream, despite how real it felt, and I didn't need a degree in psychotherapy to figure where it had come from.

I needed space.

I left my seat and headed down the aisle to the back of the plane. Most passengers in the area were fully asleep, with a few die-hards engrossed in their laptops or watching the other small screen on the back of the seat in front of them.

I arrived at the rear emergency exit and stared out through the small window at the night sky. Years ago I'd have been dressed in combat gear, armed to the teeth, wearing a parachute with my handy PNG night-vision goggles and oxygen bottle, waiting for the rear door to open so I could leap headfirst into the darkness on another fun-filled HALO jump. I could do that kind of thing once, but not anymore. Physically, I could. But deep down inside there was something broken, something that I didn't want to think about, something I had done my best to keep hidden. I'd been faking it for years. Failed racing driver? Guilty of hardly even trying. Special Forces has-been? That was me. Business owner? No cash, and hardly any clients worth speaking of, and that was gone now anyway. Hotel Owner? Don't ask. Fifth dan Ninja? Yes, but so what? I'd stopped training except for my morning routine, and I had let the thieves get away with Mike's sword. Family man? I was doing OK there, but everywhere else I was a fraud. Nothing more.

I slowed my breathing. I knew these thoughts, these unwelcome friends, these intruders into my psyche. Those who didn't know would say, *'don't listen, let them go, don't think them, think about happy things instead,'* as if all that was needed was a modicum of mind-control. But that is easier said than done. Meditation and controlled breathing help. So does having someone to talk do; someone who knows how to dig deep, who knows how to break through that barrier, that defensive wall behind which lay the darkest secrets. Julie had done that for me. Only she knew the whole, dark story.

I needed space, time, and solitude to rebalance myself.

And home, I needed to be home.

Then I saw someone at my seat. He was standing in the aisle, twenty rows from me, looking at the empty space where I had been sitting, partially lit by the reading light from the seat behind mine. I doubted he could see me, but I stepped away from the window into the shadows and observed him.

It was the man in the queue, Mr. Angry, the one whose leg I had slightly touched with my rucksack. He looked around, discreetly checking to see if anyone was watching. He was good. Only someone who knew what to look for would have been aware – someone like me. I expected the person with the reading light had fallen asleep, otherwise Mr. Angry wouldn't have opened the locker where my rucksack was. What the heck was he doing? Looking for something, obviously. Revenge, maybe? But I knew he couldn't get my rucksack out with a solid tug, and that would have made too much noise.

A cabin attendant came out from behind the curtains of the central galley. The man closed the locker. She said something to him, but it was too far for me to make out what. Then she led the man to another locker and opened it. The man nodded and said something else, politely and with a charming smile. I still couldn't hear, but if it had been me, I'd have pretended to have been looking for some locker space and would have thanked her ever so nicely for showing me.

The cabin attendant went back to the galley, apparently satisfied with his story. The man headed towards my end of the plane, searching every sleeping face as he went down the aisle. If he was still upset with me for nudging his leg, he was going to extremes to show it. He came closer. I stepped out of the shadows and came face to face with him, making it look as if I had been stretching my legs, just as he had.

"*Sumimasen,*" I said, for the second time that day, and politely half-stepped out of his way, giving him the opportunity to reciprocate.

The man grunted impolitely, kept his ground and stared at me. There was less than two feet between us. We stayed that way for several seconds, eye to eye. He was smaller than me, strongly built with no neck and cauliflower ears, which I took to be from Judo. There was a feint scar on his left cheek, possibly a knife flick that hadn't quite hit the target. I had no doubt he was tough, a streetfighter, and not to be taken lightly. I wondered if he knew I wasn't to be taken lightly either – a kick to the knee, a twist of his elbow, an *Oni Kudaki,* and he'd be limping back to his seat. But if got me in anything resembling a bear hug then I'd be the one limping back to my seat – if it were possible to limp with a crushed spine.

I was ready to start a fight. *What the hell was I thinking?*

Then Mr. Angry turned and headed back up the aisle. I followed as far as my seat and kept eyes on him until he returned to business class. As I sat down it occurred to me that it had been over a decade since I'd faced that kind of situation, and yet I was calm and was breathing normally. Shit, I hadn't even been doing that five minutes earlier.

Nonetheless, it didn't stop me from wondering what the fuck had just happened.

Nine

JAPAN

I was through immigration at Tokyo Narita airport in no time, despite the change in the law requiring returning foreigners to get fingerprinted and photographed every time we re-entered Japan. In fact, it had made things quicker for permanent residents. There were special lanes, which ironically meant you could by-pass most other travellers who still had to queue up to show their Japanese passports.

I reached luggage claim and found a spot where I could wait for my bright green and blue Samsonite to arrive. It had been Yuko's idea to buy one with an easily recognizable colour scheme. Unfortunately, the partners of other frequent flyers must have had the same idea – I picked up two identical cases before I finally put a hand on mine. I turned and headed towards customs when the sound of a voice calling my name made me look back. I'd thought it was Mike, but it was only some Gaijin hailing a friend.

Then I saw it.

At first I thought it was a trick of the eye, in the same way I'd been tricked by an English accent, but this was no illusion. I stood motionless, watching it nudge its way around the caravel. The urge to grab hold of it was overwhelming, but I could have been wrong; there must have been others like it in the world.

"No way." I heard myself say. "Not on the same flight."

The odds against that were staggering – an absurd, impossible event. But as the long black shape passed in front of me, barely three feet away, all doubts left my mind. Even through the semi-transparent protective plastic wrapping provided by ANA I knew those scratch lines, the way the tape was half-wound on the handle, the way the clips fastened, the picture of Jimi Hendrix at Woodstock on the front.

It was Michael's guitar case, and the sight of it made me speechless.

Then the man from the flight, the one whose leg I had brushed with my rucksack, Mr. Angry himself, picked it up. He brushed straight past me and walked off towards the 'nothing to declare' exit, Mike's guitar case in one hand, pushing his wheeled suitcase with the other. I followed and stood behind him in the queue, my mind racing. Should I grab it from him and shout 'thief!'? No. If I did that, I would be the one getting arrested.

Mr. Angry was called forward. He presented a document to the customs officer who studied it intently while taking a good look at Mike's guitar case. A discussion followed, but I couldn't catch what they were saying. I knew what they were taking about though; the document was obviously about the sword, our sword. That would explain why Mr. Angry wasn't on a flight earlier in the week – they needed time to get the paperwork done. Shit, if I'd told the truth to the police back in the UK, then it would have been on an international stolen goods list, and the conversation in front of me would be very different.

Mr. Angry glanced to his left, straight at me, then turned his attention back to the customs officer, who had placed a gloved hand on Mike's case and was firing off a series of questions. After all, you can't just carry a Samurai sword through customs as if it were a bag of duty-free. But then again, what did I know? Maybe that document was all he needed. I could see some kind of red stamp on it, so it must have been official, probably processed by the Japanese embassy in London. But why leave the sword in the case? But, then again, why take it out? The case was perfectly adequate for the job. Perhaps the officer was making the same point, but he didn't seem too concerned and waved Mr. Angry through.

The ruse had worked: the bastard had gotten away with it.

Then it was my turn. The same officer checked my passport, asked me several innocuous questions in passable English which I answered in my mediocre Japanese, and let me through. I walked quickly but naturally through the automatic doors to the arrival hall, as if I was late for a train rather than trying to catch a crook, and got there just in time to see Mr. Angry exiting the main doors to the pick-up area, no longer alone. He had been met by three tough looking players, one of whom offered to carry Mike's case. Mr. Angry refused to let it go – which was telling. I stood and watched, slightly concealed by a TV monitor, as they got into a black limousine that was waiting outside. The man had opened the door himself, rather than waiting for someone to open it for him. Another telling move. The other three men got in, and the car moved off quickly, but not so quick as to attract attention. And so he was gone.

Now what was I supposed to do?

Coincidences are meant to happen. That was something that Julie Branding used to say. It certainly applied here – the chances of my being on the same flight as the sword were astronomically small, to say the least. And the man knew me, I was convinced of that now. He *had* recognized me on the plane, but hadn't expected to see me there, and that's why he had come to check me out.

Come on Walker, now you're being ridiculous, paranoid.

My phone buzzed. It was a text from Yuko.

Did you arrived yet?

I'd completely forgotten to let her know. I messaged back.

Just landed, rushing now, I'll call from the Shinkansen.

She wrote back.

Ok.

My family. Christ. What if I was right? What if I wasn't being paranoid at all? If he did know me, then maybe he also knew where I lived.

As I stood there in arrivals, I felt fear. Not the childish fear of heights or the dark, but the very adult fear of the unknown. The fear of being carried along by a wave of events beyond my control, towards an unknown destiny. I didn't see myself as someone who scared easily, but beneath the fear was something else. A thought, a sense of knowing, a fragment of an understanding that I couldn't grasp. As one of my teachers had once said, it like trying to pick up a garden pea using a single chopstick. Every time I felt I had it, it went away.

Naomi was right. I knew, and yet didn't know. I had to find her. I headed towards the train station – and home.

Ten

I awoke in darkness.

It was four thirty in the morning and the sun was a good hour away. I was used to waking early, but this was a bit extreme. I tried to go back to sleep but my mind kept telling me that I should be looking for Naomi, and for that I needed to go to Tokyo, to Yamaguchi-san's shop. But before I did that I needed to think, to go deep within and try to locate that unresolved thought, that whisper of a feeling, that unrealized realization shrouded in darkness below the light of my consciousness that lay there waiting to be made free. And to think clearly, I needed to not think at all.

Yuko stirred.

"Just going up the mountain," I said, kissing her on the forehead. Yuko grunted and went back to sleep.

I got out of bed, dressed quietly in a tracksuit and went into the kitchen, where Honey, our three-year-old Labrador, was waiting to greet me. She knew the morning routine well and followed me to the hotel entrance and waited while I collected my *bokken,* my wooden sword, from my study. We went outside. I was wrong about sunrise; it would be here soon enough.

We by-passed the family Toyota and got into Octavius, my old Mini Cooper. Honey jumped into the back and I sat with my hands on the steering wheel for a while, remembering the conversation I had with Mike.

"Shall we go?" I said to Honey. She barked in response, as she always did. I turned the key – the starter motor clicked in response. I tried again, still nothing, not even a click. Mike was right, I should have a go at fixing the thing myself.

"Come on laddie," I said. He must have been listening because on the next try the starter obliged and the engine sprang into life. We moved off up the mountain road.

If there was one good thing about living in a hotel halfway up a mountain in the Japanese Northern Alps, it was the mountains themselves. The air was clean, the views spectacular, the skiing great in the winter and the summer breeze cool enough to not need air conditioning. I loved it there, and so did Yuko and Miki. But we knew in our hearts that it wasn't for us. Yuko never said anything, of course, but I could see she was missing her friends and the Tokyo lifestyle. I was missing the dojo, my small English communications business had closed, and I was wondering how Miki would be able to get to school every day in the village at the foot of the mountain once the hotel re-opened. I expected Yuko was thinking about that, too. And now that we had Mike's house, the alluring choice of living in our new home in the English countryside might be too tempting. At some stage in the next few weeks I'd have to discuss the idea with Yuko, but I suspected she'd say we'd have to fulfil our obligation to her parents, our *giri*, and stay here until the hotel was fully re-formed and in full operation. Well, I could wait if she could. And if we didn't like the idea after all, we'd sell the hotel, sell Mike's house and head back to Tokyo.

The other good thing about living on a mountain was space – lots of it, such as the clearing Honey and I had arrived at. I parked, opened the driver's door so Honey could jump out and run free, and collected my *bokken* from the passenger seat.

And so our morning routine started. I chased Honey between trees, up and down the dormant ski-slope, bounced off rocks and threw sticks for her to retrieve until she was tired enough to lie down, panting heavily. Good, stage one was over. Now it was my turn, as if I hadn't had enough already.

I started with Tai-chi as the sun rose. Perfect timing to be infused with those energy-giving rays. I loved the way the light filled our valley, the daily re-birth of the world. Then I started my Ninpo routine. This was one of the reasons I liked to come out so early. Not that anyone would likely be around to see me if I went out later in the morning, but if they were I didn't want anyone to wonder what on earth that gaijin was doing. *Was it Karate?* No, Ninpo was very different. *Was it Ju-Jitsu?* There were forms common to both arts, but they went their different ways at black belt. I had studied both, so I knew. *Was it Aikido?* No, not at all. There were similar elements, though. Wrist locks, for example, at least in the beginner levels. *Are you Ninja? Really? Amazing!* Not amazing at all, really, there are dojos all over the world, and you wouldn't say that if you knew anything at all about Japanese martial arts.

No, better not to have to explain anything to anyone.

I picked up the *bokken* and fought a pitched battle against seven armed attackers. It was always seven Samurai in my imagination, like the Akira Kurosawa movie, but in reverse. Seven rogue Samurai, bad Ronin. I was the good guy, of course, and always won. But today wasn't about winning, or losing, or having perfect form, or clearing out the cobwebs of a week without training. Today was about going within.

I put down the *bokken*, sat on the grass, crossed my legs and adopted a meditation pose. Some practitioners preferred to mediate with their eyes open, the idea being to stop the mind from assuming it was about to go to sleep and so start dreaming. I wasn't one of them. I preferred to work out the physical stress by exercising and doing my routines. Then I'd sit, close my eyes to shut out all visual distractions, and then calm my mind – or wait for it to calm itself. Meditation isn't about stopping all thoughts; instead you simply observe them, then let them drift past your awareness like leaves floating on a stream until they fall away leaving the true, deep self that lies beneath. It's harder than it sounds. Getting your mind to avoid distraction from its own random images and feelings takes years of practice, and when you have a lot on your mind as I did that morning it's even harder; especially when you are deliberately searching for something, and right now a thousand thoughts were filling my head. I observed them without following, listened without starting a conversation, and let go when they tried to drag me along.

Or rather, I tried to. But it was hard to silence those doubts, those fears, those images of Mike dying in the car, those memories of Naomi, the man on the plane, and the sword itself. I knew, though, that below all of that was… something. If I could quieten my mind, maybe I could hear its message.

But a different kind of message revealed itself.

Honey heard it first. She stood on all fours and stared at the sky, alert, growling. I opened my eyes. Then I heard it too. A distant cry, from somewhere beyond view. Honey barked softly. She wasn't the guard dog-type and tended to be more interested in visitors than worried by them. But this was no ordinary visitor.

The cry came again, nearer, louder. I could see it now, a Japanese Golden Eagle coming in low over the treetops as if on a bombing run. I'd seen a couple in the past few weeks, having seen none before that. I'd read up about them. Usually they lived as a breeding pair, but right now there was only one. It circled overhead, looking straight down at me. This was worrying. Was it going to attack? It could do if there was a nest nearby. From where I stood, those claws were pretty sharp. I picked up my *bokken*. I had something to defend myself with, but if those claws got anywhere near Honey's eyes, they could cause serious damage.

I risked a glance across. Honey was sitting, watching, calm as anything. I looked up again. The great bird banked away and headed down the hill. I relaxed. Good, that could have gotten nasty.

Shit.

The eagle turned sharply and headed straight up the slope towards me, less than ten feet above the ground, it's large wings seemingly beating far too slow to account for the tremendous speed it was going.

Christ!

I ducked to the ground as it flew inches above my head with a powerful thrust of air. That was close. So much for defending myself. I sprang to my feet, swivelled around and held the *bokken* in front of me. If it came back, this time I'd be ready. But our visitor wasn't flying. Instead, it was perched on a rock, wings folded behind its back, staring right at me. I was no ornithologist, but even a bonehead like myself could see this was unusual behaviour. Honey pressed herself against my legs for reassurance. We stayed that way for a while, three beings on a mountainside, all looking at each other in silent communication.

I decided to take the risk and stepped forward. The bird stayed where it was. Honey too – it was near enough for her. I kept going until I was no more than five feet away.

"Hey, big guy," I said, softly. I'd never been this close to such an extraordinary, intimidating creature. Then it spread its wings, let out a cry that split the valley and took to the air. I instinctively ducked again as it passed over my head. The great bird circled high again, looking down at me as it had before.

"OK, you've got my attention," I said.

The eagle flew away to the other side of the valley and began flying in circles again, this time above a distant clump of trees. Hidden amongst the leaves was the barest glimpse of a sloping roof. I'd been on this mountain hundreds of times, standing in this exact same spot, but I had never noticed it before. This was odd, almost bizarre. Undeniably bizarre. An eagle, talking to me? Is that what was happening here? Last week Peter Walker would have brushed it off as a stress-induced figment of his imagination. But the way things had been going the past few days I wanted to know.

"Come on girl," I said to Honey. "Shall we go and have a

look see?"

I opened the door for Honey to jump in. This time the Mini started first time and we were off down the mountain.

#

It took a while to find the place.

The Mini, being old, had no GPS, and with no phone with me either I followed my navigation instincts, which weren't working that well. I took several wrong turns and bumped into some dead-ends until I found the little unsurfaced lane that took me through the trees and delivered me into the forecourt of a small temple.

I was never sure of the difference between a temple and a shrine. I assumed temples were bigger and had a priest, whereas a shrine didn't. This one appeared to be somewhere in between, but I was going for it being a temple. Either way, I knew it was the right building because the eagle was perched on the roof, looking down at me once again.

"You stay here," I said to Honey, and got out of the car. The eagle flew away, its work apparently done.

I took stock. I was standing in front of a temple, on a mountain side in Nagano, having been guided there by a rare Japanese Golden Eagle. The morning was calm, the air clean, the smell of burning incense carried by the gentle breeze. Behind me was a forty-year-old Mini Cooper with a dodgy starter motor and a Labrador in the back seat. A few kilometers beyond that was my family and the life I had. Ahead was ten yards of gravel that led to the open door of an old wooden temple. If you discounted that superb creature winging its way back through the valley, then everything was normal, reasonable – just another day in Japan. Yet I knew that if I crossed those ten yards and went through that open door, then everything would change.

Everything already has changed.

I crossed those ten yards, took off my shoes and went in.

It was quiet inside the temple, and more spacious than I

had expected. I stood still on the tatami matting of the main hall, feeling like an intruder more than an invited guest. In front of me was the small platform where the various instruments of worship were carefully arranged. A statuette of Buddha sat at the back on a raised plinth, eyes closed in silent mediation. The walls and ceiling were beautifully decorated, in contrast to the four solid pillars that supported the structure. At the base of the platform was a table where the incense burned, which meant someone was there – somewhere.

"Hello?" I said quietly, with reverence.

No reply.

I stood still. There was something about temples and churches that resonated with me. I was never able to fully understand it, but whenever I was inside one I felt a connection to something outside of me, beyond myself. There were those who thought they were nothing more than brick, stones and wood, monuments to mankind's inability to let go of myth and legend and accept that there is nothing aside from the mechanical universe. I understood that view. I'd seen enough pain and destruction to make anyone believe that there cannot possibly be an all-powerful being who would let his children suffer. Which is why I could never explain to myself this feeling I had that, despite all the bullshit in the world, everything was connected – everyone was connected.

"Hello." I called out, louder this time.

Nothing.

What was I expecting – Naomi to come bouncing forward and say *'Ah, you found me'*? No, this wasn't where I was supposed to be today. I had imagined it all, starting with an eagle talking to me. Ridiculous, frankly. It was time to go, to get out of there and head back to the world I knew.

As I headed for the main entrance, a framed photograph caught my eye. It was hanging on the wall, oddly out of place, as if this was somebody's living room with the family portrait strategically positioned for guests to ask, 'do tell, who are all these people?' The photograph was black and white, dated December 1936, taken in front of the temple, and was of two rows of thirty or so individuals dressed in priests clothing, the back row standing, the front row sitting. Mostly they were men but there were three women, too. Everyone looked strong, powerful, and in a sense dangerous. This was no ordinary group of priests. And they were all Japanese, except for the tallest one in the middle of the second row. So tall, he stood out even without his western face. The names were written at the bottom of the photograph, and in the eighty or so years since it was taken the handwriting had faded somewhat, but it was clear enough to read.

I stared in astonishment. The name of man at the back, the foreigner, the gaijin, the one who stood taller than all the others, was Donald Welton.

I couldn't help myself. "My God," I said. "Lord Welton was here?"

"Indeed he was."

I span around to see a small, bald man dressed in priest's robes standing close behind me. He had crept up on me, silently, unseen. Normally I could sense if someone was doing that. It's an awareness you build up from years in the dojo, and years before that in the special forces. You had to, or you wouldn't survive. I'd had some aspects of that alertness since I was young. But not today.

"Did you know Donald-san?" the man asked, in good English.

I was complete caught off guard.

"No, I used to live near his house, in England. A coincidence," I replied, feeling even more like a trespasser, although there was nothing in that warm smile of his that was accusing me of that.

"Ah, I see."

There was something about this old priest; a calmness and serenity coupled with the same grace and strength of the eagle that led me here – and yet he was making me nervous.

"I was taking the dog for a walk, a drive, and came in."

"Ah, a coincidence, indeed," he said.

For a split second I had the feeling I had met him before. I hadn't, of course, I knew that, but there was something familiar about him. In any case, I wanted to get out of there, even if I wasn't sure why I was there in the first place.

"And she's still in the car." I was trying to sound in control, but I was just making school-boy excuses. "So maybe it's best if I take her home."

"I see. Well, of course, but you must come and visit us again, when you have the time."

"I will. I mean, thank you."

"You are welcome."

I walked away, turned to bow, then put on my shoes and got back into the car. The starter motor clicked a couple of times, but on the third try the engine sprang to life. The priest bowed gently. I nodded in return from the driver's seat and drove away. Half a mile down the lane I stopped the car and sat there for several minutes, trying to make sense of what had happened, and why I had run away with my tail between my legs so utterly defeated by a small man in a robe who did nothing.

There was more, much more I didn't know than I did. A thousand questions ran through my mind, and I kept coming back to the same answer; find Naomi. So why the hell was I sitting in my car staring at the tarmac?

"Time to go home," I said to Honey.

#

Breakfast was waiting when we got back; rice, o-natto and dried fish for me, Royal Canin for Honey. Yuko had been worried because we'd taken longer than usual, but I made some excuse about meditating on the mountainside and losing track of time.

Yuko knew when I wasn't being honest, and I could see it on her face. She didn't challenge me on it, which made me wonder how I was going to get away with telling her I had to urgently go to Tokyo that day. I had my excuse prepared, but for that I needed to pretend that an email had arrived, and since it was still early and I hadn't yet been online, that little charade would have to wait. Either way, I wasn't in the habit of hiding things from Yuko, and right now I was hiding just about everything.

"Is everything OK?" she asked as she ground the coffee beans. That was Yuko's way of saying *'something's wrong, isn't it?'*

"Of course," I lied, wondering if she had read my mind.

"You'd tell me if it wasn't, won't you?"

I'd fallen for Yuko the moment I first saw her face. I'd been in Tokyo six weeks and hadn't even found a decent place to live, although I had found the Ninpo dojo, introduced myself, been accepted on the recommendation of Jimbo the Aussie, and started training. Meanwhile I was sharing a room in a 'gaijin house,' which was a converted old wooden apartment block full of foreigners and cockroaches. It was cheap, though, and quite fun to be in, despite the unwelcome guests. In those days I'd bash them on the head with a shoe and flush the carcasses down the toilet. Nowadays, I'd pick them up and gently put them outside. I'd changed, or at least I liked to think I had.

But living anywhere requires money, so it was at the English conversation school in Shibuya where 'Peter Sensei' met the cute student who had returned from a homestay in Oxford and wanted to carry on the conversation, literally. It was against the school policy for teachers and students to fraternize outside the office, but everyone ignored it. We were married six months later, and Miki was born a couple of years after that. That was eight years ago, and a lot can happen in eight years – including your wife getting to know you as well as you know yourself. I sometimes thought she had been a *Kunoichi* in a previous life, a female Ninja, and had kept her sixth sense in this one.

"Darling?" she said.

"Yes?"

"Everything is OK, isn't it?"

I must have been miles away. "Yes, of course it is. Sorry, I was thinking about Michael, that's all."

"OK," she said, and hit the button on the coffee maker. It gurgled into life. "Miki has to go to the doctor today. I can take her, but do you want to come too?"

"Is she OK?" I asked.

"The same rash on her arm, it came back."

"She must be allergic to something."

Yuko sat down. "I ordered a special futon from the internet, just if case."

"Maybe we should order a new one for us too, just *in* case."

"I already did."

"Clever girl."

"I know."

We sat there for the next hour, talking as husbands and wives do, about this and that and everything in-between. All the while I kept one eye on the clock, waiting for the time to pass so I could have an excuse to check my email.

The in-between became a long conversation about the hotel. While I was away a quotation had arrived for a new boiler: one million yen, which was near-enough ten thousand dollars. I usually thought in dollars, the conversion was easy, and I tended to buy books and other odds and ends from the US Amazon site rather than UK one. Yuko's parents were going to pay, God bless them. The rest of the re-form project was on track, and in three months we'd open before the snows fell for the ski season, by which time we'd have found enough staff to help run the place and have decided what to do about Mike's legacy to us.

"Daddy!"

Miki came in and gave me a big hug, the start of her morning ritual. "Honey!" She gave Honey a bigger hug. "Mummy!" Another hug.

"Hungry?" Yuko asked. Miki nodded – she was always hungry.

It was eight thirty. "I'll go and do some work," I said, and headed to my study.

#

My study was on the east side of our hotel, facing up the mountain. I'd have preferred the west view down the valley towards Nagano city, but that was reserved for guests. The room itself was small without being cramped, despite my best efforts to fill it with filing cabinets, an oversized desk, an unnecessarily powerful PC with multifunction photocopier/ printer, a modern reproduction Samurai Tachi sword – my other one was in our bedroom – a kerosene heater for the winter months and a whole bunch of small unused electrical bits and pieces that I should have thrown away months ago. Perhaps it was a little cramped, but the window had a good view of the road that went passed the front of the hotel, and that was holding my attention now.

A Nissan GT-R was crawling past, the two occupants eyeballing the hotel, and I didn't think they were looking for somewhere to stay. I reckoned they couldn't see me behind the reflection of the window, so I eyeballed them back.

I could clearly see the driver, a tough looking Yakuza-type, but it was too dark inside the car to see his passenger. I'd come across this kind of player before in Tokyo – short hair and light brown suits, with minimum brains and maximum brawn. But the gangs tended not to bother with the ordinary population, and often put themselves out to help people in trouble. They were even among the first groups to arrive in the northern area of Japan after the earthquake and tsunami. We'd had one in the Ninpo dojo in Tokyo. He was a decent enough bloke, and a good training partner. In fact, I rather liked him, so perhaps I was being unfair with the minimum brain observation. The other thing I knew was that it was unwise to underestimate their group identity. Hurt one, you hurt them all, and a whole bunch of them would be out for revenge. Considering I had no adverse contact with anyone from any group, seeing a pair of them outside was troubling.

Or maybe they were simply looking for a place to hold a national gangster convention.

Then the passenger's face came into view, he was leaning forward looking right at me. I was wrong, they could see me. Were they connected to Mr. Angry, or was it just my mild paranoia? The way things had been going recently they could well be. I didn't like that thought. I didn't like it at all. The two of them exchanged words, and the car drove away down the mountain road. I took a mental snapshot of the license plate as it went.

"Mmmm. Nice car." I hadn't noticed Yuko come in. She was carrying the coffee pot. "Do you want some more?" she asked.

"Yes please."

She took my mug of off the desk and poured.

"Thank you," I said.

Now I had a dilemma. Should I go down to Tokyo and discover whatever I could there, or should I stay here? No matter who you are, whether you're a dojo grandmaster or a retired flower-pot designer, you're supposed to stay and protect the ones that you love. I considered my options quickly, differently, unemotionally – the way you're required to do when planning a mission. I'd go to Tokyo, find out what I could, race back here and call the Japanese police and tell them everything I knew, and live with the consequences of having not done the same thing with Detective Sergeant Harry Masters of the West Sussex police. I'd only be gone a few hours, and nothing would happen before then. The alternative was to stay here, but I needed to know, I had to know – and if Naomi were there, I would know.

Apparently, I had decided I wasn't being paranoid.

"Darling," I said. "I've just had a message from International Standard, they want me to go down to Tokyo today to meet the regional manager, they might want me to go to Hong Kong for their regional meeting next month."

As with all white lies it's best if it's based on a kernel of truth. International Standard had been my one big client before we came up to Nagano, and I'd conducted several team-building workshops there. I'd passed the account on to a friend when we came up to the hotel, but every now and then they'd needed extra support from good old Walker-san.

"Today?"

"He's only got time after lunch," I said. "I won't be long, just quickly down on the Shinkansen, and back again."

"There's a typhoon coming."

"Really? Another one?"

"It's the global warming, people said on the news. It's big one, too, biggest since thirty years."

I checked the weather app on my phone. "It's not coming until later this afternoon." I said. "I'll go now, I'll get the bus to Nagano station and I'll back early, so you don't have to worry."

"Are you sure? You can't change the meeting for another day? The trains might be stopped. I'm going to change Miki's doctor just *in* case."

"It has to be today. But don't worry, I'll be back in time to close all the shutters and everything. Can you pick me up when I get back?"

"Of course I can," she said. "But I prefer it if you stay."

"I know. But everything will OK, you'll see."

"Then you should hurry, bus is in ten minutes."

"I know," I said, and gave her a hug.

"Do you love me?" she asked.

"Of course!" It was just about the one true thing I had said that morning.

"Then come back quickly, please!"

"I will."

I should have listened, should have stayed, because everything was definitely not going to be OK.

Eleven

Yamaguchi-san's shop was a fifteen-minute walk from Hikifune station in the *shitamachi* area of Tokyo between the Sumida and Arakawa rivers. Even though it was far from the major shopping areas, people who knew about these things still went out of their way to go there, tourists included. There weren't many visitors to the area today, though. The typhoon was closing in on Tokyo and although the winds were relatively light and the rains hadn't yet started, it wouldn't be long before the main storm hit.

Yuko, worrying as she always did, had already messaged me. I'd told her that that as soon as my meeting was over, I'd be heading back on the Shinkansen. In fact, I wanted to get back as soon as possible. I was having second thoughts about whether it had been a good idea to come to Tokyo. A voice in my head kept telling me it was a bad decision. I should have stayed, should have called the police and sat tight, ready. But another voice kept telling me that not coming was an equally bad idea. I didn't know which to listen to. Maybe they were both right. Either way, I was here now.

I knew the area well and took a series of short cuts through the back streets. Yuko and I had lived not far from here, and Miki was born just the other side of Sumida river. It wasn't the best place to live in Tokyo, but it was close to the Ninpo dojo where I had trained for seven years and was where I was heading now – to be in the neighbourhood and not visit Matsumoto Sensei would be a travesty of the highest order, at least from my point of view. I checked my phone – I'd rushed for the bus in the morning and had neglected to put on my watch, which wasn't like me at all; it was eleven twenty-three. I'd call in, pay my respects, go to Yamaguchi-san's shop, then be heading back home by two at the latest.

I arrived at the dojo. If you watched enough TV specials you'd expect a modern-day Ninja to be a secret fighter, dressed in black from head to toe, hiding in the shadows, unseen, unheard, springing forward to assassinate their target before disappearing into the night. And if you thought that way you might be disappointed to find out that Matsumoto-Sensei's dojo was in a Tokyo side street, not far from a convenience store, opposite a bus stop, with students going in and out on a daily basis in full view of anyone who happened to be passing by. Inside there would be tatami matting, some wooden swords and knives on the rack on the east wall, some *hanbo* wooden staffs on the west wall, but apart from that there wouldn't be much to say that this was the dojo of a master Ninja, who did a bit of dentistry in his spare time. There was a Karate dojo half a mile away, and Ikeda Sensei and Matsumoto Sensei were good friends, often holding joint events to promote Japanese Bushido. Times had changed since the days of the original shadow warriors. That said, by the time you got to 5th Dan, as I had, you'd learned a few of the secret techniques that were not for public display.

I could hear sounds of training inside. Reluctant to disturb the session, I slid the door open quietly. Sensei, of course, had already realized I was there and nodded to me as I stood in the *genkan*. I bowed and waited in the entrance area as he instructed the group on the fine art of *muto dori* – knife evasion. They were high level techniques, too. Not for beginners, nor for that matter first time black belts. This was a group of advanced students, although I didn't recognize anyone there – which was unusual because I thought I knew

Sensei's best practitioners. They were good, too. Very good, and younger than me. Most were these days. Sensei instructed everyone to stop with a soft "*Yame*," and bade me to enter. I took off my shoes, bowed and went in through the threshold.

Matsumoto Sensei walked over to greet me.

"Ah. Peter-san, Long time no seeing you. How are you?" he said in his own particular English. We shook hands. Sensei was the least formal grand master you could imagine. And at five foot six, if that, he was also one of the smallest. I'd learned years ago not to let size fool anyone – he'd make mincemeat of both me and Mr. Angry with one arm tied behind his back, while eating an onigiri with the other, and with his eyes shut, too.

"I am very well, thank you Sensei," I replied. "And you?"

"Ah, I am so much better for seeing Peter-san! Have you come to train with us today?"

"No, I'm sorry to say. Actually, I'm on my way to see Yamaguchi-san."

"Ah, to buy new sword?"

"No, I'm doing some research. But I thought I should at least come in and say hello."

Sensei turned to his students. They were watching us, quietly but intently. There were ten of them, four male, six female. They were different from ordinary students – stronger, faster, more accomplished. I wouldn't want to be in their bad books. Dressed in their black Gi they also looked a lot like each other, too. I searched the faces. Was Naomi among them? No, of course not. Why would she be?

"Ah, we are happy to see you," he said. "But, please, come more often, Peter-san. I miss having my best student!"

"Well, you are too kind, Sensei," I replied. "But I don't think I quite qualify for that. New members?"

"Friends from other dojos, here to share their knowledge and to learning from each other."

"They're very good." It wasn't simply a polite compliment; they were impressive.

"Ah, but you are still the best, Peter-san."

Sensei was always like this with me. I appreciated it, but it was a bit embarrassing.

"Thank you, Sensei, but I don't think –"

"Do you still practice every day?"

"Most days," I said, which was almost true.

"Every day, Peter. It is very important. And you must open your own dojo, in the mountain, there is no better place."

"Yes, I will do my best, Sensei."

The shutters rattled with the wind, a reminder that I needed to be moving on.

"Ah, typhoon is coming," Sensei said.

"I had better get going, before it gets too close."

"Please give my regard to Yamaguchi."

"I will. Thank you, Sensei, and sayonara."

"Sayonara!" All the students said it together. I wasn't expecting that, but it made me feel welcome, as if everyone were greeting an old friend. Or, rather, saying goodbye to one.

#

Yamaguchi-san's shop was a five-minute walk from the dojo through non-descript residential back streets built during the reconstruction period after the war. The whole area had been devastated in the infamous bombing raid in March 1945. More than three hundred B-29s had dropped over 1,500 tons of incendiary and other bombs, including napalm. The first bombers had dropped their packages of death in a concentrated X pattern, which made an easy target for others to follow. Interesting letter, X; it can mean death or treasure. A hundred thousand plus had died that night. Five months later the world discovered that reasonable men could use atomic weapons, but in my mind this was a natural extension of the thinking that had started with the London blitz, carried on through Hamburg and Dresden and culminated with Hiroshima and Nagasaki. It's easy for people to look back and condemn these events as war crimes. I didn't disagree, but those people were missing the point. War itself is a crime. I knew, because I was one of its criminals.

I put those thoughts aside as I arrived at the little 'Traditional and Modern Japanese Swords' shop, tucked between two 5-storey one-room office blocks and opposite a row of old apartments. That was the thing about the reconstruction period, zoning hadn't been on many planners' minds. A thoroughly modern Kawasaki Ninja motorbike was parked nearby, adding another level of contrast that was so often the case this side of the river. Rain started to fall. I checked the weather app on my phone. The typhoon was closer than I had thought it would be. I had time, but not as much as I wanted. I went in.

Yamaguchi-san's shop was one of my favourite places anywhere. It was small and jam-packed with swords, Samurai armour, Ninja Shuriken, knives, halberds, spears, reproduction muskets and whatever else was needed to start a revolution. I never tired of calling in and could happily live there, as Yamaguchi-san did. Nobody knew more about the arsenal on display than he, and many people thought of Yamaguchi-san as an unofficial Japanese national treasure. He certainly deserved to be recognised as one. If he didn't know about Mike's sword, then there wasn't a soul on the planet who would. And if it turned out that he didn't know, then that would make me wonder about the people who had stolen it. What did they know? What did Mike know? What did Naomi know? And if Yamaguchi-san couldn't help me find Naomi, then what would I do? I supposed I'd have to cross those bridges when I came to them.

The curtain at the back of the shop opened, and out came Yamaguchi-san. I hadn't seen him for almost a year, and he hadn't changed a bit, which wasn't much of a surprise considering his favourite joke that he was the oldest thing in the building. Small of stature, with a straight back and steady legs that belied his age, he was living proof that the Japanese still had the longest lifespan in the world. Yet if I had seen him more recently then I might not have been standing there with a dumb look on my face.

"*Ohisashiburi*, Peter-san," he said.

I stared. How could I have been so stupid? Why had I seen it that morning but not made the connection? If you cut his hair shorter than a jarhead, draped him in robes and removed that tell-tale scar from his right hand, then the man standing in front of me now, Yamaguchi-san the sword shop owner, was the splitting image of the priest in the mountain temple. It was so glaringly obvious I couldn't speak.

"Peter-san. Are you OK?"

I wasn't OK at all. Here I was talking to the twin brother of a priest at a temple that I had been guided to by an eagle, a man who I had known for years and yet suddenly didn't know at all. A man whom I'd thought could help me, and now I wasn't so sure. I was struck once again by how everyone seemed to know what was going on except me. Was Naomi here? I sensed that she was, she had to be. There were too many coincidences, too many connections.

"Have you come to buy a new sword?"

Why the question? Yamaguchi-san knew why I was here; he had to know. But I had to find out what was going on. I centred myself. I'd go along with all the charades, the games, the deceptions, the concealments. It was the only way I'd find the truth of what happened to Mike, the sword, Naomi – and of myself.

"Not today. Instead, I wanted to show you something," I said. I reached into my rucksack and pulled out a photocopy of the parchment that Mike and bequeathed to me. I handed it to Yamaguchi-san. He recognised it, of course he would.

"Shall we sit and have some tea?" he said.

"Yes please," I replied.

I had crossed another threshold.

#

We sat at Yamaguchi-san's antique mahogany desk, drinking tea while the rain lashed at the window. In the time taken for me to explain what had happened in England the typhoon had made landfall. I would have to get going soon or I'd be stranded in Tokyo, and there was no way I was going to let that happen.

Yamaguchi-san had the photocopy of Mike's parchment in his hand, though he'd hardly even looked at it. I had the distinct impression he wrote it in the first place.

"And the case, it was at Narita airport?"

"Yes, I saw it. I'm sure." I had told Yamaguchi-san everything except for the part about Naomi. I wasn't yet ready to reveal that, although I had a feeling she was nearby. Better to keep my cards close to my chest until I knew more. I also didn't tell him about my visit to the temple that morning, although I assumed he had already heard about that from his brother.

"That is not good, not good."

"You know about this, don't you, Yamaguchi-san?" It was a simple question, and I was ready to hear any answer he gave. Whether it was about the sword or about anything connected to it.

He nodded. "Five hundred years ago, Taiyo, that is the sword name, it means 'Sun' in English. Sun in the sky above, not son of a mother with dirty nappy."

Yamaguchi-san's gentle humour made me smile, as it always did, even today.

He continued, "Taiyo was made for a very bad man by a very good man. My ancestor! But there was a spirit that came into the sword. A power that good men can use for good, but bad men can use for…bad."

"And people believe that?"

"Some do."

Things were beginning to make sense. "And whoever has this sword can control that power, is that what you're saying?"

Just because I trying to show understanding and insight, it didn't mean I believed in this kind of myth. My goal was simple, ask questions, dig deeper, find out whatever I could.

"Taiyo's power is to bring out what is already inside," he said. "My fear is, if Ohno already has it, then we may be too late. There is much bad inside that man."

"Who's Ohno?"

"President of Ohno Industries. He's a famous businessman, maybe you know him."

I did. Most of Japan did, and half the world beyond that. His company owned the bulk of the eastern Japan energy market, and Ohno had spent the years following the Fukushima disaster arguing loudly with government officials, prefectural governors, concerned citizens organizations and TV discussion panels that his nuclear reactors were perfectly safe and could be re-started, moreover *should* be restarted to reduce carbon emissions and combat global warming. I'd even toured three of his plants, and as my report to Doggy Barnes testified, they weren't a disaster, but neither were they shining examples of anti-terror preparedness.

"Oh, that Ohno. Yes, I know him. Or of him, I mean."

My phone buzzed. It was Yuko.

Typhoon already on Tokyo. Going more north!

I typed quickly.

Leaving soon!

I had a million more things to ask, but they would have to wait. "I'm sorry, I'll have to get going soon, Yamaguchi-san," I said, trying to sound apologetic. "Thank you for the tea, and the story about the sword."

For the first time since I had known him, let alone that day, Yamaguchi-san's smile left his face. "It is not a story, Peter-san. There is only one who can stop Ohno. We call him the Mamoribito. The one who protects, who defends. He is the true owner of the sword. He must find the sword, take it back from Ohno, before it is too late."

I had never seen Yamaguchi-san so serious. "Too late for what?"

"Ohno's belief is only the Mamoribito can stop him. He will do everything he can to destroy you first, before you can do the same to him."

That sounded ominous, but I'd have laughed out loud at the melodrama if it had been anyone else sitting on the other side of the table.

"Me? I'm not this mami… whatever his name was."

"Mamoribito. You say that because you do not yet know who you truly are."

Him too? Naomi said something similar, even Mike had alluded to it. Well, if they thought that, they were wrong. Everyone was wrong. I wasn't anything other than Peter Walker, whose unique skill was screwing things up. Even so, I was now sure those had been Ohno's men in the Nissan outside our hotel. It was time to get out of there, to get home.

"People keep saying that." The words just came out.

"Then perhaps it is so."

I stood up and hurriedly put on my rucksack. I didn't need to look through the window to check the weather outside, I could hear it, but I made a point of doing so.

"I have to go, Yamaguchi-san. The typhoon."

"Of course, you must. But you cannot run from yourself forever, Peter-san."

The only place I wanted to run was back home. I walked fast to the shop entrance. The rain was pelting down and the wind was getting up, approaching gale force. I had to move before the Shinkansen service stopped.

"An umbrella?" Yamaguchi-san was right behind me, holding a cheap plastic *kasa*.

"I'm fine." It would be next to useless in these winds, so there wasn't any point me taking it.

"As you wish."

I opened the door. There was one last question I had to ask, one I had been avoiding because I didn't want to know the answer. It could validate everything he had told me, and I wasn't ready for that. I asked anyway. "Is Naomi here?"

He didn't bat an eyelid. "Oh, she will be along, I expect,

when you need her most."

I had no idea how to respond to that, other than by saying, "Thank you for your time, Yamaguchi-san, but now I must go."

I exited into the rain rather rudely, but when you're not thinking straight then all you want to do is get back to the one place you knew you had to be, with the ones you are supposed to protect.

I started a fast walk back to the underground station. At that pace I reckoned I could cut the fifteen-minute walk down to ten at the most. From there I'd be at Ueno station in another fifteen minutes, where I'd grab the first available Shinkansen seat and ninety minutes later Yuko would be picking me up at Nagano station. I'd outpace the storm and be home in time to close all the shutters and be ready for those thugs in the GT-R. If they tried anything, as what's-his-name had famously said, they'd find out that I had a particular set of skills.

If I had stopped still for a moment and used my pathetic excuse for a brain for even a second, I would have turned around and gone straight back to Yamaguchi-san's shop and called the police. But I was moving too quickly for rational thought, too afraid for those I had left behind, too hurried, too foolish, too stupid – and that quick journey home was about to take a lifetime to complete.

Twelve

I put my head down and headed through the downpour that had suddenly descended on Tokyo. That's the thing about typhoons; one moment a light shower, the next moment a full-on, clothes-drenching deluge. I upped the pace to jog-level but kept it short of a full out run. In this weather, any weather, the sight of a man blasting through the streets would attract attention, and I preferred to remain anonymous. I didn't mind the rain. I'd had plenty of practice, if that was the right word, humping fifty-kilogram kit packs and an armoury of weaponry up and down the mountains and valleys of Scotland and Wales. In comparison, this was child's play, and on the plus side the rain would keep me from overheating.

My head, on the other hand, was on fire. I didn't see myself as having lived an ordinary life and had done things most people wouldn't even dare to consider doing, but this was bordering on the absurd. A secret lost sword with some kind of built in power? There were stories about mythical swords that had come to life to defend their injured owners, but they were just that, stories. Inanimate metal objects are precisely that too, inanimate – unmoving, non-conscious lumps of metal. Sure, I sometimes talked to my car and swore at the ruddy starter motor, but I didn't think it was actually listening to me.

And this mami-protector, the guardian of the sword?

Me? Come on, Yamaguchi-san, and Mike, and Naomi. Come on the lot of you. Mike was dead, and people were acting as if Peter Walker was the saviour of the world. How could a reasonable-minded person believe any of this? But what if it were true? Of course it wasn't true. And if Naomi was part of this, then why was she the one stealing the sword from Mike's house? Shouldn't she be keeping hold of it, to give to me? Unless this is what she meant by her promise to tell me everything when we met.

And Ohno – it was a stretch to think that a captain of Japanese industry could involve himself in something as trivial as this. He had everything he wanted, and if he'd wanted the sword all he'd have to do is offer Lord Donald Welton a bundle of cash. Unless Welton refused to sell. Mike, on the other hand, was far too practically minded to refuse such an offer.

But Mike was dead, Mr. Angry no-neck on the plane had the sword, an eagle led me to a priest in a temple who had a splitting-image brother in Tokyo whom I've known but not known for years and who says I am the owner and protector of Taiyo, and then tells me Naomi will be along when I needed her most.

Maybe the only person who wasn't convinced was me.

I stopped still. Shit, where was I? I had gone straight past the turning to the underground station. How could I have been so distracted, so unaware? I had trained for this, was good at it, and yet was making rookie mistakes. But when you've fucked up what you don't do is to rush, to panic and make decisions you'll regret later. I could see the top of the Tokyo Sky Tree, the tallest structure in Japan, fingering the clouds high above the buildings a kilometer ahead. That gave me direction and bearings. OK, so I wasn't so far of course, and didn't need Google maps to tell me where I was.

My phone rang. It was Yuko. I ducked under the awning of a fish shop for cover from the rain. "Hello darling," I said, calmly as if everything was under control.

"The typhoon is speeded up. Are you on your way?"

"Just about to get on the underground. I'll be at Ueno station twenty minutes. I'll message you when I'm on the Shinkansen."

"OK, be careful."

"I will," I said as I noticed a black Lexus SUV, parked fifty yards away, sidelights on, windscreen wipers beating back the rain. There were four passengers besides the driver, and they were all looking my way.

"I'll be back soon, don't worry."

"OK. Miki is waiting for her daddy."

"I know, me too. I'll see you soon."

I hung up. There's a golden rule I had, everybody in the regiment had, everyone in the dojo had – if it feels wrong, it is wrong. I had taught this in a series of self-defence classes for women that I ran for three years in Tokyo. I had lived it in the mountains of Afghanistan where it had kept me alive in situations when I should have been dead. And when five heavies in a car are watching you it qualifies as beyond merely feeling wrong – this was obviously, evidently, glaringly wrong.

The rest of the street was empty. Shop owners had already shut up their stores in readiness for the typhoon, and who ever lived in the area was either back home or still in their offices waiting for the order from their companies to get back home. The rain was heavy and the wind strengthening, but not yet enough to disrupt travel. I expected my travel was about to be severely disrupted. I glanced back up the street away from the SUV. There was another one, behind me, parked about a hundred yards back. I couldn't see inside but I didn't need to.

Fuck.

There were two side streets leading off the main road I was on. One led towards Sky Tree, the other went in the opposite direction. Although I was familiar with the area, I didn't know this part of it. It didn't matter. I had to act, now. The obvious choice was the Sky Tree route – it would lead to shops, offices and the underground entrance, and nearby there would be a Koban – the ubiquitous small police stations that were literally everywhere. They were part of the reason Japan was so safe. Safe, that is, except for today.

It also didn't matter who the heavies in the cars were. Ohno's men? They must have been, if Yamaguchi-san was right. It did matter that neither of the cars was a GT-R, but if I called Yuko to warn her she'd be frightened as anything. Besides, there was no time for that – the cars were starting to move, and I didn't think they wanted to invite me to Starbucks for an Iced Americano.

I ran towards the street that led to Tokyo Sky Tree. It was narrow, but big enough for the SUVs. If I was wrong, then I would be no more than a dumb gaijin gunning for shelter. If I was right, I'd be in a public space in seconds and beyond their reach. The cars sped up. I wasn't wrong.

Shit!

I was completely wrong; the street was a dead-end.

I glanced over my shoulder. The two SUVs were heading right towards me. There was a narrow pedestrian passage off to my right, I made for it just as the SUVs arrived, their occupants spilling out on to the wet tarmac behind me. One of them was carrying a sword – it was Mr. Angry himself. Christ, he had a nerve to be so open like that, even in the middle of a typhoon. I sprinted faster as shouts filled the air. I was wearing jeans and sneakers, had a light rucksack on my back and could move quickly. They weren't slow, but in suits and slippery-when-wet office shoes they'd be no match for me. I'd outpace them easily.

I hit another dead-end.

Fuck.

The passage split right and left at the T-junction. In those situations you decide and go with it. I chose left. The passage ahead was long, narrow and straight. A quick glance behind showed the right-turn option was barely ten yards long before it hit another dead-end. That quick glance back also showed two of them were gaining on me. I'd gotten that wrong, too: in a chase, sneakers and experience were apparently no substitute for youth and black dress-shoe-look-alike trainers. A hundred yards ahead I could see the lights of a main street. I'd be there in a little over twelve seconds, maybe less: quick enough to get clear of my pursuers.

Wrong again. Two players suddenly appeared fifty yards in front of me. They must have thought ahead and positioned men at strategic points – that took some planning. Unless they simply sent people in multiple directions. Either way, it wasn't important. I could outpace that sword, but if they had firearms, I'd be a sitting duck. One of them reached inside his jacket. They had firearms.

What the fuck was going on?

I darted left into a narrow side street. The rain suddenly became heavier, so heavy I could see barely the end of the alley. Downpour wasn't the word; it was like running through a waterfall. Christ, how could conditions change so quickly? At least it worked both ways: my new friends would have the same problem, and I doubted they had humped their way through the Brecon Beacons in any kind of weather, let alone this.

I kept going as fast as I could. Ahead was another dead-end. This time I realized why – sections of the neighbourhood were being re-built, and each dead-end was the border wall of a building site. Good. This was made for me. In the regiment we got pretty good at vaulting obstacles, and in the dojo, at the higher grades, we got better. I kept going at a full sprint and ran vertically up the metal wall, a virtually impossible technique if you hadn't trained for it. The wall shook precariously under the onslaught but held firm. I grabbed the top, which thankfully had no barbed wire to deter intruders, vaulted over and rolled out as I hit the ground. I would have loved to have seen the look on those faces chasing me, but I was no mood to wait and find out.

I had no more than thirty seconds before someone found a way in after me, but I needed to take stock. The site was bigger than I had expected and had been abandoned for the day due to the typhoon. There'd be a guard somewhere, most likely in a prefabricated hut near the main entrance, but through the rain I couldn't see where that was. The building itself was fifteen or so stories high, and evidently going higher, though as of now it was a framework of steel beams and unfinished floors. Construction equipment of all kinds was everywhere. Good, that would provide cover if things got out of hand. But I wasn't going to let that happen. Cover everywhere also meant barriers everywhere. I couldn't just sprint madly through all of this, especially through the building itself, which was unlit and in the diminishing daylight brought on by the thick low clouds that could be a real problem. Still, it meant plenty of places for concealment if I needed them.

I should have listened to Yuko. I should have stayed at home.

I was panting heavily. I worked to control my breath, which would also help to control my mind. I had a choice; run, fight, or hide. There were too many of them to fight, even if I used the shadows. I could hide, but they'd only need to search for five minutes before they found me, and they'd make sure the guard didn't call the police. Vaulting that fence didn't seem a good choice after all.

A shot rang out. A bullet ricocheted nearby. Shouts followed, indecipherable through the wind and the rain. The bastards must have found a way in. I'd spent too long thinking, evaluating, instead of doing. Another rookie mistake. I was full of them today.

I needed cover and somewhere to hide. Mr. Angry's men could be anywhere between me and the main gate, and I needed a run-up to vault the fence again, by which time I'd be firmly in someone's sights. The building was the clear choice. I sprinted up four flights of metal steps, each loud, clanking footstep sending a signal, *'here he is.'* I'd be getting myself killed in no time at all if I continued at this rate of mind-numbing stupidity. At least it was dark here; I could hide in the shadows and then climb down the outside of a corner section while they were looking for me somewhere else.

The clatter of heavy feet came resonating up the stairs. I sprinted for the far corner, confident that the combination of near gale force winds, driving rain and the racket from their own footsteps would conceal any noise I was making.

Then I felt a sharp crack to my head, and everything went black.

#

I'd been shot.

I was going to die here, in this unfinished building, my life wasted, my existence terminated, my potential unfulfilled, my family left to fend for themselves. I'd die a failure, running from myself, running from the hurt I had caused, running from what I could have been. I'd die the death of a fool who could have been so much more than he was, but who gave up believing in himself. And, worse than all of that, I'd die not knowing why I died.

But I wasn't dead. I could still hear the rain and feel the wind on my cheek, could still smell the paint and adhesives, could still sense my heart beating in my chest. My awareness returned. I picked myself off the floor, but only as far as my knees. I touched my forehead, there was blood but not the raw flow that would have been made by a bullet. I looked up. I'd run headfirst into the low telescopic arm of some kind of lifting equipment that had been practically invisible in the darkness.

So, I wasn't shot, not yet, but I would be soon. A few yards to my left stood two of Mr. Angry's men, drenched from the rain, pistols drawn and pointing straight at me. I tried to stand.

"Don't move!" the taller one shouted.

I stayed on my knees. I was still groggy and wasn't sure I could move very far anyway, and at this range shit-for-brains there could hardly miss. Which made me wonder why he hadn't pulled the trigger already. I didn't have to wait long to find out.

"Let's do this," said the smaller one, in Japanese.

"We must wait for Tanaka." The taller one was obviously the senior of the two.

"Why wait? Let's get this over with."

"You heard what he said. It must be done with the sword."

"Why? A dead man is a dead man."

Did they think I couldn't understand their language? Or were they so confident in themselves that they didn't care? It didn't matter, I was fucked.

"Put down your weapons!" The voice came from behind me. I turned my head. It was Mr. Angry, who I took to be Tanaka, along with five more of his crew. Eight against one, with the eight armed and the one on his knees.

"Stand aside."

Tanaka's men did his bidding, forming a semicircle behind him. Tanaka raised the sword above his head. I could see now that it was *the* sword, Mike's sword, our sword. Taiyo. It was like a scene from Merry Christmas Mr. Lawrence, only a lot, lot worse. I was going to die here, this day, after all.

Tanaka looked me in the eye. "Now we say goodbye to you!"

Then he raised Taiyo high and swung it down straight towards my unprotected head.

Thirteen

From almost the first day you enter a Ninpo dojo you learn sword evasion techniques. Some are simple, such as swivelling to one side and letting the sword swing down harmlessly in the empty space that you left behind. Other techniques involve rolling way, ducking, stepping back, jumping and raising both feet in the air – all depending on what angle the blade was coming from.

When you reach the higher grades, you don't expand the range of evasion methods. Instead, you perfect them whilst learning to disarm your attacker and prise the sword from his grip. When you start learning the more secret methods you realize that many of them are advanced variations of what you learned the first time you got hit by a bamboo sword. I could do all them, could teach all of them. And when the time came, if I could ever be that ready, I'd sit in meditation and wait for Matsumoto Sensei to silently approach me from behind with a real sword and attack with the deadly 'killing Ki.' Those who sensed this would survive and become true Ninja. Those who didn't sense it, well, it would be their last day on planet earth.

Whichever technique you chose to use, it had to be natural, instinctive, immediate. You didn't selectively choose, either, because that would mean the mind was getting in the way. It should happen unconsciously, like walking or breathing. What you should never do is kneel and watch the sword come at you, a deer caught in the headlights, and do nothing.

Which is exactly what I did.

It happened in slow motion. Tanaka's arms were high, his form good, the blade held straight. His eyes were fixed on me but looking though me at the same time, as Musashi Miyamoto, the famous Japanese swordsman had written in The Book of Five Rings. Tanaka uttered a sharp cry, a *kiai*, then swung silently, using his core rather than his shoulders to deliver the strike, with strength and power instead of effort. All the while I watched as the instrument of my death hurtled down towards me. I knew a hundred ways to avoid the blow, but I did nothing. I was rooted to the spot. No part of me would move, no muscle would respond, no nerve would twitch, no fibre would listen to the torrent of commands screaming from my sub-conscious. It was as if I was observing a dream in which I was dead already.

But in his hurry to end me, Tanaka's awareness failed him. As the sword passed over his head, the tip struck a low hanging bundle of electrical cables and jammed solid. Tanaka tugged at the sword, but it wouldn't come free.

Wake up!

I lept to my feet, sprang forward, grabbed hold of Tanaka's hands and kicked hard to his chest. He flew backwards, releasing his grip on the sword, and clattered to the floor. Taiyo was in my hands now. I pulled downwards. It came free, immediately, effortlessly.

I moved instinctively before I heard the shot. The air shimmered as the bullet missed by millimetres. I was on the gunman before he could fire again, striking him on the hand with the hilt of the sword, sending his weapon spiralling across the metal floor. It didn't get me far though, as all the others had drawn their firearms and were aiming at me. I stood still.

"Hold your fire!" It was Tanaka.

He got up. It was still eight against one, but this time the one had the sword. We faced each other, a Mexican standoff.

All they had to do was to squeeze their happy finger and I'd be gone. Even if I rushed forward swinging wildly, they'd cut me down instantly. So what was stopping them?

"Give me the sword." Tanaka said, in accented but good English.

"Fuck you," I replied.

"Give me the sword and your family will not be hurt."

If it feels wrong, it is wrong.

I should have listened to myself. I didn't believe him, though. If Tanaka and his team had been tracking my movements closely enough to ambush me here, they wouldn't need to ransom the ones I loved. Yet if they wanted Taiyo, then why didn't they shoot? They weren't going to, that's why. The tall one said so himself; *'It must be done with the sword.'* In which case they could put a bullet in a knee and make it easy for themselves. So, what was stopping them? And what the fuck was I supposed to do now?

The answer, when it came, was as silent as a whisper, as formless as a shadow, as elusive as a ghost – and as devastating as the typhoon that was raging outside.

A shuriken, the Ninja five-pointed star, flashed through the air. It struck one of Tanaka's men in the arm, causing him to cry out in agony and drop his weapon. I rolled to one side as multiple weapons fired. But in the semi-darkness they shot blindly, not knowing where to aim. More shuriken spun through from the shadows, hitting more men, causing panic as their pistols came crashing to the floor.

"Stand your ground." Tanaka shouted, but it made no difference.

Then the shadow itself was upon them. It moved fast, effortlessly, silently. The last two still holding their weapons fired at the emptiness as the form ghosted between them, pure luck preventing them from hitting each other. The shadow was carrying a crooked-hanbo and hooked the taller one behind his leg, sending him spinning, then used the same weapon to hook the last remaining man by the neck. He was down. They were all down, expect for Tanaka – the only one who had been brave enough to stand his ground. The shadow kicked away the nearest pistols. The situation was under control.

I'd never seen anything like it in my life. But I knew who the shadow was. I'd seen her move before, not like that, but I recognized the figure, the shape, the underlying grace and power. It was Naomi, dressed as a Kunoichi, a female Ninja and was, absurdly, carrying an umbrella, not the hooked-hanbo I'd thought it was. As Yamaguchi-san had foretold, she was there when I needed her most.

"I was wondering when you'd be turning up again," I said in my best 007 voice, but I doubted I'd ever be so grateful to see anyone ever again.

"We must go, Peter-san," she said.

"You will not get far, Mister Mamoribito." It was Tanaka, yet another who believed these stories about me. He would do, I realized, if he was on Ohno's team.

I took a step forward and put the tip of the sword to his throat. For the first time since we had met, he looked scared. They all did. "What have you done with my family?"

Naomi put a hand on my arm. "Peter, leave him," she said.

"I want an answer, Tanaka."

"No, Peter." Naomi pulled gently at my sleeve. "We will find them, but we must leave this place, now."

"Naomi, I need to know."

"Trust me. But we must hurry." She tugged at my sleeve again, harder this time. "Peter!"

"Ok," I said, realizing that trusting her was the better option.

Naomi turned and ran. I followed as she led the way down the stairs. Behind us Tanaka screamed, *"After them, you idiots!"* But they'd have to be quick to catch us, and with those shuriken injuries I doubted they had the speed, or the nerve, to do so.

As we hurried off the bottom step a security guard was nervously approaching, dressed in a clear plastic one-sheet to fend off the rain, phone to his ear. He must have heard the shots but not fully realized what they were – the wind was causing all sorts of cables and loose bits of equipment to clatter against each other – but he'd been brave enough to step out of the relative safety of his hut and check. Or possibly he had seen a group of heavies charging up the stairs, one carrying a Samurai sword. What he would make of a long-haired Japanese woman and some gaijin rushing past, with the gaijin carrying that same sword and the woman wearing Ninja clothing and carrying an umbrella, was anybody's guess. Either way, the phone in his ear meant the police were likely on their way. I admired his courage.

Naomi shouted as we raced past, *"Don't go up there!"*

I was pretty sure he wouldn't.

The main entrance to the building site was partially open, with a chain covering the gap. Naomi maintained pace and somersaulted over it, discarding the umbrella on the other side when she landed. I slowed, lifted the chain and went underneath, wondering if there was anything this incredible woman wasn't capable of. I followed Naomi as she took a convoluted path through the little alleys and passages that littered this part of Tokyo, a route I suspected was to provide some obscurity from prying eyes – I was carrying a sword, after all. We raced up steps, vaulted over fences and darted along the side of small rivulets whose natural embankments had long-ago been concreted to match the city that was growing around them. I had no idea where we were going, but wherever it was, it was away from Tanaka and his men.

The rain was torrential, the wind fierce, urging us to take shelter, but that didn't slow Naomi down. Nor me. We ran for five minutes before we exited from yet another narrow pedestrian passageway onto a street wide enough for two cars. Naomi stopped in a covered doorway that formed the entrance to a small one-room apartment block.

"We must wait here," she said.

"OK," I panted.

Naomi gently pushed my hand behind my back until the

sword was concealed behind my right leg.

"People may see," she said.

"Good point."

A police siren passed nearby, then another. I couldn't see them, but I had a good idea where they were heading, although they'd be too late – Tanaka and his men would be long gone by the time they got there.

A middle-aged salaryman came out from the Seven Eleven store across the street, carrying an umbrella, which turned inside out as soon as he opened it. I laughed; I couldn't help it. What else did he expect in the middle of a typhoon? The man walked towards our doorway, head down against the wind and rain, the now-useless umbrella still in his hand. If he lived here, then why bother with the umbrella?

Naomi put her arms around me and pulled herself closer. "Pretend we are lovers, sheltering here from the storm."

"OK," I said as Naomi buried her head under my chin.

I put my free hand around Naomi's slender waist and held her tight. We were both soaking wet, our clothes sticking to us like waterlogged sheets. Vapour rose from our embrace despite the warmth of the equatorial air brought by the typhoon – we'd been running hard, and the heat of bodies was enough to overcome the one hundred percent humidity surrounding us. I could feel the toned muscles in Naomi's back, her breathing against my chest, her gazelle-legs pressed against mine, the light caress of her fingers on the back of my neck. Any more of this and I wouldn't be able to keep up the pretence.

The man stumbled past our doorway and headed down the narrow passageway next to the building, where there was some shelter. At least that explained why he thought he needed an umbrella, although it still wouldn't do him any good. A pair of large headlights was approaching.

"He's gone, but there's a bus coming," I said. "And there's a bus stop about twenty yards from here."

"We must wait."

Our faces were inches apart. For the first time I realized Naomi's eyes were dark green and had an incredible ability to see right through to one's soul – my soul. Who was this extraordinary woman who had saved my life? I hardly knew her, yet there was a connection between us, more than physical proximity, something deeper. If she'd asked me to take her to infinity and beyond, I'd have dropped everything and climbed aboard the nearest interstellar cruiser. But I had a family that I loved, a wife and child who needed me, and a million questions that needed answers.

"Naomi, what the hell is going on?" I asked.

"Soon you will remember, then all will become clear."

She was doing it again. "Why do you always talk to me in riddles?"

"Because of who you are."

"I'm Peter Walker, and we've already had this conversation. Now, please tell me, in simple English, what's happening?"

"There is no time. They have your family. You must go to them, now."

"Why? Why take my family?"

"You know why."

"No I don't." I may have understood the words that Yamaguchi-san had said, but knowing and understanding are not the same thing.

The bus stopped and began to discharge its passengers, one of whom sprinted straight past us into the apartment block, handbag covering her head, unaware that we were there.

"How did you know," I said as the apartment door closed, "that I needed you?"

"I was in Matsumoto-Sensei's dojo, training with my cousins. But I concealed myself, then followed you," she said, doing that thing with her eyes again. "And I already knew you would come."

"Were you training with umbrellas?"

"Uncle gave it to me. You should have taken it yourself."

So, Yamaguchi-san was Naomi's uncle. Make that her great uncle. What next?

The bus moved away, windscreen wipers furiously ineffective against the rain. Behind the bus was a Subaru WRX, the street version of the Impreza rally car. It stopped outside the Seven Eleven. The driver got out and bolted into the store, his head low, as if that would make a difference.

"You must go," Naomi urged. "They need you."

I didn't require persuasion, but home was close to three hundred kilometers away, and I was sure Shinkansen operations would soon stop – and anyway, hopping on board with a samurai sword in my hand would raise more than a few eyebrows. My mind raced as I figured out what to do.

"Come with me, Naomi," I said. "I need you."

"I cannot. This, you must do alone. And the true Mamoribito does not need me to protect him."

"For God's sake, Naomi, I'm not this bloody mammyburito."

"Mamoribito. Ma-mo-ri-bi-to. Your Japanese is terrible. Mamoru means protect. Hito means person. Together, Mamoribito, the one who protects."

"Does that matter right now?"

She kissed me, harder this time than before.

"What was that for?"

"They need you. Now go!" She pointed to the Subaru. The driver was still inside the Seven Eleven. He'd left the engine running, the lights on. People in Japan were way too trusting. "There! Take it!"

"I can't just steal it," I said, although I'd been planning on doing just that.

"Then borrow it. Now go!"

"Ok. Ok."

I released my hold on her, took the rucksack off my back and took a step forward into the rain. There was one more thing on my mind. I looked backward over my shoulder.

"Thank you, Naomi, for saving my life."

She smiled. "When we meet again, I will tell you

everything."

"You said that last time," I replied.

And with that I ran across the street towards my chariot of fire.

Fourteen

You're supposed to capture a vehicle stealthily, approaching from an unseen quarter, ideally a blind spot behind a pillar beyond the view of the driver or his mirrors, crouching below the line of the windows and quietly opening the door before climbing gently on board to avoid creating a give-away wobble of the suspension.

I ignored that and jumped straight in, throwing Taiyo on to the passenger seat along with my rucksack. Not bothering with the seat belt, I slammed it into gear and blasted away, the intelligent four-wheel drive system struggling to cope with the demands of its unintelligent driver. I glanced at the rear-view mirror – the owner was running down the street after me, waving his arms and shouting. He fell to his knees with his head in his hands. The poor bugger must have really loved his car.

"Don't worry, you'll get it back," I said as I took a sharp right hander that would take me to the motorway on-ramp that lay a short distance north of Tokyo Sky Tree.

During the short dash across the street from the shelter of the door where Naomi and I had stood, I'd figured out the quickest way home, my actions upon arriving there, where and when I would call Yuko, what I was going to tell her, and alternative actions in case any of those didn't work. It was the fastest I'd ever put together a mission plan, and I'd have at least four hours on the motorway to figure out where it was all going to fall to pieces, but those hours were part of the plan, too. What wasn't part of the plan was the soft cry I heard coming from the rear. I pulled the mirror down and across. A young woman was sitting there, right behind my seat, with a baby in her lap, sheer terror on her face, too scared to scream.

I stopped the car next to a Denny's. *"I'm sorry,"* I said, in my inadequate Japanese. "*It's an emergency. Please wait in there.*" I pointed to the restaurant. It would provide shelter until her husband arrived. The woman gathered her bags and got out without saying a word. I felt awful scaring her and then forcing her out into the storm, but it was a short walk and she would soon be safe and dry.

When mother and child were inside, I took off my rain-sodden jacket and covered Taiyo with it – there were pedestrians sheltering under a nearby bus stop and I was exposed enough as it was. I didn't bother setting the GPS. I knew the way and it would waste precious time figuring out the Japanese interface and dialling in the route, and I could track my position by looking at the screen anyway.

I fastened the seat belt and moved off, slowly, so as not to attract attention.

The entrance to the inner Tokyo motorway system was three hundred yards dead ahead, and was still open, despite the storm. Good. I drove through the automated gates and whispered a quiet thank you to the car owner for having an ETC card on board to pay the toll, plus having the foresight to fill up the tank. I'd pay him back later, somehow. It did mean the police could track my movements, though, but I had a hunch they'd have a lot more on their minds tonight than a stolen vehicle. My one worry was if they set up a license recognition protocol on subsequent toll gates. I was in a Subaru WRX, albeit an older model, and with a big power bulge on the bonnet and an even bigger spoiler on the boot it was hardly inconspicuous. But I could outdrive and outrun anything they had. And if they did give chase, well, I might need the help of the Japanese boys-in-blue anyway, so

I could just keep going and lead them straight home.

I leant over and retrieved my phone from a jacket inside pocket. I called Yuko. She always had the phone next to her, but there was no answer. I called again and let it ring. Still no answer. I called the hotel landline, praying that Yuko's phone was somehow acting up. No answer. My heart sank; I knew there was no longer any point trying.

#

Twenty minutes later I was on the Kan-Etsu Expressway, the main artery that led all the way to Niigata on the Japan Sea coast. The motorway was half-deserted: only mad dogs and Englishmen would be out in this kind of weather. I wanted to go flat out, but the typhoon was overhead and it was all I could do just to keep it in one lane. The rain was beyond torrential, and even with the wipers on the fastest setting I could barely make out a hundred yards of road. It was going to take everything I knew, every ounce of experience, every grain of concentration to get back in one piece, let alone break any records doing so. But when you're desperate, you take desperate measures.

It was two hundred and fifty kilometers to Nagano, then another twenty-three up the mountain to our hotel. On a normal day in normal traffic and normal weather I could do that in a sensible four hours. Today was the least normal day of my life, and I didn't have four hours, but there wasn't a damn thing I could do to go any quicker. I was dangerously quick as it was – at one hundred and twenty-five kilometers per hour I was already three times faster than the emergency signs were telling me to go. If I could have seen another ten yards, I'd have added another ten to my speed.

There was nothing I could do, except drive, think and pray.

#

Eighty intense but uneventful minutes later I entered the first of a series of tunnels. We'd driven this route every other weekend for the best part of six years taking Miki to see her grandparents, and I knew it well. The tunnel was long, straight, and empty – I hadn't seen another vehicle for the last thirty kilometers. I put my foot down, and even though I was soon doing one-ninety I could relax. I let it all sink in, the whole day, from the mountain eagle in the morning, through the battle of the construction site and the almost erotic embrace with Naomi afterwards, to the tiny baby sleeping in its mother's arms in the back seat – and all points in-between.

I knew what had happened, but I understand very little of it. Was I this Mamoribito? Of course not – I would know if I was, and I didn't know, even if everyone else thought they did. Shit, even Tanaka thought he knew. I just wanted to know why the fuck he wanted to kill me. I needed to find someone who could tell me, who could lay it out all clearly, unambiguously. But that would have to wait – my family were in danger, and I had put them there. If there was any proof needed that I wasn't the Mamoribito, then it was my own stupidity. How could I have been so blind, so inept, so-

Christ!

The end of the tunnel was approaching fast, and with it the violence of the typhoon. I'd been too wrapped up in my own thoughts and hadn't been paying attention to what was going on around me. I pumped the brakes in a frantic attempt to slow down without locking the wheels and aquaplaning into something hard and unyielding – too late, we blasted through the exit into a solid wall of rain. It was like driving through Niagara Falls, but with less visibility and no life jacket. I had no clue where the road was or where I was in relation to it. We hit a pool of water. I hadn't seen it on the road, but I could feel it under my hands and see its effect as spray surged past the side windows.

The car turned sideways. Christ, we starting to rotate. I jumped hard on the brakes and clutch to force the spin into

the smallest possible area, instinct from racing on dry tarmac. Not the best thing to do in the wet, and the worst thing to do in this kind of wet, but it was too late – we were committed. We revolved three times before coming to a stop. Taiyo, covered and protected by my jacket, stayed lodged firmly between the passenger seat and door. If it had been flung around, I'd have saved Tanaka the trouble of cutting me in half. We sat there, car, sword and driver, in the middle of the motorway, facing who knew what direction, glad to be alive but scared shitless.

I did a quick debrief. I had decelerated for the exit, but I must have still been doing at least one fifty when I charged into the storm, and that was bordering on insanity, even in this brilliant car. Slamming the brakes on had fortuitously resulted in a tight spin that kept us away from the crash barrier that formed the last line of defence before the rock of the mountain. Instinct can indeed be your friend. But there was no time to sit and congratulate myself on my amazing driving skills; I had to get moving before another fool did the same thing and smashed into us. Ahead I could make out two feint orange lights which I knew to be the next long tunnel. Three full rotations and still facing forward, and still alive. I patted the steering wheel. "Thank you," I said, and moved off.

I kept the speed at a reasonable rate and did a double check on the petrol gauge. The tank was three-quarters full, and although the GPS showed Nagano City was still a hundred plus kilometers distant, it was more than I would need. That said, I wouldn't get there at all if I lost concentration again.

This brilliant car.

It suddenly struck me – how had Naomi known about the car? She had led me straight to it, as if she'd been expecting the Subaru to be there, but that what have required an impossible level of planning ahead. Was she psychic, clairvoyant? Or just lucky? She might be all three. God, I wished she had come with me. And if it meant getting kissed again, then that was a risk I would be glad to take. Naomi had a thing about me. Christ knew why – I certainly didn't. I was going to have to work out that little problem at some stage before I started having a thing about her.

I exited the tunnel at more controlled speed that was still too quick for the conditions, but I was past worrying about little things like that.

#

Sixty kilometers later, the chances of getting home quickly, or even at all, suddenly became bleak.

It was thirty minutes since I had narrowly avoided totalling both the car and myself. Thirty minutes I'd spent thinking things through, planning and re-planning what I'd do if Yuko and Miki were still safely in the hotel with a broken telephone system and a failed cell phone network; what I'd do if they were being held hostage there; what I would do if they weren't there at all; and what I'd do if Mr. Angry's men tried to re-acquire me there – which I would if I was them. I prepared myself for all eventualities, including ones I didn't want to think about. My desperation level was rising, too. I kept seeing Miki's frightened face as men with guns crashed uninvited through the front door.

Every second of delay made it worse – but the flash of police patrol-car lights five kilometers ahead had turned all my carefully laid plans upside down.

I slowed to the required speed limit. Was I going to have to stop? There was nowhere to go, and the next exit was roughly were those lights were. Precisely where those lights were, I realized, as I got closer. Temporary barriers were extended across both lanes of the motorway, and a red warning message was pulsing on the overhead electronic signalling system. At this distance I could just make out the kanji for *yamakuzure* – landslide – which explained the road closure, and although it meant they were unlikely to be stopping traffic to search for stolen vehicles, this stolen vehicle in particular, it also meant that I would have to either take the old road that ran roughly parallel to the motorway or the very local road through the mountains – as if either would be any less likely to not have a landslide of its own.

I'd faced the same choice a couple of years earlier when there had been a flood. The same exit, too – the Japan Highway Corporation should do something about incident prevention. I decided on the mountain route, gambling that other traffic, light as it was, would steer clear of that. It was technically a shorter route to the hotel and on a good day in the right conditions it could be faster, but you'd have to be going rally-driver quick to make it into one. Not an option I'd usually take, except today it was the only option worth considering. On the other hand, if there was even a solitary truck ahead of me on those narrow, twisty roads I'd be in trouble.

With no feasible alternative, I headed down the exit ramp. The police lights stayed where they were. Either they hadn't been looking for the Subaru or hadn't seen the license plate through the rain diffused glare of my oncoming headlights. Either way it didn't matter. My mind was set on one thing, and one thing alone – getting home.

#

I drove flat out.

My luck was holding – the mountain road was deserted. The Subaru was built for this wild, white-knuckle driving – and so was I. Maximum throttle, maximum braking and controlled four-wheel drive power slides through tight hairpins gave me the feeling that I was flying, going quicker than any part of the journey so far. I wasn't in fact, not compared to doing a steady hundred and twenty on a half-empty two-lane national highway, but at least I felt my destiny was in my own hands.

The rainstorm was easing, and although the wind was still strong it was less of a handful in the lee of the mountains than it had been on the open Ken-Etsu. A flash of lighting lit up the clouds, but it was a long way off and the car would act as a Faraday cage if we got hit. I wasn't worried, not about the weather.

The kilometers dialled down, forty, thirty, twenty, ten. It was completely dark, the twilight negated by the thick cloud cover. My plan, if that's what it could be called, was to leave the car a safe distance from the hotel and use the cover of both the storm and the night to climb in through the unlocked boiler room. I wouldn't have time to do a full external reconnoitre, save for checking if the GT-R was in the car park, but that didn't matter. If they were expecting me, which I had to assume that were, concealment would be my weapon – the rest of it I would handle once I got inside. If the bastards were armed, well, I had Taiyo and knew the hotel like the back of my hand, and if they had –

Fuck!

I slammed on the brakes – far too late. We smashed straight into the rockface at the far edge of a tight right-hander. I'd done it again, losing concentration at a crucial moment, applying too much power too early for the four-wheel drive to cope. We'd aquaplaned straight into the side of the mountain.

Come on Walker, focus, for Christ's sake!

As I reversed a nasty, teeth-grating scrape came from the front left. I stopped, angry with myself for being so careless, and opened the driver's door. The wind was stronger than I expected and nearly blasted the door clean out of my hands. Stepping out into the rain was another pleasant surprise – as if my getting out of the car was a signal for the taps to be set to full. A bolt of lightning split the night, no more than a kilometer away judging by the time it took the thunderclap to arrive. King Lear and his fool had nothing on this idiot.

In the soft illumination of a roadside light I could see that the front left of the car had taken the full impact of my little escapade with the mountain. The damage wasn't as bad I had feared, but with the front offside compressed like that the car was undriveable. I tugged hard at the wheel arch. The metal stubbornly resisted, but with a foot hard on the tire and applying all the force I could muster I moved it clear of the wheel. Far from perfect, but it would do.

I got back into the car and took a moment to settle myself. I breathed deeply, re-setting my *Ki*. I should have done that earlier, after the tunnel, but now was better than never. The GPS showed about five kilometers to go – another ten minutes or so and I'd be home. I removed Taiyo from under my jacket and held it across my lap. "What are you?" I asked, though I doubted I'd welcome the answer.

Another lighting flash lit up the area, followed instantly by a colossal crash of thunder. That was close. I was right in the middle of a thunderstorm, taking the lead role my own private horror show.

Then everything got completely terrifying.

A fist-sized stone landed on the bonnet with a resounding thud, making such a deep indent that it must have fallen from way up above. Another one crashed on the road in front of the car. I looked up through the windscreen.

Oh, Jesus!

I'd never seen a landslide before, let alone been sitting in the path of one. Everything happened in slow motion. Smaller rocks and stones cascaded around the car as a burst of lighting illuminated the scene above, camera flashing a thousand tons of boulders sliding down the side of the mountain straight towards me.

Get out!

With one hand on Taiyo I opened the door, simultaneously jumping and falling out of the car as the full force of the landslide hit. The noise was incredible, obliterating everything. All my thought, my awareness, my entire sense of self was lost in the cacophony surrounding me. I had one impulse – to survive. A large rock collided with a larger boulder and cartwheeled straight towards my face. In pure adrenalin-fuelled instinctive terror I leapt over the crash-barrier into the darkness beyond.

I fell through the trees towards the sheer cliff of the valley below. I let go of Taiyo and desperately grabbed at a branch, any branch. I could see nothing, absolutely nothing in the blackness. Panic gripped me as a thousand wooden fingers clawed at my clothing and skin. I kept tumbling onwards and downwards, unable to stop myself. A thick bough slipped through my fingers as the line of trees ended.

I was falling in free space.

This is the end.

A lightning bolt split the night. In that instant I saw everything; the stream that cut through the valley below, the majestic beauty of the mountains above, the storm-blown forest strobed into position by the flash. I felt the wind in my hair, the rain on my face and sensed the single heartbeat that measured the slice of time I had been gifted to understand the most important lesson that anybody could possibly learn – I was alive!

Then I crashed into a tree and felt a hand grip the hilt of Taiyo as I swung under the branches, my legs dangling precariously a hundred yards above the floor of the valley.

I pulled myself up and lay face down on the trunk, shaking with adrenalin. A series of lightning flashes showed how close I had come to disaster. I'd free-fallen twenty-feet, no more, but they were the longest twenty-feet of my life. The tree that had saved me was the last one before the precipice, growing alone below the trees above, perpendicular to the cliff face, as if it had been waiting its whole solitary existence for me to call upon it for help. Taiyo must have fallen ahead of me and lodged itself across the branches of my tree. I couldn't explain how my hand had found it, nor the incredible sliver of improbability that had resulted in it being there for me to grab hold of.

I checked myself for injuries. I had plenty of them, but they were relatively minor scratches and soon-to-be bruises.

Nothing was broken. I looked up. The streetlight was visible through the trees, blinking in and out of existence as the wind buffeted the branches, and before then there were plenty of small rocky protrusions for me to grab hold of. Not an easy ascent, but I could do it. I pulled the belt from my jeans and made a make-shift shoulder strap for Taiyo. I'd have to be careful not to dislodge it as I climbed, but compared to everything else that had happened tonight, this was going to be the easy part.

#

Thirty minutes later, as I clambered exhausted over the crash barrier, I had long since changed my mind about it being the easy part. At least I was still in one piece. The Impreza, on the other hand, had disappeared under the gigantic pile of rock, mud and debris that had surged down the mountainside, the pale light from the streetlight barely able to illuminate the full extent of the devastation. If the owner were here, he'd definitely be on his knees. Maybe I should do the same and beg for his forgiveness.

I stared at the incredible scene, conscious that I'd had a lucky escape, but at the same time wondering if I hadn't caused the landslide by smashing into the mountain in the first place.

It was five kilometers to our hotel. My phone, jacket and rucksack were still in the car. I was soaking wet, covered with cuts and scratches, with a Samurai sword strapped to my back, standing in the middle of thunderstorm, itself part of one of the biggest typhoons to hit Japan in the past thirty years. People I didn't know were trying to kill me. Other people I hardly knew were telling me that I didn't know who I was. The one thing I did know was that my wife and child were in danger, and I was standing by the side of the road staring at a mound of rubble.

I turned and headed up the mountain road towards home as fast as my aching legs could carry me.

Fifteen

The lights were on in our hotel, giving a sense of normalcy, of nothing out of place, of life going on undisturbed, unhindered, troubled by neither the typhoon nor the guests that must have surely been the owners of the Honda hatchback that, apart from Octavius, was the sole occupant of the visitor car park. Except that the hotel wasn't open for business, the guests were uninvited, and life was anything but normal.

The best part of six hours had passed since I'd left Naomi outside a convenience store in downtown Tokyo. Six long hours lost in the struggle to get where I was now, concealed in the mountain forest, with everything I loved less than thirty yards distant, but now a lifetime away.

I'd had a flash of hope when I noticed our family Toyota wasn't there, thinking that perhaps Yuko had managed to flee, but Ohno's men must have taken it along with Yuko and Miki – and to find them I'd have to make myself into the alluring bait that the piranha Ohno couldn't resist.

The architects had placed the boiler room away from the main part of the hotel, primarily for safety reasons but also to make it easier for the kerosene delivery trucks to fill the tank. Good, it would give me cover and a way in, although I wasn't worried about being observed as the lighting here was non-existent and no-one would hear me above the wind, even though the storm was subsiding.

I dashed across the open area to the back of the hotel, where I quickly found the length of discarded drainpipe that I'd left there from an unfinished repair weeks earlier. I carefully put Taiyo inside the piping. The irony of what I was doing wasn't lost on me, but it had occurred to me that whatever was going on in Ohno's twisted mind, he wanted both me and the sword, together. I expected his men were armed, I would be if I were them, but I had a few ideas on how to deal with that eventuality, most of which included the sword on the wall in my study – provided I could get there undetected.

I opened the boiler-room window and climbed in, thankful that the broken lock was another unfinished item on my to-do list. It was pitch black inside, but I knew my way around and kept my fingertips touching the wall to guide me to the door, which opened with a subdued grinding sound that I hoped was inaudible to anyone more than ten feet away. I stopped and listened in case I was wrong. It was deathly quiet, save for the wind rocking the shutters on the guest rooms. Yuko must have closed them herself, another job I had failed to do today.

The corridor that led to the main part of the hotel was dimly lit, and empty. Guests, when we were ready to accommodate them, would leave their outdoor shoes at the entrance and wear slippers inside the building. I was going to do nothing of the sort, but my trainers were still wet and I'd have to tread carefully to avoid squelching my presence to anyone nearby. As for the trail of footprints I'd leave in my wake, well, there wasn't anything I could do about that.

I moved forward slowly, keeping lower than the window line, timing my movements with surges in the wind to cover the sound I was making. The door at the end of the corridor led to the main kitchen. I could see through the frosted glass that a light was on. I crouched, listening, waiting – then slid the door open an inch and a half, enough for me to see the whole kitchen, which was silent and deserted. The only hiding place was between the freezer and the fridge, and the likelihood that anyone would squeeze themselves into that tiny space wasn't worth considering.

I'd made the same journey multiple times in the past few months, in and out of the boiler room, back through the kitchen, back again to the boiler room, trying vainly to fix the thing, which had proved way beyond my capabilities. Each time Honey had been waiting for me – so where was she now?

I waited for a stronger gust of wind, slid the door fully open and went in. I had two choices; take the far exit through to the lobby or the nearby exit that led to the guest dining area. The lights in the dining area were on, as were the lights in the main part of the hotel – I'd seen both when I had been outside. Neither route offered any advantages, but I couldn't stay where I was – the lack of hiding spaces in the kitchen also meant being badly exposed. I had to assume they were expecting me. So, where would they have laid their little trap? Upstairs in the front entrance? Too open and too obvious, and Peter Walker-san could run back out of the front door if he needed to – but it would give them a clear view of the car park and they could choose their ground. I wasn't coming in through the front door, though, and I expected they were smart enough to figure that one out for themselves.

What about downstairs? With twenty sets of chairs and tables, the dining room offered plenty of opportunity for concealment, but it was hard to escape from if things went wrong, which would also make it easier for them to confine me in there. The logical route was to head upstairs, past the main breaker box and cut the lights. I had considered that idea on the drive up, but having left my handy night vision goggles back at the barracks it wasn't my first choice – it would even things out, though. The fact that they hadn't done the same thing meant they were unlikely to have brought their handy night vision goggles with them either.

I took a step towards the main stairs and stopped dead in my tracks, my eye caught by something lying motionless on the dining room floor. Not something; someone. Someone

precious, irreplaceable, beautiful, loving, and above all, loyal.
Honey.

It was obviously a trap, but I didn't care. I walked across the kitchen and into the dining room, not bothering to conceal myself or hide the sound of my footsteps. I knelt next to Honey, my knees in the pool of blood that surrounded her. She had been shot twice at close range. Poor, brave Honey. Defending her home and family, mercilessly killed for no reason. You can tell a lot about someone by the way they treat animals, and this told me everything I needed to know.

I sensed movement behind me. I kept still, tears clouding my eyes, my hands on Honey's lifeless form, stoking her soft hair. I heard two clicks, the unmistakeable sounds of someone releasing the safety and cocking the hammer on a handgun.

"Don't move!" It may have felt like a command to him, but to me it signalled amateurs trying to be professionals. I stood up and turned around.

"I said, don't move!"

There were two of them, both armed with Colt Delta Elites nervously pointed in my direction, not what I would have thought to be the weapon of choice for this crew. There had only been one set of clicks, too, so it was odds-on one of these fools had neglected to release his safety. From this angle I couldn't be sure which. Did they even know how to use their weapons? Even if they didn't, at this range they were hardly likely to miss.

One of them had a phone in his free hand. He dialled and spoke in Japanese.

"This is Suzuki. He is here but does not have the sword." Suzuki listened for instructions while the other one glared. *"Understood!"* he barked into the phone like the loyal soldier he was. Suzuki addressed me, "Give me a sword. No sword, no family."

I kept silent and motionless, all the while planning, rehearsing, imagining. Come a couple of steps closer, my friend…

Suzuki took a step forward. "Give it me!"

"I don't have it," I said. "It fell down the side of the mountain."

"You lie! You have it!"

"Pull the trigger, shit for brains, and see for yourself." I was buying time, trying to destabilize him, to put him off balance. The one glaring at me moved to his left. I could see both weapons now, and both hammers were back. I'd been wrong about the clicks.

"Suzuki!" The voice come though the earpiece.

Suzuki put the phone back to his ear, taking his eyes off me for a split second. That was all the invitation I needed. I sprang forward, grabbed his pistol while pivoting on one leg, turning the business end away from me as I ripped it from his grip. Unbalanced, Suzuki fell backwards as the second man fired, his aim disturbed by Suzuki falling through his line of sight. I leapt over a dining table, keeping one hand firmly on the front edge and using my momentum to turn it on to its side as I crashed through two chairs, sending them flying. Rounds blasted into the thick wood, the crack of the shots reverberating around the confines of the dining room, splinters flying as the soft lead bullets almost penetrated through to the other side – my side. At close range the noise can be deafening, and if you've never experienced it before it can scare the wits out of you. I was plenty scared, despite having heard it before, and in a smaller room, too, but adrenalin was scorching through my veins and at times like this training takes over. I leapt again, just as a round tore through the weakening wood, and fired a single shot in mid-air.

I had no idea what training manual that move was from, but it worked. The gunman, hit in the arm above the elbow, screamed in pain and dropped his weapon. Suzuki was still on the floor, cowering – he was as scared as I had been, minus the adrenalin.

"Suzuki! Suzuki! What's happening?" It came from the

earpiece of Suzuki's phone, which had spun out of his hand when I'd cartwheeled him to the ground.

I ignored the phone and picked up the Colt. Now I had both. I pulled the magazine from the one that Suzuki's accomplice had dropped and put it in my back pocket, then put the weapon on the table next to me. In the unlikely event one of them made a grab for the gun, it wouldn't do either of them much good.

The injured man was holding his arm tightly, blood seeping through his fingers, in obvious pain.

"You," I said to Suzuki. "Take off your tie, take off his jacket and then tie his arm." Suzuki did as he was told, his colleague wincing in silent agony. He was tougher than he looked, unless his arm had already gone numb.

"Suzuki!" The voice was anxious.

I picked up the phone. "Suzuki-san can't come to the phone right now, he's indisposed," I said, and put the device face up on the table in loudspeaker mode. It had gone quiet at the sound of my voice, but I wanted whoever was on the other end to know who was in control here.

"Now, take off your own jacket, put it on the floor."

Suzuki did my bidding.

"Turn around, both of you." As they did, I could see there was nothing in their back pockets; no phone, no hidden ammunition, no knives. Whatever they had was in their jackets.

"In there, please, gentlemen," I said, pointing to the kitchen. It wasn't a request. I followed them in.

"That door. Open it." I nodded to the pantry. There was a large, chunky padlock on the door, one of Yuko's insistences that I'd thought pointless at the time but now I welcomed her great foresight. Suzuki twisted the key to undo the lock.

"In you go," I said.

Suzuki put his hand on his partner and shook his head. "His arm is injury."

Suzuki didn't have great English, but I wasn't going to

hold that against him. I was, however, perfectly willing to shoot them both were they stood for what they had done to Honey. The fact that I hadn't already was a careful calculation based on what I would have to tell the police later.

"Go in," I said.

Suzuki turned around. "No."

He'd probably been thinking that whatever happened I wasn't going to pull the trigger, or maybe he felt the need to show his boss that he wasn't going to give in so easily. I fired two quick shots at the floor between their legs, one bullet each. That shook them up.

"Ok, ok." Suzuki led the way in. I padlocked the door. It wouldn't take them much time and effort to break through the old hinges, but I didn't plan on still being there when they did. I checked their jackets and found a set of car keys and two wallets complete with driving licenses, but no second phone.

I returned to the dining room. The phone was still on the table where I'd left it – it was hardly likely to have gone anywhere. The line was still open. I picked it up and listened, hoping to catch them unaware, discussing their next steps. There was silence on the other end. Silence, that is, except for the soft breathing of a man waiting to hear something. He'd given up calling out Suzuki's name. I expected he was waiting for me. We stayed that way for a while, my second Mexican stand-off of the day.

"Is that mister Peter Walker?" said a voice. He was smart, this one. He must have heard the scrape as I picked up the phone. His tone was different from Mr. Angry's. The English was better, too, with a slight British accent. You can tell a lot from a couple of words, in this case it was enough to know that this was a man whose voice I'd heard a hundred times on the news, whose outspoken views on energy generation and foreign affairs polarized debate everywhere he went, a man whose wealth, power and reach far exceeded anything I could bring to the table. It was Ohno, the President of Ohno Industries. Naomi and Uncle Yamaguchi had been right. Of course they had. If only I'd listened.

I knelt down beside Honey, stroking her gently. "Fuck you, Ohno." I was in no mood to be polite.

"Oh dear, such manners," he said. "Indeed, this is Takashi Ohno. Now, I would say that we both have something each other wants. I suggest we conduct an exchange."

"You do anything to them, Ohno, and I'll hunt you down."

"Oh, I think not, Peter. I can live without Taiyo. It's not ideal, but I can do it. But you, I think you cannot live without the ones you love, can you?"

I already didn't like the way this conversation was going. Ohno held all the aces, and I all I had was a pair of jokers. "Where are they?" I said.

"Bring me my sword."

"It's not yours, Ohno."

"If you say so. But I will exchange it for your family."

I instantly disbelieved him, but I could see no alternative. "Where?" I asked.

"We'll send our location to the phone you are holding. It is not far from where you are now, an hour's drive at most. I suggest you do not contact the police. We will know if you do."

Ohno may well have had people everywhere, but that didn't mean I was going to take him at his word. "How do I know I can trust you?" I said.

"Well, I could ask how should I know if I can trust you?" he replied.

"Because I'm not full of shit."

"Well, let's say that depends on your point of view. We'll meet soon, Peter. I look forward to it."

The line went dead. I wasn't a trained hostage negotiator, but I didn't have to be one to know my performance on that call was nothing to be proud of. Ohno had won that exchange. I'd gifted it to him, given him everything he wanted; my anger, my fear, my emotion blocking my ability to think logically, clearly, strategically. I understood now, as if I ever needed to, the power that someone can have over you when they have everything you hold dear in their hands.

The phone buzzed with a text message containing a google map URL and the words, 'be there within an hour.' I opened the link. It was a map of a hydroelectric power station thirty kilometers to the north east at the foot of the dam at the Kakizakiku mountain man-made lake, in Niigata. I knew that lake, it was a popular place for family Sunday walks. I opened the satellite view and zoomed in. The plant looked old, built years ago. Part of Ohno's power empire, no doubt.

I considered my options. There weren't many. Heading back to Tokyo to find Naomi was out of the question. Conducting a clandestine attack on the power station and rescuing my family – sure, if I had a platoon of highly trained and ridiculously armed elites to help me out. Call the police? It would take too long to explain, and even then they wouldn't believe me. Plus, I had to accept that Ohno probably did have people there. I ran through more scenarios, but all of them led nowhere. No, there was only one thing I could do, only one course of action I could take.

#

I carried Honey into the back garden at the rear of the hotel so she could see the mountains. I didn't have time to bury her properly, so I covered her gently using a pile of stones that were ready for a garden wall that I'd scheduled for the following spring.

"Goodbye, sweet girl," I said.

I placed the wallets and car keys of our uninvited guests under a different pile of stones. I'd come back for them another day and hand them over to the authorities. Then I went back into the hotel, changed my clothing, and briefly searched around for Yuko's phone. It was nowhere to be found, which wasn't particularly surprising. I picked up the keys to the Mini from my study, along with a sports rucksack, into which I placed the two pistols, having replaced the magazine in the one I'd left on the table. I headed downstairs. Back in the kitchen muffled voices were coming from the pantry, and although I couldn't make out what Tweedledum and Tweedledee were saying, they didn't seem too concerned about their predicament. Neither was I.

I opened the top draw by the sink and took out two tea-towels, placing them in the rucksack. Then I went back to the boiler room, this time exiting through the door to the rear of the hotel and retrieved Taiyo from the drainpipe. I was ready.

Octavius the Mini was waiting for me, like the loyal servant he was, in the corner of the car park. I took the pistols from the rucksack and wrapped each with a tea-towel. I lifted the backseat and put one in the space underneath, the other I put in the driver's door pocket. Finally, I placed Taiyo and the rucksack on the rear seat and got in. It took three turns of the ignition to convince the starter motor to do its thing.

I looked across the car park to the hotel. It had been our life for the past year, and our guarantee of a brighter future. All that was gone now, replaced by a sinister cloak of darkness descending upon everything I held dear.

The wind was still blowing, the rain was still raining, but both were easing and would be gone in an hour, two at most. I glanced at the phone; nine thirty-three. By midnight the storm would have given way to the clear night sky, my family would be safe, and I would have met that obligation that every man must fulfill, the foundation upon which life itself is built and which manifests as the deep, unchangeable, immutable instinct to protect those that he loves, whatever the cost to himself.

I drove away, unsure if I would ever return.

Sixteen

I'd taken Yuko and Miki to the Kakizakiku mountain lake the previous spring to walk amongst the cherry blossoms that lined the waterside. At that time I hadn't known a lot about the hydroelectric power station, but now I knew that it was built at the base of the dam that had been constructed in nineteen sixty-three to stem the flow of the Kakizaki river, and provided 270 megawatts of power with a flow rate of 70 cubic meters per second – or so it said on the public information board at the main entrance. The sign also said that the power station was being reconditioned, and would open again in three months, which explained the trucks and construction equipment in the car park.

I drove through the gates and parked under a broken light. They were watching me, obviously, but I still preferred to stick to the shadows. I sat there, thinking, analysing, planning. If I did somehow manage to get away, I'd dip below the line of the car park wall, edge through the gap in the fence and make my way through the dark spots between the lights back to the Mini. From there, well, I'd make it up as I went along. I had been so far, so I might as well keep going with that tried-and-tested strategy. Even so, a voice was whispering inside me that I'd made the wrong choice. No, not whispering – yelling.

I ignored it. Coming here was the right decision. It had to be.

There were seven non-construction vehicles there, including a black limousine which I took to be Ohno's. The GT-R was there too, its sharp lines menacing in the night. The rest were people carriers and SUVs. Octavius could outrun them all on these twisty mountain roads, perhaps even that GT-R. That still necessitated me getting out, and I gave myself a fifty/fifty chance of that at best.

A nearby loudspeaker crackled into life. "Welcome, Peter. The main entrance, please." It was Ohno.

I picked up Taiyo from the backseat and got out of the Mini, leaving the keys in the ignition. "Where's my family?" I shouted towards a nearby security camera.

"I'm sorry, Peter. We can see you, but we cannot hear you. Now, drop the bag, please, and bring the sword. If you wouldn't mind."

I opened the car door and put my rucksack on the back seat. This had been one of the scenarios I'd considered on the way, an obvious move on Ohno's part. They'd search the rucksack, find it empty, then check the rest of the car, where they'd find the pistol in the door pocket soon enough. I doubted they'd think to look for the other one.

It was about thirty yards to the entrance of the power station. I walked slowly, deliberately, taking it all in. Five large diameter pipes ran down the long slope from the dam at the top of the hill behind the station – the water feed for the generators. Somewhere below my feet would be the run-off that led the water down to the river, or maybe it led to the lower reservoir from where it would be pumped back up at night to repeat the cycle. I had no idea. The building itself looked large enough to house several turbines and generators, five of them judging by the number of feeds. It also looked its age, although it wasn't in bad condition. Everything appeared normal. So why here?

Yuko and Miki were elsewhere. There was no reason that I could think of, strategic or tactical, for Ohno to bring them here. But then again, I could see no reason for any of this, so what the fuck did I know.

The main door opened. It was Tanaka, this time armed, as were the six men that followed him. They must have headed here straight after leaving me at the construction site, taking the other branch of the motorway and so avoiding the landslide. The six men formed a semi-circle behind me, keeping their distance. Interesting. They were scared of me, or at least had their reservations. Several had makeshift bandages on arms and legs that spoke of shuriken injuries, so that could be a pretty good reason why. Those four and five-pointed metal stars aren't designed to kill, instead they inflict pain – quite a lot of too, I hoped. People drop things when they get hit, such as swords and pistols, or can't walk properly, so you can escape fast into the night. I wasn't escaping anywhere fast, despite half-expecting Naomi to jump out of the shadows and take them all down for the second time, but she was nowhere to be seen. Of course not, she wouldn't be. I was on my own.

"Inside." Tanaka gestured towards the door. I did as I was told, and followed him into the building, Taiyo in hand.

The reception was spacious, with three sets of glass swing doors, all leading to different areas of the main building. To my right, a stairway provided access to what I assumed was the second-floor office area; but that was just an uneducated guess. There were six lounge-style seats for visitors, and a more spartan office chair for the receptionist behind the front desk. Except tonight the only receptionist was the one standing on the second-floor balcony.

"Ah, Peter-san. At last we meet," Ohno said, as he descended the stairs.

"Where is my family?" I knew they weren't here, but I needed to have some sense of keeping the initiative.

"Oh, they are waiting for you. But first, Taiyo, if you wouldn't mind."

"My family first."

"My sword, please, or my men will shoot." Ohno was half-way down the stairway. The face was familiar, unsurprisingly, considering the number of times he had been in the media. What I hadn't been expecting was how fit and powerful he was. He must have been at least seventy but looked fifty at most and moved with a grace and fluidity that belied his years. But it was the dark, fierce intensity of those emotionless eyes that got to me. I sensed danger, real danger: the kind that makes the hairs on the back of your neck stand up when everything seems just fine.

"You won't shoot me. You'd have done that already."

"Most astute. But that is why you came, isn't it, Peter, to trade your life for theirs. Most noble. Now, return to me my sword, and I'll let them live."

Any thoughts I had of escape vanished. There would be no way out of this, no magic road to freedom, no second chance for life, no negotiation, no winning goal at the final moments of the decisive game. This was the final, and I had lost. I could see that from the way his eyes fixed on mine. Despite what he said, Ohno wouldn't let Yuko and Miki live, I knew that he wouldn't. I'd gladly trade my life for theirs, but there would be no trade, no deal, no exchange. I had walked straight into a literal dead-end. Naomi was wrong. Yamaguchi-san was wrong. They were all wrong. I was no Mamoribito, no protector of others, no guardian of the sword. I was a fake, a fraud – a complete, utter, reprehensible fool.

I had nothing left.

Tanaka approached cautiously and took Taiyo from my grasp. I gave it up easily, totally defeated. Tanaka offered the sword to Ohno in the correct manner, as if this was nothing more than ceremony.

Tanaka stepped back.

"At last," Ohno said, as he examined the sword in much the same way I had done at Welton Hall. I interpreted that to mean this was the first time he had hands on Taiyo since it was returned to Japan.

Then he turned to Tanaka and ordered, "You know where to take him."

I didn't like the sound of that. Not at all.

Seventeen

The main turbine room was chilly, stark, and unforgiving.

I could see why they brought me here. Apart from the thick, heavy stainless-steel main doors and the small emergency exit, all of which were locked, there was no way out that I could see. The room itself was large, more aptly a hall than a room, and had clearly been designed to withstand a massive flood from a broken feed-pipe or a damaged casing, the thick concrete walls more than capable of withstanding the full force of the flow from the lake above.

There were five turbines in the room, each connected to a separate input flow from the dam, each of which would bring huge volumes of water rushing down the hill to spin the blades that in turn span the generators above my head. I couldn't see those generators directly, but I knew they were there, in the room above this, connected by fifteen-foot shafts to the turbines on the floor where I stood. Each assembly looked like the axle of an enormous truck, turned on its side, each wheel being either a turbine or its associated generator.

One of the turbines was partially disassembled, it's feed-pipe inspection hatch ominously removed. It wasn't the only removed hatch either. They all were, on all five turbines. Shit – this didn't look good. The hatches were wide enough for someone to get inside, but they would be impossibly slippery to climb. And even if you could, they would only lead to the reservoir sluice gates. I put that idea out of my mind. What about the run-off pipes? They'd be going downhill, towards the river. It could work, and I'd take my chances if I could find a way in. But for that I'd have to remove their inspection hatches, which were still firmly bolted in place, and there was no way I could enter through the open feed-pipe hatches and climb through the turbine blades to the exit pipe.

Scrap that idea.

I sat down on the concrete flooring. There was no use thinking this way – it wasn't going to lead anywhere. I knew why, though. It gave me something to do, something to hang my hopes to, a distraction from the reality of these four walls, this prison, this tomb.

So why was I still alive?

Tanaka and his team had purposely avoided shooting me at the construction site. It had to be done with the sword, they'd said. The two back in the hotel had different ideas, but Tanaka hadn't been there to control them. They had Taiyo. Ohno held it his own two hands. If slicing me in half was so important to them, why hadn't they done it? Why bring me down here, to this dungeon, in a non-operational hydroelectric power station? I thought of Yuko and Miki. I hoped to God I was wrong, that Ohno would let them live.

Christ, what was I thinking?

Let them live so they could tell the story of what had happened?

How could I have allowed things to come to this? I should have gone to the police straight away when Mike died. I could have put a stop to this right at the start. Why had I let Naomi talk me into taking the Impreza? I should have gone to the Japanese authorities then, instead of listening to her. They could have sent a car from Nagano and been at the hotel in thirty minutes. I'd walked into this, with my eyes wide shut.

I wept. Not the silent tears of a man yearning for his past, but the full, desperate sobbing of a man who had lost everything, and been the cause of it all. I was not this

Mamoribito. I was a nothing, a nobody, a fool. A thousand times a fool.

A loudspeaker crackled into life. I stood up. A ceiling mounted video camera turned towards me.

"Ah, there you are, Peter." It was Ohno. "Distressing, it is, I know, to have come so close, only to have failed at the last. It's strange, though, don't you think, that my men were afraid of you. They believed you could stop us, or even destroy us. One man. I too was fooled by the legend. For a while. Never mind, you still have your use, for which I am grateful."

"Let my family go, Ohno."

"I'm sorry Peter. I can see that you are talking but I cannot hear you. The refurbished plant will of course have microphonic facilities in key areas, but not today. Did you know this installation was once the largest of its type in Japan? No, of course you did not know that. Why should you."

I glared at the camera so Ohno could see me looking him straight in the eye.

"I wonder what you do in fact know, Peter. I expect they told you that you are the Mamoribito. I had thought so too, particularly after you defeated my men in Tokyo. Or was that the Kunoichi? Yes, that was her, and you were merely a spectator."

I moved as close to the camera as I could.

"But no, you are not who we thought you were. The true Mamoribito would not have willingly given me Taiyo and then allowed himself to be imprisoned in his own grave. You are not he."

"Fuck you, Ohno," I said, exaggerating my lips movements to leave no doubt as to what I was saying.

"Ah, polite to the last. But do not despair, you will die a hero's death, having gallantly failed to prevent the terrible act of sabotage that brought such devastation upon Japan. But it must be done, Peter, to avoid an even greater tragedy falling upon the world entire. The people are so asleep, you see, and they must be awoken."

What the hell was he talking about?

"Goodbye, Peter. We shall not meet again."

The lights went out. All of them, including the emergency lights. It was completely dark, pitch black.

"Ohno!" I shouted in the darkness. "Ohno!"

There was only echo.

#

I stood still, listening, waiting for the sluice gates to open and release the full, unchecked flow from the dam towards the turbines, and me. Immense torrents of water would soon burst from the open inspection hatches and flood the area. It wouldn't take long for the turbine hall to fill, during which I would feel the fear building as the water level rose, until panic set in as I realized there could be no escape, no respite, no sudden release except for death itself. Of all the ways in my years on earth I could have met my maker, I never thought it could have been this way. I sat down again on that hard, impartial floor.

"I'm sorry. So sorry."

I said it for Yuko and Miki, for Mike and Julie, for Naomi and Yamaguchi-san, for Matsumoto Sensei, for lost friends, for those innocents who haunted my dreams, for anyone who had ever believed in me, for anyone who had ever put their faith in this flesh and bone, this disappointment, this unrealized potential, this unresolved enigma of a man who could not return that trust.

But most of all I said it for myself.

Time passed, perhaps minutes but it felt like hours, and although my eyes had adjusted to the dark, I couldn't see a thing. If hell is the absence of light, then I was in hell. Nothing was happening, not yet, but it would be soon. Ohno would give the command, and that would be it. Despite the hopelessness of my situation, I couldn't help asking myself how flooding the turbine hall of a hydroelectric power station would unleash devastation upon Japan, as Ohno had put it. It wouldn't, obviously. This couldn't be the only event, there must be something else. But if I could figure that out there wasn't a damn thing I could do about it anyway.

I did the maths, more to give myself mental distraction than anything else. I'd always thought in a combination of yards, miles and kilometers. I couldn't help it – it came naturally to me, despite knowing that I should stick to one system or the other. I did the conversion; the sign at the plant entrance had said the plant used seventy cubic meters a second. At around 200 gallons per cubic meter that would be, shit, come on, think… 14,000 gallons per second, near enough. Christ, that was 840,000 gallons per minute. Factor in me getting the gallons per cubic meter on the low side, and we're at a million gallons flooding through those open hatches every sixty agonizing seconds.

Fuck.

I needed to relieve myself. I laughed, even at a time like this the body still has to do its thing – but it wouldn't amount to any more than a tiny stream of protest against the rivers that would soon burst from those open hatches. I stood up, as one does, moved a few feet and sprayed the wall. But that simple movement was enough to change everything.

I became aware of a faint glow at the far end of the hall. It must have been hidden from my line of sight by a generator housing, or axel, or some other piece of equipment invisible in the darkness.

Where there is light, there is hope.

I headed towards the light. It was still pitch black and having already banged my thick head hard enough at the construction site I took it slowly past the pipework until I was close enough to the light source to walk unhindered.

The glow was coming from the ceiling above the last turbine, number five, the one that was partially disassembled. I had to take care not to step on the panelling and other parts that lay scattered around the floor; it was if everyone had downed tools and gone for a tea break. There was a small opening at the base of the generator – another inspection hatch that had been removed. Light was hardly pouring through, but there was enough to convince me that the panelling encasing the generator must have been opened in the room above, where the power was still on. Perhaps the whole unit was being overhauled, or just the bearings at the top of the shaft needed greasing. I couldn't tell. It didn't matter. What did matter was that there was a way out.

I looked around. The maintenance team would need a way up there, but if there was a mobile access platform anywhere, I couldn't see it. Never mind. All I had to do was climb the shaft, squeeze myself through that little hole and either worm my way through the gap between the stator coil and the magnets, or clamber through the coils, or squirm through the mounting assembly in the middle or just fucking do whatever it took to get through.

I shook my head, sighing deeply. There couldn't be a way through. These types of machines are built with incredible precision and tight tolerances. A rat couldn't get through. I was either going to get stuck and drown when the sluices opened or get cut in half as the turbine span the shaft with me part way through the inspection hole, or be shredded into grated cheese by the magnets inside the generator.

Well, so what? At least it would be better than standing here feeling sorry for myself. I took off my belt and fastened the buckle to form a loop. I'd tried climbing coconut trees when Yuko and I honeymooned in Fiji, and the shaft was about the same height and diameter as those trunks. The fact that it was made from stainless steel and not bark might be a bit of an inconvenience, but my trainers had good, grippy soles and I would take hold of the thing as if my life depended on it – which it did. There was another technique I could have used, but that required a pair of *shuko*, which were hand-held iron climbing claws used by the Ninja to scale castle walls, and which were equally good for climbing tree-trunks or deflecting sword blades. They wouldn't have been as effective on a column of pure steel, though, and I'd anyway forgotten to slip a pair into my rucksack on the way over. I smiled, almost laughed. At least I wasn't having a sense of humour failure – that really would have ruined my day.

I clambered over the feed-pipe onto the turbine assembly, avoiding the open areas where the panels had been removed. At my feet, the blades in the housing were large, sharp, and dangerous – and despite their being stationary I didn't fancy falling onto them. I looped the belt around my ankles. In Fiji, our Polynesian instructor had jumped onto the trunk and shimmied upwards like he was born to it. I hadn't quite managed to do it as well as he had, not being born to much of anything, but I had climbed that damn tree and had coconut milk for breakfast.

I placed both hands on the shaft and hopped forwards and upwards, gripping the steel with the soles of my shoes, with the belt pulled tight across my ankles and pushed firmly against the metal. My knees were frog-splayed outwards and I didn't feel particularly secure, but I was on. I held on tightly with my palms and extended my legs. I went up the shaft, just as I had back in Fiji. I pushed upwards again, without slipping – ye gods, it was working.

I made it to the inspection hatch at the bottom of the generator in seconds. I held my position, reached up, grabbed the rim with both hands and pulled my shoulders up through the opening, to be met with a wonderful, glorious sight. The magnet assembly wasn't there! It must have been removed as part of the refurbishment, and in its place was a huge, gaping hole, big enough to drive a bus through. A small bus, of course, but it meant there was nothing in my way. I wasn't going to need to mutate into a mouse to squeeze through the tiniest of gaps, I wasn't going to get stuck like a cockroach in a spider's web or be chopped to pieces by a water-powered cabbage slicer. I was going to make it, to survive, to prevail.

Then a shrieking klaxon shattered the silence, and I felt a blast of air as the sluice gates opened a hundred yards above my head.

#

The journey from absolute elation to abject terror was instantaneous. I pushed hard with my feet, pulled with every ounce of strength I could muster and flew so fast through the opening that I crashed headfirst into the hard-coiled stator wiring that lined the generator housing. How I managed to do that was beyond comprehension, but when everything is at stake you find reserves of power and coordination that can transform you into an Olympic gymnast.

There was no time to sit and wonder at my athletic genius. I had to get out, fast. Ignoring my aching skull, I removed the belt from around my ankles, got to my feet and checked for a climbing route out. As I stepped onto the stator I couldn't help glancing downwards through the open hatch. The access for the turbine feed-pipe was directly below me, and the huge blast of air from it and the four other pipes was incredible. It could only be seconds before the water followed.

Less than that, as it turned out.

Driven by some five hundred feet of vertical pressure, a huge column of water surged out of the feed-pipe access and smashed into the bottom of the generator housing, blasting straight though the opening that I had jumped through. The flow slammed me backwards, cracking my head for the second time on the stator and almost knocking me clean out. Somehow I held on to both the thick wiring and consciousness, but in my half-dazed state I could only watch as the generator, shuddering like a toy seized by a massive trembling hand, flooded around me, the inflow from below overpowering the meagre outflow trying to drain back out. The mounting for the magnet was revolving too – there was still plenty of pressure to spin the turbine blades despite the hole in the pipe. If I hadn't been knocked back by the flow, I'd have had a foot torn off by those rings. Above everything was the surging, thunderous roar of water pounding the thin metal walls of the housing. Christ, I'd never heard such a terrifying sound in my life. It was like being anchored at the base of Niagara Falls inside a bathtub, and I'd had plenty enough of Niagara for one day.

The water level was approaching my neck. Dazed or not, it was time to get out. I took a firm grip on the stator writing, hauled myself upwards and tumbled out on to the relative safety of the generator hall floor, soaking wet, blood flowing down my white t-shirt from the crack on my head, my whole body shaking.

I had made it, I had survived, I had prevailed.

I was alive.

Eighteen

The escape route I had fast-planned on arrival had been the right one, and from the gap in the car park fence it was clear that the vehicles that had brought Ohno and his men were gone, the exception being the GT-R. The Mini was still where I had left it, obviously needed to place me at the scene, but how Ohno intended to show that I was a gallant anti-saboteur hero was beyond me. I didn't care – my concern was saving my world, Yuko and Miki.

The two from the GT-R were standing, elbows resting on the roof of their car, eyes on the power station. The noise from the flood was audible despite the thick concrete walls of the turbine hall, but it wouldn't be loud enough to fully cover any sounds I made. There were no sirens, no klaxons, no emergency warning lights. Apart from the muffled sounds of flowing water, which could easily have been mistaken as coming from the river itself, there was nothing to indicate anything was wrong.

I forced the gap open wider and squeezed my way through the fence. I stayed low, keeping to the darker areas between the lights, and quickly made it to the Mini unseen. The GT-R was twenty yards away. All it needed was a scrape of a hastily opened door and they'd be on me before I had a chance to retrieve the second pistol from under the back seat, assuming they hadn't already done that themselves. But me and Octavius were old friends and I knew how far the door would open before the hinges creaked, and where to find the little mechanical pusher to stop the interior light from coming on. I took my time – the trick in these situations is to do things slowly, carefully, fighting the urge to jump in and get moving.

The keys were still in the ignition, thank God, but the pistol in the door pocket was gone. I'd check for the other one later. I left the door on the latch, I didn't want to risk the clack of shutting it fully, but it was enough to keep the interior light off. A quick glance through the passenger window confirmed that the two players were still watching the power station. Good, they were unaware of my presence. That would change soon enough, but I would have a few seconds lead and I was banking on that being enough, despite their four-wheel drive and four hundred horsepower advantage. In any case, I had the advantage of surprise, experience, and determination.

I put on the full harness seatbelt. Usually I only did the lap strap, but today was different. I re-checked the GT-R. They still had their backs to me, and if they did turn around, I was inside a dark car, which itself was in an unlit area. I'd be practically invisible.

I dipped the clutch, selected first, released the handbrake, and placed one hand on the steering wheel with the other on the ignition key, heel-toeing the brake and accelerator. The car park exit was straight ahead, and beyond that the mountain road promised escape, freedom, and above all, hope. No, not hope. Hope was too small a word for it. Hope was a word for those who no longer believed in their ability to affect change, to impact the course of their own destiny and of those they loved. Hope was a word for those who needed someone to save them, to rescue them. Yuko and Miki were waiting for me, and I was going to find them and bring them to safety.

Then time stood still. I was hit by the realization that everything I had ever done in my life had led to this instance, this moment, this fleeting second of existence. My racing career, my time in the Territorials, my trauma in Afghanistan, the death of Julie, my long years in the dojo, the love of a family, the connection to Naomi, knowing Yamaguchi-san and his shop, seeing Tanaka on the flight, the eagle that had guided me to the temple, the finding of Taiyo, the fall through the mountain trees, the playground fights at school, Mike's crash, the swimming lessons I'd had as a child, the chance meeting on the beach in Thailand that had led me to the Tokyo dojo, tumbling down a hillside in the Brecon Beacons with fifty pounds on my back during selection, the trip to England last week, the Samurai dream on the flight, my kindergarten first love, the smell of freshly baked bread that was Nanna's specialty. Everything was connected; all actions, all coincidences, all obstacles, every happening from the least significant to the intensely harrowing, had led me to where I was. Without them, I would not exist. Without the challenges and trials that I'd had to endure, I would not be here.

The realization passed. I checked the GT-R. No change, they still had their backs to me, although one of them now had a phone to his ear. The storm was gone, the full moon shone brightly in the cloudless night sky, the insects sang their love songs. Octavius sat on his haunches, poised, prepared, willing. I was ready. We were ready.

"All right laddie," I said. "Let's show them what we've got."

I turned the ignition key.

Click.

I tried again.

Click.

"Come on Octavius, not now, for God's sake."

I turned the key again.

Click.

We were parked on a slight upwards incline. I couldn't roll forward and start us up that way. I tried again.

Click.

"Mike, where the fuck are you when I need you!"

Then the passenger door opened and the inside of the Mini was flooded with light.

#

I knew at once what had happened. Ohno's men had heard the metallic clunking of the starter motor, and being unable to see inside the Mini, one of them came to investigate. We stared at each other for a split-second. He hadn't been expecting to see me, or anyone else for that matter, which explained why he wasn't holding a handgun. He reached inside his jacket to rectify that little mistake.

"Come on!" I shouted as I turned the key. The engine sprang to life. I floored the accelerator and released the clutch in one movement. We rocketed forward, sending the man spinning in our wake. He fired two quick shots, one of which went shattered the passenger window and went straight though the front windscreen – it must have missed me by inches, if that.

We powered through the open gate and onto the narrow mountain road. I didn't need to look in the mirror to know what Ohno's men were doing. They'd be in the GT-R, starting that daunting engine and engaging that four wheel-drive beast in the pursuit of Peter Walker and his brave little Mini. But we were a team, and they could go to hell. I flicked on the headlights and all the rally lights. With everything on full beam, the road ahead lit up like an oil painting, as if the path to freedom was illuminated to the exclusion of all else.

When everything is at stake you're supposed to slow things down and take your time, to think before acting rashly. That wasn't me, not tonight. I threw caution to the wind as I flung us down a short straight and blasted into the tight hairpin bend at the end, tugging the handbrake to send us sliding through sideways, the front wheels hard over in opposite lock, tyres squealing in protest. The Mini could take it, it had to.

I kept my foot hard down on the accelerator, keeping the

revs high and stretching those four cylinders to their limit. We powered onwards, hard and fast. Despite the full throttle intensity of my driving my lines were ideal, my gear changes flawless, my anticipation and timing approaching perfection. The connection I felt with Octavius was unlike anything I had known before. We were one, man and machine.

The road straightened, the treeline cleared, and I could see three choices in the moonlit valley ahead; keep going on this road, turn on to the faster, straighter road that ran beyond the farms, or take the tighter road up the mountain. All would lead to my destination – Naomi – and I knew where she would be.

A set of bright lights suddenly filled my rear-view mirror. *Shit.*

I was wrong about the GT-R. Whoever was at the wheel knew how to drive and had caught up with me quicker than I had expected. Of course they had – that was the nature of the brute that could outrun anything. We were on a one-kilometer straight and they were closing fast. The GT-R came closer still, until I could barely see anything ahead through the dazzle of its powerful LEDs. I pushed the mirror to one side. I didn't need it anymore. I knew they were there.

Then they rammed us. When you are three times lighter with one quarter of the engine power, you feel it. Octavius shuddered, but we kept going. They rammed us again harder, maintaining contact. Christ, they were going to push us off the road. We were helpless. There was nothing I could do to outrun them, I couldn't brake, couldn't turn away, couldn't jump clear. It was all I could do to stop us spinning out of control.

We bounced over a hump in the tarmac, sending the Mini airborne and breaking the connection with the Nissan as we thumped back down to the road surface. It was all I needed to gain a few yards. There was a right fork ahead, just before the corner at the end of the straight, a narrow one-vehicle passageway that led down to the farms. It was concealed by a hedge which is why I hadn't seen it earlier, but it meant neither had the GTR. I took it, at full speed, slamming on the brakes for what I knew must be a tight turn ahead. We left the Nissan on the road above our heads as we slid through the corner, bouncing off the hedge-line at the side of the road as we came through the apex. Not quite such a perfect line, but we were still alive.

The road straightened out and I was back hard on the throttle. To call it a road was a misnomer, it was no more than a track between rice fields, and I could have done with the security of that four-wheel drive system to take us through the residual floods following the typhoon. Water splayed upwards from the Mini's front wheels as we charged through huge puddles, the steering lightening as we started to aquaplane – but little Octavius held true.

I risked a glance to my left. The mountain road followed the line at the edge of the rice fields, two hundred yards away, running parallel to the track I was on, and would intercept the larger road that lay the other side of the two farmhouses ahead of me. We were still fifty yards from the T-junction between those farmhouses, but the Nissan had already turned right onto that road, heading in our direction. My God, that thing was fast.

I slammed on the brakes and took us hard right through the junction, drifting style, almost spinning, but once more Octavius held true. The Nissan was a hundred yards behind us, the four cylinders of the Mini screamed in protest as I gave it everything. We'd never be able to outrun it like this – I had to get us back onto a mountain road. They were all mountain roads, but the one we were on ran through the valley and was straight and fast, perfect for the GT-R. I knew there was an exit soon, I'd spotted it earlier, just before the GT-R had tried to push us off the road, but right now I couldn't see it.

The Nissan was closer now, barely ten yards away, lights on full dazzle. We were doing ninety miles an hour, way beyond the local speed limit, and almost at the Mini's own limit. We bounced wildly over each imperfection in the road, but they were probably cruising along in second, the super-adaptive computer-controlled suspension unbothered by anything. Shit, the next time I had a spare eight million yen I'd get myself one of those things.

They rammed us again, but this time I was ready and had more revs in hand to move clear, albeit by inches. We wouldn't be able to escape another ramming, though – there was nothing left. I needed that exit point, now.

There!

Fifty yards ahead a smaller road forked left, leading back up the mountain on the other side of the valley. We took it at full speed, with the Nissan right behind – he'd obviously anticipated my intentions. It didn't matter. This was a narrower, twister road than the one we'd been on before, for which the Mini was far better suited. Here, the Nissan would be too big and powerful for its own good. It might have been helpful if the GT-R diver had the same thought, but he kept hard on our tail as we charged up the mountain. He was good. I had to be better.

I was.

We started to pull away. Not a lot at first, but with each tight hairpin and series of S-bends we inched ahead. I was stretching that little engine to the limit, and beyond. If I wasn't careful, we'd start overheating. I glanced at the gauge; we already were. Octavius could take it, I was sure, and I knew he wouldn't give up on me until he was totally spent. Regardless, we couldn't go on much longer this way. I had to get clear, and then lose them somehow.

As we climbed higher, I could see the light of the pre-dawn sun. Was it sunrise already? I'd been in that damn turbine room longer than I'd thought.

I worked to retrieve the map of the area that I had deep within my mind. I'd driven this route before, months ago, when Yuko, Miki and I had visited the lake, as a nice country saunter back home. I wasn't sauntering now. If I was right there was a fork ahead, on the other side of the mountain, and a couple of additional forks after that. If we could get far enough ahead, with a bit of luck we could lose them.

The road levelled out, and then declined – were on the descent, a few more fast corners after this next one and we'd have a chance. I checked the side mirrors, the GT-R and its crew were more distant now, the light from their headlights no longer directly behind me. I hadn't lost them completely, but-

Christ!

A huge twenty-ton truck edged around the corner ahead, filling the road as it strained its way up the hill in low gear, its massive bulk an impenetrable obstacle set to utterly overwhelm the Mini. The driver slammed on his brakes. I did likewise but he had the advantage of only having to slow a few miles per hour, whereas we were still doing seventy. It was way, way too late. I'd been too busy checking the mirrors to notice the approaching headlights. We were going to slide straight into him and obliterate ourselves on that gigantic front bumper.

There was a gap, the narrowest of chances, between the monster truck and the valley-side of the road. There was no crash barrier to bounce off, but if I got it right we could make it through. I nudged the steering wheel but got it all wrong. The Mini was under full braking and heavy on the nose, the back-end light, the car unstable. I'd done it again, just as I had with the Impreza on the motorway. For the second in the space of a few short hours, car and driver started to spin. If I'd have been looking ahead, as I should have been, none of this would now be happening, but it was too late for regrets. Instinct took over and I corrected the movement, but instinct isn't always your friend. The Mini swerved in the other direction, I'd overcorrected the spin and was losing control. I desperately tried to manoeuvre us through that gap, but we were weaving strongly, unable to stop in time, unable to steer effectively, our fate in the lap of the gods.

We almost made it, but at the last second we clipped the

front of the truck, hard and fast, the impact from hitting that immovable behemoth sending us spiralling off the edge of the road into the cool morning air.

Nineteen

There's a scene from the movie Monte Carlo or Bust where two British Army officers accidentally drive their vintage Lea-Francis off a ski jump in the middle of winter, and the senior officer, calmly pointing to the slopes below, orders the driver to "land there." They succeed, of course, because in movies you can break the law of gravity and do whatever you want.

I had no such luxury.

We rotated around the center axis of the Mini, spinning like a helicopter leaf at the mercy of the wind through two full circles before we smashed sideways into the solid, immutable mountain, fifteen feet below our launch point on the opposite side of the hairpin bend. We dropped another five foot to the road, thudding onto the tarmac with an almighty crash that broke the glass in every window.

I sat, immobile, hands gripped hard on the steering wheel, every muscle in my body clenched tight, every nerve fibre twitching to the extreme. I shook violently, my eyes focused on the road ten feet ahead, barely able to comprehend the fact that we were still alive.

The sound of metal impacting metal spilt the air. I looked through the remains of the shattered driver side window. It all happened in slow motion. The GT-R had done the same thing I had – I understood it now. The curve leading to where the truck had stopped was tight enough to create a blind spot, nothing hazardous for anyone travelling at normal speeds, but positively lethal to anyone charging along at the rates we had been going at. Perhaps they'd been distracted by the sight of the Mini flying off the road, but in any case they'd left their braking too late and had hit the truck in the same place I did. The GT-R, being heavier but with more powerful brakes, didn't fly off the road. Instead it toppled off the edge and slid inelegantly backwards down the side of the mountain until it pummelled into the trees fifteen yards below, coming to a halt in the safe embrace of those welcoming branches.

The truck driver was still inside his cab, staring at the scene in bewilderment. He wasn't the only one. We made eye contact. I waved, not a cheery hello, but as way of saying I was OK. The two in the GT-R weren't OK at all, but I wasn't going to worry too much about how they would find their way out of their predicament. They probably wouldn't without the help of an emergency rescue team, complete with ropes, pulleys, cranes and whatever else they needed to affect a rescue. Good.

Blood was flowing down my forehead onto my shirt. I couldn't find the rear-view mirror, it must have fallen off in the crash and disappeared under a seat, so I manually assessed my head. I had two cuts, one from the turbine room, and the other presumably from the smack into the mountain. Apart from that I was brand new. As for Octavius, his loyal heart was still beating with each stroke of that little four-cylinder and his wounded body was intact, but the passenger side was severely damaged. If we'd hit that rock face on my side, well, I might not be as intact as he was. I undid the safety harness, leaned over and pulled up the back seat. The pistol was still there, wrapped in its towelling. I used it to punch a hole in the windscreen, then tied the towel around my head.

"Oy!" The truck driver was out of his cab, phone in hand, calling out to me and the GT-R simultaneously. *"Are you alright?"* he shouted in Japanese.

I waved and nodded.

He shouted again, *"I'm trying to call the police, but the signal is bad."*

It must have been the mountains, which was unexpected as they'd expanded the number of transmitters years ago, or it could have been damage from the typhoon.

The truck driver started walking around, trying to find a spot where his phone would work. He'd have to drive to the farms in the valley to pick up a signal or use one of their landlines. Perhaps that was where he had been heading, but the damage to the front wing from the two hits was too much – he'd have to walk. We could be stuck here for hours, by which time the two goons in the GT-R might well have figured their way out.

Either way it raised the question; should I stay and wait for the police, or should I keep going? I'd need them, for certain, but whether they believed me or not would be another thing. And factoring in Ohno's claim that he had people there meant waiting around for them to arrive wasn't my best choice. In any case, it could take a long time to figure everything out, time that Yuko and Miki didn't have.

I needed to get moving. I put the Mini into first and released the clutch. Somehow, incredibly, we moved forward. The drive shafts were still in place, the suspension still working, the wheels rotating as they should, with enough steering to keep us on the road. How Octavius had survived was a miracle. We headed downhill, away from the incident, and sped up to about twenty when a loud clanking started, accompanied by a strong vibration pulsing through the steering column. I slowed us down, the clanking subsided, the vibration lessened. We clattered onwards for fifteen minutes or so, the shaking increasing all the while, the steering loosening, the brake pedal becoming worryingly spongy. At least there wasn't any traffic – Octavius and I had the road to ourselves.

I reckoned we were about twelve kilometers or so from the temple. Naomi would be there, I knew she would. She had to be. How I knew that was a good question, but it was the only thing that made sense. The problem was at this pace it would take us an hour or more to get there, an hour during which I'd be too exposed. I doubted the road would be empty for too much longer, and all it needed was a concerned farmer to drive past and that would be it.

Then Octavius made the decision easy for me. My brave little friend, the saviour of my life, the loyal companion who would keep going until he could go no more, gasped his last and died by the side of that mountain road. It was then that I noticed the fumes. I got out and checked under the car – the petrol tank had been holed, but it hadn't registered earlier. Those twin blows on the head must have affected me more than I'd realized.

I patted Octavius on the roof. "Thanks, little friend," I said. "I owe you one."

The sun was beginning to peer over the low shoulder of the mountains at the far end of the valley. If I kept its rays to my back I'd get near enough to the temple, and from there I should be able recognize the area and find my way. Twelve kilometers by road. I could do that with a full pack in two hours, and with a light rucksack I could run it in a lot less time than that, although my aching head meant I wouldn't be able to maintain full pace – a fast walk would be the best I could manage. I knew I could do it. Besides, I had no other options.

I retrieved the rucksack, put the pistol inside, and set off.

Twenty

Compared to a seventy kilometer slog across north Wales with a fifty kilo Bergen on my back, the journey to the temple should have been a morning stroll. But it was hard going, and I've had gladly taken the long drag any day of the week.

My head throbbed with every step of the way – hardly surprising considering what I'd been through. If I ever got the chance to design a special forces selection program, this would be the final test. My neck ached too, from the whiplash when I hit the side of the mountain, and I knew from experience it would be worse in the morning. To top it all a sharp pain was shooting up and down my left leg from a cut that looked for all the world a bullet graze, which must have happened when goon number one took a pot-shot in my general direction back in the power station car park.

I was off the mountain road now, yomping, as the Paras liked to say, on the ski slopes of Shiga Kogen, empty of both snow and people in the off-season. Although I hadn't seen any vehicles the thought of a passing tea farmer spotting a wounded gaijin hobbling along, his head bandaged and bloody, with a heavy scowl on his face, played on my mind. Worse still, if someone discovered me collapsed by the roadside with a pistol in my rucksack, well, that would have put the cat amongst the pigeons. So, when I'd come across the signpost for the Yamada Bokujo ski resort, I didn't need a second invitation. At least I knew where I was. As I pushed onwards and upwards it occurred to me that I'd skied here in March, when it had been a lot easier to get up the slope in one of those chairs that now dangled tantalisingly above my head. God, a quick sit down on one of those would be wonderful. But you can't give in to those thoughts, you can't say to yourself, *'I'll just rest here for a while, five minutes, no more.'*

If I stopped once, I'd stop twice.

The morning sun was bright and warming, and my clothes had dried out an hour ago. Had it been that long already? More than that, nearer two. Shit, I hadn't had any fluids for far too long, which was ironic considering all the water I'd been deluged with in the past twelve or so hours. No doubt the blood loss wasn't helping either. I removed the towel from around my head. It was soaking red. I re-tied it, but I needed stiches – and before that I needed to re-hydrate. But I was near the top of a ski run, and there was nothing here, no year-round vending machine, no friendly smiling concession owner offering me a Sports Drink.

You know what Ninja means, don't you? The exact translation? It means 'One who endures.'

"Yeah, that's me," I said, recognizing the first symptoms of dehydration, which for me had always been disjointed thoughts and weird self-talk. Shit, if that were true, I'd be in a constant state of needing something to drink.

I had to keep going. I set myself small targets. That tree, that fence post, that clump of grass. After a while my leg stopped hurting. I knew it had simply gone numb, but I welcomed the release from the pain. That respite didn't last long, it was over as soon as I jabbed my toe on a rock and fell forward into a half-roll. Instinct again, except this time it was my friend. As I sat there on the grass, I realized it was the same spot where I had lost a ski and tumbled in the snow seven months earlier.

Coincidences are meant to happen.

I got up, as quickly as I could, which was slower than I wanted to, and stood facing down the valley, taking in that extraordinary view. I'd seen it many times before, the western alps lit up by the rising sun in the east, but never like this. The air was perfectly clear, the sky empty of clouds, visibility unlimited. As I stood there alone in that beautiful landscape, I became aware of myself, my true self, and the connections that existed between all things, living and inert – the consciousness of the universe. I'd had the same feeling before in the car park at the power station, but this was bigger, something on a vast scale that was truly infinite. I was at the intersection of two worlds, part of each universe yet separate, belonging yet unbelonging.

The awareness left me. I wanted it back, wanted to know, wanted to understand, to be in that place again, but I couldn't take myself there. Apparently, these things were beyond my capacity to control. I'd have to wait for the next invitation.

So be it.

I set off again, promising myself I'd take a five-minute breather at the top of the slope, knowing that I would need to break that promise as soon as I got there. It turned out that I didn't need to. On reaching the non-descript wooden hut that served as the operator's cabin for the ski lift, I realized I'd got the direction right but the distance wrong. At far end of the valley below, shrouded by plumes of mist as the sun liberated the moisture from the surrounding earth, stood the temple, less than a kilometer away. I'd made it. Of course I had, it was nothing more than a Sunday stroll in the mountains, anybody could do that.

I headed off-piste.

#

Naomi was waiting for me at the temple entrance. She sprinted the two hundred yards up the road to where I had collapsed to my knees, overcome by exhaustion, fluid loss, the pain in my leg, head and neck, and the emotions that flooded over me from seeing her face again.

"I've got you," Naomi said as she put her arms around me and helped me to my feet. "Grandfather!" she shouted to the temple. "He is here! Grandfather!"

Grandfather was already on his way. It was the priest I had met yesterday, the one I'd realized was related to Yamaguchi-san, the sword dealer.

"Come, Peter-san," he said, as he put a shoulder under my arm. "Let's get you inside."

Then everything went black.

Twenty-One

I awoke to find Naomi gently wiping my forehead.

I was dressed in a yukata, a kind of lose fitting one-piece kimono, lying on a futon on the floor of a tatami room somewhere in the temple complex. I didn't know how long I had been unconscious, but it was enough time to strip and re-cloth me, and to clean me up too.

"There you are," she said, as she stopped wiping. "We were worried. You took so long to find your way to us."

"I got stuck in traffic. How long have I been out?"

"A few hours."

Christ, more time lost. I grabbed her wrist. "I have to go, Naomi. They have my family."

"I know," she said, releasing my grip. "And we will get them back for you. I sense they are unharmed. First, you must recover your strength." She leant across me and grabbed three large cushions from a small alcove, her breasts inches from my face. I did my best to pretend not to notice. "You should sit up."

It wasn't a suggestion. Naomi positioned the cushions between my back and the wall. I tentatively fingered the bandage around my cranium.

"We've treated your wounds," Naomi said.

I took 'we' to mean Naomi and her grandfather. I checked my left leg – the upper calf was also wrapped with a bandage. "So I see," I said, disguising my wonder at where the pain had gone.

"It was a bullet. Just a graze, though."

"Thank you," I said, this time with less disguise. I rubbed the back of my neck, not looking forward to the whiplash that would surely set in soon. It was slightly greasy – an ointment of some sort had been applied. Maybe that explained the mild ache instead of throbbing pain I had been expecting.

Naomi moved closer, pressing her thighs against mine. She began to wipe my forehead again with the softest of towels. Or maybe it was her touch that was soft. Either way it wasn't necessary – there couldn't have been anything left to wash away by now, but I wasn't going to stop her.

"You said you'd tell me everything," I said.

"Grandfather will, soon." Naomi put down the towel and turned to a small teapot and sake cup on a tray. She poured, then handed me the cup. "You must drink this. It will make you feel better."

For such a small amount the aroma was pungent. "Are you sure?"

"A secret Ninja recipe. Very powerful. But drink it quickly, it tastes like shit."

I smiled. I hadn't been expecting that kind of talk from her. "I need some water first," I said. "I'm a little dehydrated."

"Drink first, then water."

"Yes ma'am."

Naomi was wrong about the taste; it was a lot worse than that. It had an immediate effect, though, as if I had been injected with a miracle drug. "No wonder that stuff's a secret," I said.

"Now you can have water."

There were five two litre bottles in the alcove. Naomi reached for one of them, again brushing herself against me. I may have passed Territorial SAS selection, served in Afghanistan, become a fifth dan Ninja, survived a flood, spun off a mountain road and generally gotten through hell in the past few hours, but I wasn't sure I could take much more of this.

"Here." She passed the bottle to me.

You're supposed to sip it, but I gulped half of it down in one go.

"Too much, Peter. You must regulate yourself."

An interesting choice of words, but I was done, for now, at least.

"Tell me what happened," she said, "after you left me in Tokyo."

"I didn't leave you, Naomi. I wanted you to come with me."

"I couldn't. The journey was yours to make, Peter, and alone. And besides, the Mamoribito does not need my help."

"Yes he did. Does," I said.

"So you know who you are?" she replied.

"I'm Peter Walker, that's who I am."

"That is just your name."

"Haven't we had this conversation already. Twice?"

She smiled. "Maybe. Now, please, tell me everything."

So I told her about the rush through the typhoon, the rock fall when I crashed the Subaru, how Taiyo saved me when I jumped over the roadside barrier, the battle at the hotel, how I buried Honey, the way I gifted Taiyo to Ohno at the power station, the escape from the turbine room, the chase with the GT-R hot on my heels, the spin off the mountain road, the long walk across the ski resort, and the way seeing her face at the temple was the best thing that had happened to me all day.

"And yet you still doubt you are the Mamoribito?" she said.

"I gave the sword to Ohno, Naomi. And he has my family."

"I already said, we will find them. Together."

We looked at each other in silence. There was something here, something beyond my understanding that I could not explain. Naomi knew what it was, though, I was sure of that.

"Naomi, back at the house, in England, at Welton Hall,

you said it wasn't meant to be that way. What did you mean?"

She sighed, the deep heavy sigh of one who has done something they will forever regret. "It was Michael's idea," she said, genuine sorrow in her eyes. "The sword would be stolen, and you would find it again in Japan. The coincidence would have convinced you, or so we thought. But then, at the house, we heard you, one of your dreams that Michael had told me about."

They must have heard me scream. I didn't know whether to laugh or be embarrassed. Had he also told her why I had those dreams? I hoped not.

"We realized you were going to wake up sooner than we had planned," she continued, "So we had to move quickly. We ran to the car, then you chased us, both of you. It wasn't what I was expecting."

"What were you expecting?"

"That Michael would wake you up, and you'd follow us together, in his car, but we would get away after the long straight road. And when you got back to Japan, Uncle would invite you to his shop to see his new collection. You would discover Taiyo there, and begin to make the connection."

"Sounds complicated," I said, which was my submission for understatement of the year. "Was Michael's crash part of the plan, too?" It was hardly a fair question. I regretted it instantly.

"I had to stop. I couldn't... I got out of the car, and then-" Naomi stopped in mid-sentence, remembering.

"And then?" I said.

"I was betrayed by a friend, the worst of all betrayals. He drove away, with Taiyo, leaving me there. Which is why I went back to the house, so you would find me, so we would find each other. Actually, I didn't know what else to do, which is not like me. Not like me at all."

"Was he one of Ohno's men?"

"I failed to sense it then, but, yes, I know now."

Whoever it was had managed to hide that from Naomi. She was human after all, and not yet the goddess that Michael had taken her for. So did you, Walker, I reminded myself.

"At the house, why did you let me chase you like that?" I asked.

"So you would want to catch me, of course."

I smiled – I should have figured that out for myself.

Naomi offered me the half-empty water bottle. "More?"

"Please." I drank the rest in one go. The look on her face said it all. "I know, I have to regulate myself," I said.

She took the bottle from me and set it aside. "What do you see, when you have those dreams?" she asked. It was an innocent enough question, but I wasn't prepared to answer it. The smile left my face. Naomi let it go. "When you are ready," she said.

Would I ever be ready? One day, perhaps, but before then there were too many riddles to solve, starting with the one that was troubling me the most.

"I still don't understand why Michael did what he did," I said. "Do you?"

It was Naomi's turn to shake her head. I realized then it was a question that would probably never be answered. Maybe Mike had changed his mind; maybe he was too drunk to think properly; maybe he had a deep, subconscious death wish and wanted to be reunited with Julie. Or maybe he had lost himself in the charade and taken things a step too far. I knew that I would never know, and the guilt of not knowing burned my soul.

Naomi sensed my anguish. "It is best not to think on what might have happened," she said. "We can only think on what we must do now."

"I know that Naomi," I said, although I was doing both. "But why not just give the sword to me? Why the charade? You too. You could have said something at Welton Hall."

Naomi sat back. "The Mamoribito cannot be simply told who he is, because he will not believe. Like you didn't, even still don't. Instead, he must find out for himself. We knew it wouldn't be easy for you. Michael said that you had lost confidence, lost belief in your cause, lost faith that the world was just, and that you were broken by the war that you had fought."

"Doesn't sound much like a Mamoribito, does it?"

She started wiping my forehead again. "The Mamoribito is who he is because of what he has lived through. He knows the pain of others because he has suffered pain himself. He knows he must defend others because others have defended him. He knows others are afraid because he knows fear himself. He knows that strength must be used to help, to guide, to protect, not to subdue, because he has seen for himself what happens when power is wrongly used. He knows what it means for someone to lose their way, because he himself has been lost in darkness. And yet he goes on, despite all these things, because of who he is."

It may have sounded like a passage she had memorized from some secret Ninja parchment, but coming from Naomi it had an effect. I looked at her. It was hard not to, considering she was inches from me, but it was even harder not to be drawn in by her astonishing beauty. Michael must have been as affected by Naomi as I was, yet from the way she had asked me about my dreams it appeared he hadn't told her – if he had then she would know I couldn't be the Mamoribito, not after what I had done.

"At Welton Hall, you were on a motor bike," I said, wanting to lighten the mood. "Did you steal it?"

Naomi glared at me as if I'd accused her of a high crime. "Of course not," she said. "I borrowed it, like you and that car."

"I hope you left it in better condition than I did." I touched a finger to the towel she was using to wipe my forehead. "Is my head still dirty?"

"I'm trying to sooth your spirit," Naomi replied, stopping. "Isn't it working?"

Why would I want her to stop? "It's working. You're a pretty good nurse, Naomi."

"Actually, I'm a doctor. Not a nurse."

"You are?"

"You think a girl like me can't be a doctor?"

"Of course you can," I said. "You can be anything you want to be."

She started wiping again. "Now you sound like my mother."

"Is she a Kunoichi, too?"

Naomi shook her head. "She was, is, a professor of mathematics. It's where I get my planning capabilities from. When they work, that is."

I was suddenly struck by how many players were involved; Naomi, her uncle, her grandfather on one side, with Ohno, Mr. Angry and all their men on the other – and with me at the center of it all. With everything that had happened I wondered if I wasn't dreaming the whole thing. Was I going to wake up any minute and find myself back at Mike's? I'd have to be in coma for this level of hallucination, and I didn't need to pinch myself to know that I was fully wide-awake.

"Naomi," I said. "How did Mike know this thing about me, when I didn't know myself? It was you, wasn't it. What else did you tell him? And what else did he tell you about me? And who is Ohno, really? And how does he know about the legend of Taiyo? And why does he care so fucking much? And how many more people know about me, the sword, and all of this?"

Naomi put a finger to my lips. "So many questions."

"And so few answers."

Naomi kissed me. Gently, softly, tenderly. It was the kind of kiss that can make you give up everything you ever had, or ever would have, just to feel those lips upon yours once again.

"Naomi-chan, please." The voice came from behind her.

Naomi broke off the kiss. Neither of us had noticed her grandfather enter the room. "Grandfather, I…"

"Your methods are unconventional, Naomi, but at least he is recovering. Some tea, please, and then we have many things to discuss."

"Yes Grandfather." Naomi stood and left the room.

The priest sat in Naomi's place.

"I didn't see you there," I said.

"A true Ninja conceals his form in the shadows, only revealing himself at the time of his own choosing. I am Yamaguchi, grandmaster Ninja, head of the Yamaguchi Ninja family, protector of the true spirit of Ninpo, and guardian of the sacred sword, Taiyo."

"And Naomi's grandfather."

"Indeed I am. You must forgive Naomi, Peter-san, she can see things that are hidden from the rest of us. It was she who first sensed your return."

"I see."

"Do you not feel a connection to her?"

"I sensed something," I admitted, my second submission for understatement of the year.

"Naomi has been waiting for you. We all have, since you joined the Matsumoto Dojo in Tokyo. My nephew. And you met Naomi's cousins there too, yesterday, preparing themselves."

"Big family," I said.

"Indeed we are."

"But Sensei, I'm not a member of the family. I'm not even Japanese."

"Where you were born is of no matter, Peter-san. You are the Mamoribito, and you have returned to fight the evil that men do in this world. The evil that one man does, and whom others follow."

I knew who he meant. "Ohno," I said.

"Yes, Ohno. For five hundred years my family has fulfilled our sacred duty to protect the sword, until each time of the Mamoribito's return, your return, when the danger is greatest, as it is now. Whatever Ohno is planning, you must stop him, before it is too late."

"He has my family, Sensei. It won't take long until Ohno realizes I'm still alive, if he doesn't already. We need to call the police. I should have done it before, but they wouldn't have believed me, it would be my word against Ohno's. They might believe you, though."

"Me?" he said, feigning shock. "A lonely priest on a lonely mountain top. Why would they believe me?"

Indeed. Why would they? I had no answer for that.

Sensei continued. "But I understand how you feel, Peter-san. A man's family is the core of his being, his whole existence, what he lives for, and what he must fight to protect, even if that costs him his life." Naomi returned with the tea. "Ah, Naomi-chan. Thank you."

Naomi served, then took her place beside her grandfather.

"Sensei. I'm sorry," I said, still unconvinced despite all that had happened to me, around me. "But I don't think I'm who you think I am, who everyone thinks I am."

"The truth is, Peter-san, you are not who you think you are. Naomi, would you mind?"

Yamaguchi Sensei pointed to a photograph on the wall. Naomi retrieved it. It was the same one I saw on my previous visit.

"There used to be so many of us," he continued. "But now, so few. Donald Welton was a student here before the war. A good man, honest and true, unlike the world at that time. My father took him into his confidence and asked him to take the sword back to your country, to keep it hidden. You were born close to the sword, to be ready when the time came. Last year I sent Naomi to look after Donald in his final days, and to find a way to bring the Mamoribito to see the light of who he truly is."

Sensei placed the photograph on the tatami matting, next to him.

"Sensei, please don't take this the wrong way, but this isn't my fight," I said. "I'm sorry, but it's the job of the police, or the army. Not me. My job is to protect my family. That's all."

"You must fight him, stop him!" Naomi almost screamed it out. She was full of surprises. Her grandfather raised a hand. Naomi composed herself.

"Peter-san, why did you come here?" he said. "If you are

not who you are, then why not go straight to those in authority?"

It was a good question, the answer to which I wasn't sure of myself. "I don't know. Like I said, I thought no one would believe me, and I needed to find Naomi, she could explain everything."

"And how did you know she was here?"

"It just made sense to me," I said.

Sensei sipped his tea, the epitome of calm. "Do you not see, Peter-san? You came because your spirit knows the answers to everything you seek are here. Your whole life has led you to this place. You know this to be true, but you still hold on to who you think you are. But that is not you, Peter-san. Yes, you can go to the police, the army, I will not stop you. You can be safe with them, no need to worry about Ohno. Let someone else worry. Let another person fight while you stay at home.

"Who will you send in your place? Naomi? Me? You know that is not the way of the true Ninja. He will face danger, he will suffer what cannot be suffered, will endure what cannot be endured. The true Ninja fights the evil that men do and keeps the world in harmony and balance. We do not send our brothers, our sisters, or our sons and daughters to do this for us. We do it ourselves. And, yes, sometimes there is sacrifice. For others, Peter-san, always for others. Never for ourselves. The road is open for you, Peter-san. Turn left or right, you must choose which path to take."

Did I really have that choice? I could have gone to the authorities at any time. It would have been easy, all I had to do was make a phone call, or flag down a patrol car, or wait with the truck driver. So what if Ohno had people there? The entire Japanese police force couldn't have been under his influence. I would have been able to explain myself. I'd have been a reliable witness, Japanese special forces would have rescued my family, and everything would have been OK.

So why was I here?

"But, Sensei," I said. "I would know, wouldn't I?"

Sensei put down his tea. "You must clear your mind. Only then will you see the truth."

#

Yamaguchi Sensei led me through a narrow corridor to a dark, quiet area at the far corner of the temple. He slid back a wooden door to reveal a small, windowless five-tatami room, lit by a single candle on a table set against the far wall. In the middle of the floor was a cushion. Apart from that, the room was bare.

Sensei pointed to the cushion. "Sit, sit," he said.

I sat. Sensei circled a finger, gesturing for me to turn around and face the wall. "Meditation posture, Peter-san."

Now I understood where he was going with this. I faced the wall and crossed my legs.

"Now, calm your mind, release all thoughts. When all is quiet, then you will see.

"Ok."

"Not OK. Hai Sensei is the is the right word. You know this, Peter-san."

I did know it, of course. "Hai, Sensei," I said.

Sensei reached inside his sleeve and sprinkled powder on to the candle. The flame danced and fizzled. "To help you see," he said, and left the room, sliding the door silently he went.

I closed my eyes. The effect was immediate. I wasn't mediating, I was dreaming – a deep, powerful, tangible vision that filled my mind as separation disappeared, individuality was transcended, uniqueness no longer a part of who I was. Darkness gave way to light, until…

Empty, formless, pure nothingness. Trees slowly emerge, bathed in moonlight. A mountain forest. An eagle cries, soaring through the sky above. I know him. He leads the way across glass slopes until…

A kimono-clad woman rushes past, carrying twins in her arms, weeks old. Mounted Samurai give chase. She stumbles. The first child spills from her grasp. A Samurai picks up the baby, others close around her. She stands next to a cliff face, a sheer drop. There is no escape. She jumps, still holding the other twin. The Samurai turn away.

The foot of the cliff. An old man, strong and powerful, gently takes the second child from the mother's protective grasp. His countenance says; I will protect him.

The second child grows as part of a Ninja family. The first child grows as part of a Daimyo's household – a Samurai. Each receives a sword; Taiyo for the Samurai, a plain sword for the Ninja – the Mamoribito. Opposites, yet equals.

They battle across hundreds of years, light against dark, despair against hope, brother against brother – reborn. They cannot exist without each other.

The Kunoichi, is there. Naomi. She fights alongside the Mamoribito. He is me. I am him. He lives and dies, sometimes in old age, sometimes in youth. As does the Kunoichi. Birth, battle, sacrifice, death, and rebirth. But also beauty, love and family – things worth defending. The circle goes on and on, repeating itself, never resolving, never-ending, until…

Yuko and Miki cower in a dark corner, scared, waiting for me to come to them.

I woke up, panting heavily. The candle flickered, then stood still. I sensed someone behind me. I rolled fast to my left as the glint of a blade slashed down through the space where my torso had been an instant before. I slammed into the wall and quickly stood in *kamae*, one hand forward, the other held over my chest.

It was Yamaguchi Sensei. He had crept into the room, sword in hand, and had brought it down behind my back, silently, unseen, unannounced. He too was in *kamae*, with one foot forward, the other angled sideways, the tip of his sword inches from my heart. Had I not moved, had I not sensed his presence, I would have been killed. It was the ultimate test of a Ninja warrior, reserved for those at the highest level, and something I thought I could never aspire to – until today.

"Now you know," Sensei said. "You truly are the Mamoribito."

Twenty-Two

I hadn't noticed the motorcycle earlier, but I'd collapsed when I entered the temple grounds and so I hadn't noticed much of anything. It was a Kawasaki Ninja, the same one that was parked outside Yamaguchi-san's sword shop the day before. I should have realized then that it was Naomi's.

"Nice bike." I said to her. "Did you borrow that one too?"

"No, it's mine."

"A Ninja."

"Of course. What else would I ride?"

Was that a deliberate double-entendre? With Naomi anything was possible, and the way she looked in her riding leathers was, well, maybe I should stop thinking those thoughts. I'd had plenty to think about since the vision anyway.

Naomi picked up the jacket lying across the passenger seat. "For you," she said, handing it over. It fit, unsurprisingly. Naomi seemed to know everything about me.

I still had a thousand unanswered questions. Was I the Mamoribito? Did I even know what that meant? Was it real or just legend? Others believed that I was, I could see that, and it explained Ohno's behaviour, and the fear his men had of me. No, not of me, not of Peter Walker, but of the Mamoribito. Was it a true vision, or was it a figment of my imagination, designed to help me understand? I'd had friends who'd travelled to the Amazon to experience Ayahuasca, the hallucinogenic, psychedelic brew that had brought them to a new level of consciousness, or so they'd said. For them it was real, and both had shrugged of their PTSD, coming back transformed, leaving their old selves behind. They'd urged me to try it for myself. It occurred to me that I had, or at least Yamaguchi Sensei's version of it.

I didn't feel so different, Peter Walker-san was still alive and well in this world, as he had been for the past thirty-eight years, but something had changed inside; I had a purpose, a mission to accomplish, a calling to live up to, a responsibility to fulfil. But that and a thousand more concerns would have to wait their turn. It had been too long since Yuko and Miki were taken from me, and Naomi thought she knew where to find them.

"Also for you," she said, handing me a helmet.

"You brought one for me, very prescient of you."

"You should know that about me by now, Peter."

"Indeed I should. Can you see what will happen from now?"

"No," she said. "It doesn't work that way. I see some things, others are hidden. I don't know why."

"Life wouldn't be much fun if you always knew the answers to everything."

"Oh, life is always fun," Naomi said, looking past my shoulder. I turned to see Yamaguchi Sensei exit the temple, carrying a bag of the kind that kendo practitioners sling over their shoulders on the way to the dojo, with their wooden swords inside.

"For you, Peter-san," Sensei said as he handed me the bag.

I had been waiting for this, but it was evident from the look on her face that Naomi wasn't expecting it. After all, I still had the pistol, which was now safely hidden in the rucksack on my shoulder, so why would I need anything else? But Naomi wasn't aware of what was inside. I opened the bag and pulled out a plain, non-descript sword. It was the opposite of Taiyo – the blade had no pattern, the hilt was black, there was no signature by the craftsman. It was so ordinary, so uncollectable that if it had been hung on Yamaguchi-san's shop wall in Tokyo it would have stayed there a long, long time.

"Do you know what this is, Peter-san?"

"Hai Sensei. It's the other sword."

"There are two swords?" Naomi asked. Apparently, this was one of those things that had been hidden from her.

"There are always two, Naomi-chan," Sensei said. "Left and right, up and down, light and dark. Yin and Yang. Good and evil. Without the one, we cannot know the other. Peter must possess both. Only then can there be peace. He knows this, has seen this. Have you not, Peter-san."

"Yes, Sensei, I have."

"It is said the one that takes first blood can banish the other's spirit for a thousand years. It is why Ohno tried to kill Peter with Taiyo, and not mere bullets. Until he came to believe that you are not the Mamoribito, that is. A mistake he may come to regret. The truth is, the swords are bothers, not enemies. If only Ohno could see."

I put the sword back into the bag.

"Look after him, Naomi. He will need you, when the time comes."

"Hai, grandfather," she replied.

Naomi put on her helmet, got on the bike, and motioned for me to do the same. I adjusted the *hachimaki*, the band that was protecting the wounds to my head, and donned my helmet. I sat behind her with my rucksack on my knee and the sword bag across my back. If anyone spotted us, we'd be two people on a bike heading to the dojo for morning training.

Naomi checked her phone. "My cousins are on their way."

"How many?"

"All of them."

"Good."

Naomi handed me her phone. "You do know how to navigate, don't you?"

"A bit," I said, with as much irony as I could muster. Was

it always going to be this way between her and me? I checked the app. Ohno's mountain residence was twenty-five kilometers to the north east, and where, If Naomi was right, Yuko and Miki were being held.

"I've deactivated the password," she said. "Just shout in my ear."

"I thought you knew the way."

"I have never been invited." Naomi said, as she fired up the engine. "Let's go."

We moved off so fast I nearly fell off the bike. I put a hand around her waist to steady myself, which wasn't easy considering my rucksack was between us.

"Turn right at the end of this road," I shouted above the roar of the exhaust. "And then straight for ten kilometers."

"I know that much!" she shouted back.

Yep, it was always going to be like this between us.

#

Ohno's mountain residence wasn't the kind of place you'd expect from one of the wealthiest industrialists in Japan. I had assumed it would have been large, traditionally designed but recently constructed, semi-fortified with security cameras everywhere, maybe a guard or two, and a helicopter landing pad in the car park. In short, a living fortress that would have taken all my planning and concealment skills to get into.

The house was nothing of the sort. It looked like a normal mountain retreat, the kind that anyone could have had built if they'd had saved enough money through a lifetime of hard graft. It wasn't particularly big either, although the way it was nestled in the surrounding trees may have hidden its true size.

Naomi must have been reading my mind. "Not what you were expecting?" she said.

We were by the side of the road, hidden by the trees that overlooked the building. Buildings, if you counted the small wooden shack one hundred and fifty yards down slope from the main house.

"Not exactly," I replied. "How about you?"

"I have seen it before on Google Earth," she said, with a wry smile. "So I had some idea."

"Of course you did," I said. I'd tried to do the same thing on the way over, but either there was no cellular coverage in this area, or the network was still down. Either way, something wasn't working right. On top of that Naomi was keeping something from me. So was Yamaguchi Sensei. I'd sensed it at the temple and had been thinking about it on the way.

"You know a lot about Ohno, don't you, Naomi."

"It is my purpose."

"To study Ohno?"

"In part," she said.

"And the other part?"

"Making sure you don't mess everything up. I thought that much was obvious."

"You could say that," I replied. "But I think there's more to Ohno than you're telling me."

"Perhaps. But our aim now must be to uncover his intentions, and then stop him, whatever they may be."

I could wait for the missing story about Ohno – that would come when Naomi was ready to tell me. I studied the target. We were about twenty yards above the level of the house, from where the thick forest of indigenous trees would provide plenty of cover. A stony, unsurfaced access road led up the slope to the road we were now on, exiting thirty yards to our left. A path led from the house to the shack. I assumed it was a shack, as all I could see of it was the roof. But the most telling point was the absence of any vehicles. I doubted Ohno would have sanctioned leaving the place unguarded for too long, so we could expect visitors soon.

"You're sure they're here?" I said.

"Yes. But there are no guards."

"I expect they went shopping and will be back soon enough."

Naomi gave me one of her looks. "Shopping?"

"You'll get used to the humour in time, Naomi."

"I don't think we have that amount of time."

She was right, joking or not. "How long until your cousins get here?" I asked.

"An hour, maybe less. It's a long drive from Tokyo. They will go to grandfather's temple first."

"Too long. We'll separate. I'll take the house. You take that shack thing over there. When you're done, come to the house. And if you need me, shout. Loudly."

"Is there another way of shouting?"

I gave her a look.

"You'll get used to the humour. In time," Naomi said as she started rummaging inside my rucksack, which was positioned between us. She pulled out three shuriken. I didn't know she had put them in there.

"Here." She passed them over. "You might need these."

"Only three?" I refrained from adding that only two were bladed. The other was the blunt, rounded type.

"It will be enough. And I need some, too."

"Yes ma'am." I said, although with the Ninja sword strapped across my back and a loaded pistol in my belt, I felt well-armed enough already. Naomi placed shuriken in hidden pockets in her jacket body and sleeves. I placed my shuriken in my own inside jacket pockets.

I moved a little closer to her, there was something that she needed to know. "Naomi, back at the temple, I had a vision, in the meditation room. I saw everything, who I am, who you are, why we are here, and what we must do."

"I know," she said. "Grandfather told me. It's called the *Mamoribito no Yume* – the dream of the Mamoribito. Only the true Mamoribito can see it. And not die afterwards, either."

I smiled. "Yes, that was a little extreme."

"You saw us, together, didn't you?" Naomi said.

"Many times, across many different lifetimes."

"But not this one."

I ran my fingers through Naomi's long, straight black hair and kissed her on the forehead.

"Not this one," I echoed.

"It is not important," she said, although I knew it was to her.

It was important to me too, but my priority was my family. After that, I'd go to the police and tell them everything. With any luck I'd find evidence in the house. And if there was nothing there then Yuko's testimony should be enough to persuade the authorities to act. That's how I saw my role in this, Mamoribito or not. Even if twenty of Naomi's cousins turned up there was little we could do beyond rescuing Yuko and Miki. There was little more we *should* do, either. If we did, we'd risk getting arrested for taking the law into our own hands, and I doubted the "I'm the Mamoribito" defence would go down particularly well in court.

"Do you still not believe?" Naomi said.

Was it the look on my face, or was she reading my mind again? "It's been a long week," I replied. "There's a lot to take in."

Naomi looked me straight in the eye. It was her way of being deadly serious. It worked.

"Peter, there is something you must understand. The Mamoribito had been sleeping for more than two hundred years. Grandfather's father thought he would come, before the war, but the Mamoribito didn't come. He sent the sword to England, to be kept safe, so that anyone seeking its power wouldn't find it. Still, the war came and millions died. And the Mamoribito is here now, in you, as you are in him. You must ask yourself why. Why is he here, why now?"

I'd been asking myself a lot of questions recently, including that one. "And you think this time it could be worse than that?" I said.

"I don't know. Not for sure."

"Naomi, you're an amazing, fantastic, incredible, mysterious woman," I said. "But it's a bit of a stretch to go from a flooded hydroelectric power station to starting world war three."

"Is it?"

"Yes, it is. But you think it's possible, don't you?"

"Why else would I be here, reborn, fighting with you now?"

I had to smile. "Fighting alongside me, you mean."

She smiled back. "That too."

I was beginning to appreciate her sense of humour. "We need to go. I'll take the house and you -"

"The shack, I know. It is my place to give you all the glory, while I pick up the scraps."

I kissed her again, for luck. "Let's go," I said, and moved off through the trees.

Naomi called out, softly "Peter!"

I stopped, keeping low. She came closer and kissed my cheek.

"Be careful," she said.

"I will."

#

The house was quiet, well-appointed as an estate agent would say, and bigger on the inside than the outside, as these kinds of places often were. It hadn't been difficult to gain entrance. In fact, it had been remarkably easy to climb through an open window on the ground floor. At first I'd thought it must have been a trap, but then I'd realised that they weren't expecting visitors and had been careless. It also meant they weren't expecting anyone to get out either, which implied that Yuko and Miki weren't here. Was Naomi wrong about that? I tried not to think about what could have happened to them. If they were here, I'd find them. Or Naomi would, in the shack down the slope.

I moved quickly through each downstairs room, not bothering to conceal myself. There was no-one there, but it wouldn't be long before someone returned from wherever they had been – and I doubted it was a trip to the local shopping mall.

As I moved upstairs, I called out, "Yuko, are you here? It's me, Peter." I stopped and listened, more hoping for than expecting a reply. Nothing.

I continued to the upper floor and checked each of the four bedrooms. All were just that – bedrooms. The fifth room was different. Bigger than a study, it resembled a small city office, but with a glorious panoramic view of the valley and the mountain peaks beyond. It was the kind of room where you could sit for hours and watch the world unfold, lost in that space between reality and wonder, in quiet contemplation of what lay beyond the limitations of physical existence.

I pictured Ohno sitting at the large mahogany desk, in the large leather chair, staring out of that window, deep in thought. But something wasn't right with that image. I sensed the room had a purpose, and it wasn't just for gazing at the scenery, but apart from the furniture there was nothing here; no whiteboard for capturing thoughts, no computer for developing elaborate spreadsheets that would take down the world's financial systems, no paper filing system containing the hidden secrets of his shady business dealings, no communications equipment from where Ohno could control his industrial empire. On the surface it was a room with a view, and that didn't seem the kind of thing Ohno would build for himself. Or maybe I was getting him all wrong, and this was simply his mountain retreat where he retreated into the mountain that was himself.

No, this was the place.

A large *kakejiku,* a hanging scroll, stretched from ceiling to floor on the wall to my left. Yuko and I had four in our hotel, all done by her mother in large-brush style, with stylized *kanji* that I could seldom read nor understand. This one was a painting, a winter view of the snow-covered peaks that formed the Japanese alps, with smaller characters that were incomprehensible to me. It looked old, and valuable, too. The hook from which it hung was on a metal slider that ran from corner to corner above my head, meaning the *kakejiku* could be moved from side to side. I pushed it gently towards the window to reveal a door. Now we were getting somewhere.

There was a lock on the door, a mechanical push-button combination of the kind you might find protecting stock rooms and garden sheds, and despite what most people think they aren't that hard to defeat, given enough time. Hotel safes can be beaten with a bag and a strong magnet if you knew what you were doing. I'd done it myself in a little over ten minutes with a safe in our hotel that no one knew the combination for. The old-style mechanical version that Ohno had on this door would take longer, and I didn't have the two to three hours it would take to break the code.

I pulled the pistol from my belt and shot out the lock. Easy.

#

I opened the door and found the light switch. The room was compact, windowless and dark, not the kind of space you'd expect a maniac to use for plotting to overthrow the world, but that depended on how many spy movies you'd been watching, and I didn't see Ohno as a maniac. Cold, calculating and borderline malevolent, yes. Mad, no. He was planning something, though, and obviously did things with a purpose. I was here to find out what that purpose was.

To my right, a large map of the Kanto area of Japan covered the wall. Concentric circles centred on a small coastal headland, less than thirty kilometers to the north west of where I was standing. It wasn't on the list of plants that Doggy Barnes had asked me to survey for his report, but I knew it well enough. It was the Joetsu nuclear power station, one of four that Ohno Industries had operated until the 2011 tsunami had caused havoc at Fukushima, causing all of Japan's reactors to be shut down until deemed safe for restart. The Joetsu, along with all the others, had not yet received permission for a restart, much to Ohno's public discontent.

Photographs of the station adorned the opposite wall, together with several of the hydroelectric plant, the one that Ohno had deliberately flooded with me still inside. Both were highlighted on the map, with two lines leading to the nuclear plant, each crossed by a large red "X," yet another use of that fateful letter. The concentric circles on the map reached all the way to Tokyo and were annotated with a series of numbers with the letters Bq, and you didn't need much imagination to figure what they were: radiation fallout estimations in Becquerels. On the table in front of me was a scale model of the power station, complete with fences and miniatures of security cameras.

Jesus Christ.

Ohno was going to destroy the reactor and cover eastern Japan with radioactive fallout. That's why he had flooded the hydroelectric power station. Despite being under reconstruction it could have been back on online in a matter of hours. From there it would serve as the emergency power supply that would ensure the circulation pumps on the reactor kept going, even if a massive tsunami had swallowed up the whole complex and swamped the underground back-up generators.

That was the cause of the Fukushima disaster – not the tsunami itself, but the total loss of electrical power due to the generators being under water, and with the local power lines down there was no way for the coolant pumps to do their work. Meltdown ensued, thousands were evacuated, lives and livelihoods were destroyed. Ohno was going to create a different kind of tsunami, but it's effect would be just as devastating.

My mind raced. You wouldn't want to blow a hole directly in the reactor containment vessel itself, as some people might think. If you did that not only would you need a truck load of explosives – those things are designed to withstand a direct hit from a Jumbo jet – but you'd risk killing yourself in the process as radioactive material splattered all over the place. No, the thing to do was to destroy the pipes that circulated coolant and disable the systems for lowering the control rods, leaving the reactor jammed on full power. It wouldn't take long for the fuel to superheat and melt its way through the casing floor, and after that eat through the foundations of the building into the Earth itself, by which time things would have gotten very bad indeed. And even if the molten fuel was successfully contained, all you had to do was use some of that C4 to blow a hole in the thin building walls and then you'd be looking at a mass-evacuation and a fifty kilometer exclusion zone. Even if you didn't know what you were doing, you could put C4 everywhere and disable everything in sight. The result would be the same.

I was wrong. Ohno was a maniac.

The people are so asleep, Peter, and they must be awoken. Whatever his reason for saying that, whatever his rationale, whatever his purpose, this was insanity. He had to be stopped, and it would take an army to do it – a real one – and for that I needed Naomi.

I went back into the study and looked through the window towards the small shack. The roof was visible through the forest, but there was no sign of Naomi. Then I spotted her concealed amongst the trees by the side of the path that led to the shack, about halfway along, her back to me, observing. Had she seen something? She must have, but it wasn't like her to hold back and wait. She wasn't particularly well hidden either, as if she wanted someone to see her. Then it dawned on me that this was Naomi's way of shouting without shouting.

"Naomi," I said, softly. "Up here."

She turned, saw me at the window and gestured vigorously for me to join her. But before I could move, an SUV came down the gravel road, shot straight passed the house and headed for the shack. Naomi ducked into the trees, out of sight of both the car and me.

"Peter!" I felt, rather than heard Naomi's voice.

I rushed downstairs and had the front door open in an instant, and though I was moving fast, time wasn't. It was as if I was watching myself on a slow-downed video or a dream where the observer within is screaming "hurry!"

I saw everything, including those things I couldn't see.

The car stopped at the shack, two of Ohno's men got out, both armed, the tallest of the two carrying a petrol can, the other a length of rope. They didn't notice me exiting the house behind them. They couldn't even if they had turned around – the path itself was not straight. But I saw them, felt them, heard them, understood them.

They unlocked the door and entered the shack. It was more of a lodge than a shack, as I now knew, with space for people to sit, drink, eat, and see the morning sun rise over the distant peaks. With no telephone, and padlocks on all doors and windows, it was also the perfect place to imprison the family of your enemy, or to firebomb them out of existence to crush the hope and spirit of the one person you believed could have stopped you. I knew all this, and yet the lodge was still not yet in direct sight.

Naomi sprinted out from the trees. She had seen Yuko and Miki within the lodge but had decided to remain hidden until I joined her – a precaution in case Ohno's men returned. She'd been right, but even Naomi had been unable to see their true intentions until they arrived.

I watched Peter Walker run. I saw him, his shape, his form, his physicality – me but not me. I saw the lodge and the people within, felt their fears, sensed their thoughts, understood their hopes, their dreams, their reasons. For an instant I was one with them, separated, yet together. I saw Yuko and Miki cowered in a corner, frightened beyond their senses, unable to cope.

The Kunoichi covered the distance to the lodge swiftly and silently. She burst through the open door and slammed into the tallest of the two men, sending him and his petrol can flying. The other shot at Naomi instinctively, hitting her in the arm. She somersaulted sideways in the way only Naomi could, and in one movement twisted the gun from his hand, kicked him in the head and dropped him to the floor.

The taller man was already back on his feet, had pulled his own pistol from his belt and was holding Miki with the barrel at her head, arm around her neck.

"Enough!" he shouted.

Naomi stood still.

"Put it down!"

Naomi slowly placed the pistol at her feet.

"Kick it away!"

Naomi kicked the pistol a short distance across the floor.

I was thirty yards away.

The man with the gun on Miki had his back to me. They all did, except Yuko. We made eye contact. I knew she was scared, knew that she didn't understand what was happening, knew that she had already given up hope of life – but in the instant when she saw me, Yuko knew that she and Miki were safe. Her nightmare was over. I was there, as I had always said I would be, to love and protect, to keep from harm, to shelter and safeguard until my dying breath.

Then that knowing, that sensing, that connection left me. I was Peter Walker again, running as fast as I could.

But now I knew for certain.

I am the Mamoribito.

Twenty-Three

The one with the gun on Miki heard me first. It's not easy to run silently when you are going flat out – unless you are a Kunoichi, which I was a long way from being. Either that or he followed Yuko's stare. Probably it was a combination of both.

He turned just as I blasted through the door. For him everything must have happened in a flash, his movements a natural, instinctive reaction to a charging rhinoceros approaching at breakneck speed. For me, things happened in slow motion. The man moved the gun away from Miki and tried to get a shot at me, but I was upon him before he managed to get me in his sights. I caught him under the chin with my left arm as I knocked the weapon from his hand with my right, grabbing his wrist as I did so, pulling him round and over and slamming his face to the floor with my own momentum. It was a technique that I had never learned, never practiced, never been shown, and yet it came as naturally to me as walking.

The second man was reaching for his own weapon, the one that Naomi had torn from his grip but had been ordered to kick away. I reached inside my jacket, pulled out the blunt, spherical shuriken and launched it at his left temple. He tried to turn his head, but he wasn't fast enough. The metal ball slammed into the spot right behind his ear. He went down, instantly. It would have killed him if I had thrown it harder, but even though he was about to murder my family I had no desire to take his life. Thirty years in prison would give him time to reflect on his sins.

It was deathly quiet. The two men were down, Naomi was saying something, but her voice had left her. Yuko and Miki were screaming silently, their voices inaudible above… above nothing. There was only void, filled with silence. There was no story, no motion, no frame of reference for me to relate myself to – as if all understanding of reality was lost, replaced by a mirror world of pure energy, pure thought. I was there, present, yet formless – a symbol of my true self that existed on another plane, an unexplored dimension of truth that carried with it a separate vibration, a new frequency that manifested as physicality purely through the desire to be, the wish to exist. I understood everything, could see everything, could go to any place I wanted through the simple affectation of will, of desire, of purposeful decision. I was above and beyond, yet subservient, giving, sacrificing. I existed as all points, all infinities, all coordinates, all instances. I was one with everything, everything was one.

Then it was gone.

"Peter!" It was Naomi.

Yuko was hugging me, in tears, as was Miki. I held them both tightly.

"Where were you?" Naomi asked.

"Right here," I replied, although from the way Naomi was looking at me, I knew I had been anywhere but right here.

Naomi had blood on her sleeve. "You're hurt." I said.

"A scratch, nothing more."

"Peter, are you OK?" It was Yuko, typically more worried about me than herself. She touched her fingers to my face; heaven knew what kind of state it was in.

I looked down at those big brown eyes of hers, now filled with tears. Everything, my whole life, my entire world, was safe in my hands. I could barely dare to contemplate what they had been through; the fear they had felt, the not-knowing, the not-understanding when strange and violent men had called at the hotel, killed Honey, and taken them both into the night. They had both suffered terribly, not physical pain, but the mental anguish that goes along with helplessness. No, anguish was too small a word for what they had been through. Terror, pure terror. I knew what this kind of experience can do to someone; the nightmares that lay ahead, the distrust of others, the fear of the simplest things such as going outdoors. But for now, at this moment, in this instance and every instance from here on, I would safeguard them from danger, shield them from pain, deliver them from fear, guard them while they slept, and protect them with my life.

Yet to do that, I would have to let them go.

I kissed Yuko on the forehead. "I'm Ok. And I'll explain later," I said. "Go with Naomi, she'll take you somewhere safe." I turned to Naomi. "Use the car, take them to your grandfather. Here." I took off my head band, the *hachimaki*. "For you arm."

"I am fine," Naomi protested.

"Don't argue, Naomi," I said as I bound her wound.

"I will come with you, wherever you are going."

"Later. First, I need you to look after my family. Then call your cousins, have them meet me at the Joetsu nuclear power station. It's on the north coast, not far from here. And call the police, the army, anyone you can think of. If they need convincing, it's all on the second floor." I gestured towards the house. "And give me the keys to your bike."

"Why there?" Naomi said, as she handed me the keys.

"Because Ohno is going to blow the reactor and flood the whole of eastern Japan with radiation."

"My God."

"Better call him too."

A groan came from behind me. I looked around at the two players lying on the floor. One was still out cold, the other was waking up. Naomi slipped passed me and slammed the man hard on the side of the temple with the inside of a clenched fist, sending him instantly back to unconsciousness.

She picked up the shuriken and placed it in an inner pocket. I wouldn't be needing that one anymore, apparently. Then Naomi grabbed the rope that the smaller one had been carrying.

"Help me," she said. We quickly tied them up, although I figured they weren't going anywhere as it was.

"Why's he doing this, Naomi?" I asked, as we finished.

"Who?"

"You know who I mean," I said.

Naomi hesitated. "I'm not sure."

"But you know more than you're telling me, don't you." It was a statement, not a question. "And for Ohno, it has to be more than me and Taiyo."

"Grandfather made me promise, Peter."

"To not tell me, you mean."

"When the time is right, I can reveal everything. But not before. I'm sorry."

"And when will that be?" I asked, although it had already occurred to me if I could slip back into the void then I'd find out for myself. But whatever and wherever the void was, it wasn't somewhere I could consciously decide to go. I'd have to figure things out here, in the physical world.

"Soon," Naomi said.

I'd have to take that for what it was. Whatever promise Naomi had made to Yamaguchi Sensei, she wouldn't break it, although obviously things weren't as she had anticipated.

"You weren't expecting this, were you, Naomi," I said.

"No, not like this. And not this soon. We thought we had more time."

"Is there something I should know, before I go out there?"

Naomi shook her head. I believed her. She might have been the most extraordinary women I had ever met, but lying to the Mamoribito wasn't one of her traits. I pushed a little harder, just to make sure. "Or should I take my family back to Tokyo now? I could do that, should do that, actually."

"That is for you to decide, Peter."

Naomi was right. What I did next was up to me, but we

both knew that I had already decided what to do. Maybe later, when the void opened again, I'd understand why.

"Just make sure they're safe," I said. "And bring the cavalry as soon as you can."

"The cavalry?"

"You know what I mean.

"No I don't."

"Google it. Time to go," I said.

"Peter, where are you going?" Yuko asked. I was glad to see that she was recovering from the shock, but it meant that she needed to understand what was going on. "And who is this girl?"

"She's Naomi, and she will explain everything," I said. "But now, I have to go."

"No, wait, I don't understand."

I kissed Yuko and Miki, who was trembling and unable to speak. She was going to need the kind of help that only a trained professional could provide. Before then, though, there were more urgent matters.

"Something is happening, and I have to stop it," I said.

"I still don't understand."

"I'm not sure I do, either," I replied. "Not yet."

Twenty-Four

The Joetsu nuclear power station sat at the base of a smallish mountain that bulged out from the north coast into the Japan Sea. I didn't have any direct knowledge about the Joetsu itself, but I could see that it was a single reactor design, fairly small as these things went, and probably built when the industry was starting up in Japan. As such it wouldn't be anything special, unlike the infamous Monju fast-breeder prototype, stationed a hundred kilometers or so to the west. That was built in the mid-nineties, but due to a series of accidents had only generated electricity for an hour or so since then and was now shut down for decommissioning. The biggest waste of money and time you could think of.

Neither was it like the Fukushima plant, with its four reactors, two of which had leaked hydrogen after the total system failure caused by the Tsunami, resulting in three containment buildings blowing up. No, not caused by the tsunami. The tsunami triggered the event, but the real reason was human failure. The failure to believe that a giant wave could hit despite the geological evidence, the failure to build a sea wall, the failure to move the back-up generators above ground to a height that would place them above even the highest upsurge, the failure of those in control to countenance that their own analysis could conceivably be wrong. The failure to think, to prepare, to get ready. But above all, the failure to act. I'd followed the shenanigans after the earthquake in 2011 and then more recently, as part of my work for Doggy, I'd read the full IAEA report on the accident. It was a chilling read, too.

I parked Naomi's Kawasaki by the side of the narrow mountain access road, three hundred vertical feet above the reactor building. Everything was quiet, as things usually are at a nuclear installation, even when they're working at full capacity. Of course in that case you'd expect some movement of people and vehicles, but this reactor, as with all the others in Japan, had been shut down since the earthquake while the government decided what to do about restarting the industry. But there should still be a maintenance crew there, or maybe the whole crew was still employed on site. There were several cars and trucks parked in the front and rear car parks, but there were still plenty of open spaces for more vehicles. So maybe not a full crew, then.

I took stock. It taken me a little over thirty minutes to get here from Ohno's mountain retreat, which meant that Naomi would soon arrive at the safety of her grandfather's temple, if she hadn't already. If her phone had picked up a signal she would have called ahead to her cousins, but if not, well, then they would have no way of knowing until they too arrived at the temple. But I wasn't worried about them. A small group of Ninja warriors might sound a good thing to have at my disposal, but in reality we needed the army, the navy and whoever else had both the firepower and expertise to stop Ohno. The Japanese Special Forces would have teams prepared and ready for situations such as this, and I doubted they'd appreciate Peter Walker running around with a sword strapped to his back pretending to be the saviour of the world, much less a bunch of black-clad non-military combatants slinging their shuriken around with wild abandon. At best we'd get in the way, at worst we'd get ourselves caught in the crossfire.

But I had to do something, especially because as much as I trusted and loved Naomi, I couldn't take the chance that whoever answered her emergency call would think she was a crackpot. Even if they did believe her, it would still take time for the quick reaction teams to get here. Every second of delay could be critical.

It would be dark in a couple of hours. I liked the night but couldn't wait that long. I started the walk down to the main gate, about a kilometer away. The forest lining the road would conceal me from view, and with no roadside cameras I could have been driving a main battle tank and no-one would have been any the wiser. Shit, if this was the UK, the head of security would have been fired for such a lapse – you don't give potential attackers free reign to approach unseen. Those trees should have been cut down years ago, or perhaps no-one had thought it was necessary while the reactor was offline. Or maybe they were simply there to stop the plant from spoiling the view of passing tourists, and I was barking up the wrong tree, literally.

I was closer to the gate now, and the down-slope treeline was about to end. The last eighty yards were open space, with no places for concealment. This was better – the security guy could have his job back. I couldn't see anyone at the main gates, but it didn't mean nobody was there, or no one was on lookout. But the way forward was sideways. I walked across the road to the treeline on the mountain side, which was still in place. Running would have attracted attention, and if Ohno's men were watching the rapid movement could have caught their eye, like a hawk hunting for a mouse in the summer wheat.

I moved forward until the road turned back towards the plant. This part of the road ran parallel to the stony beach, and the trees offered me cover until I was at the shoreline. So far so good, but there was still the problem of the gap between the end of the cover and the security fence surrounding the plant, which had cameras situated every ten yards or so. The security guy was going up in my estimation. I could wait until nightfall and walk across the tarmac unseen, as I doubted those cameras were infrared, but by then it could be too late, even if the whole Japanese military had arrived.

Then I noticed three small rubber boats moored to the beach at the nearest point to the security fence. I hadn't seen them earlier because they were below the line of the concrete waterfront that formed the barrier between the plant and the sea. They bobbed in and out of view as waves graced the shore, and were the kind of boats that Marine Commandos used – small, fast, with muffles on their propellers to hide the sound.

Why would Ohno need boats? He owned the plant and could drive in through the front gates. Then it hit me – it was part of his deception. First the attack on the hydro plant, then the attack here. Well, if the boats were hidden by the waterfront, then that was my route in.

Keeping low, I stepped up the rocks onto the concrete walkway and down the other side to the stony beach, from where I couldn't see the fence and its cameras – but it meant neither could they see me. I could have led a team of twenty in an unobserved attack in broad daylight from here. Minus two points for the security guy. Speaking of daylight, it would be darker sooner than I had predicted, maybe an hour away, probably because I had been halfway up a mountain when I'd made that assessment. I still couldn't wait that long, but I'd welcome the darkness when it came, even if all the lights came on. I was good at working my way through the shadows they would create, which I might have to when I was making my exit.

I made my way to the rubber boats, or combat rubber raiding craft to give them their proper name. All three had markings in Korean, both on the engine and the rubber of the boats themselves. I didn't speak the language, but I recognized the alphabet. Twenty yards away there was a gap in the security fence. A pair of wire cutters lay on the ground, as if carelessly dropped during the raid. Not dropped, of course, not to my eyes. I doubted anyone investigating the incident would be fooled either, but you could never know about these things. So, that was Ohno's plan; conduct a false flag attack and blame the Koreans for the resulting mayhem and all that could escalate into. Why he'd want to do that was anybody's guess. Well, whatever his reasons, whatever his purpose, he'd been found out. But it wouldn't amount to much if he could blow the reactor. I had to make sure he didn't do it, and make sure I didn't end up as missing in action either.

I climbed up the beach side of the waterfront and peered over the top. All was quiet. There were twelve vehicles in the car park at the rear of the reactor. Together with the three boats and the cars parked out front it implied there were between fifteen to twenty in the raiding party, plus whoever had arrived by road. Or fewer than that, or more – I had no idea. Shit, my mission assessment capabilities had atrophied beyond rusty into abject feebleness. I closed my eyes. Nothing came to me, no void, no message, no vision to show me the right thing to do, the right path to take. I opened my eyes again. I was on my own. The path was mine to decide.

I scrambled over the top of the waterfront, headed down the other side and was quickly through the gap in the fence. With a strong sense of deja-vu from the events at the hydro plant, I headed across the rear car park to the main building, using the cars as cover. I felt terribly exposed but moved with some confidence that there was nobody watching the security camera video feed. Or was that just wishful thinking?

I stayed hidden behind the vehicle nearest the main building while I watched the small rear entrance for two minutes. Nobody came out looking for me, so I could have been right about their lack of concern of discovery. It was a strange plan, as the likelihood of a Korean raiding party arriving by boat in the afternoon was ludicrous – they'd have to arrive at night under the cover of darkness. Unless they planned to leave one or more of the boats behind as evidence. Once the reactor was blown the whole area would be too contaminated for anyone to investigate on foot, but any one of those Korean-marked craft would easily be picked up by a helicopter camera, wherever they were to be found. So maybe that was it, unless I was missing something. Shit, I didn't know, and it didn't matter that I didn't know. All that mattered was to prevent anything from happening until the cavalry arrived.

There was nothing for it but to keep moving. I walked the last few yards to the door, all the time fighting the urge to sprint like a maniac and attract the attention of whoever was supposed to be watching the security feed. The door had an electronic entrance key, but I had a suspicion it wasn't operative. It wasn't. The door opened silently with no creaking hinges nor alarm bells splitting the air. A small mercy, but another minus point for the security guy. Except, of course, it must have been the security guy who had disabled the systems in the first place – minus fifty points for him. How Ohno had managed to recruit so many willing players for his team was beyond my meagre capacity to compute.

Ahead of me was a radiation monitoring station. Resembling a cross between a metal-detector at an airport and a hospital x-ray machine, it consisted of three individual frames with automated Geiger counters designed to scan for unwelcome isotopes. There was no barrier. I could have walked straight through, but I didn't want to risk setting off any alarms by not following procedures. I took the sword off my back and held it to one side as I stood inside one of the frames to let it scan me. A sign in front of me warned, 'Alarm will sound if scan interrupted.' A green light blinked; I'd passed the test. It was a useful indication, too – some systems were inoperative, others were still in place. I stepped through the detector, took the sword from its bag and used the strapping that ran from the scabbard to the hilt to secure it over my shoulder and on to my back. I dropped the bag to the floor.

I was in the long corridor that ran from the detectors to, well, that was the problem – I didn't know where it went. Christ, I'd broken every infiltration rule I knew. I'd approached in daylight instead of darkness, I had no plan of the building to work from, had minimal weaponry, was alone with no immediate backup, save for Naomi and her cousins and, with any luck, the Japanese Army – all of whom could be hours from getting here. On top of all that I was probably breaking a thousand laws and would either end up in jail or a bullet in my thick skull.

Then I saw my reflection in the glass of a pair swing doors. The room they led into was unlit, and the light from the corridor bounced straight back at me. It wasn't a perfect mirror, but it was the first one I had encountered for two days and was reflective enough to show the damage to my head and face. It looked worse that it felt, possibly because Sensei's magic potions were still having an effect, but I could see why Yuko had been so upset. Blood caked my hair, the bruises surrounding my left eye were black and blue – it was a wonder it hadn't closed – and there was a gash on my cheek that had either been made by a bullet at the hydro plant or had happened when Octavius and I had careered off the side of that mountain. It hadn't registered with me at the temple, but I was going to have one hell of a scar. With the Ninja sword strapped across my back I would have passed a Call of Duty audition with flying colours.

At least I was still alive, and although I didn't fancy walking down a corridor with no exits and bumping into someone with an AK-47, there was only one thing for it; I had to keep moving. My intention was to get to the doors at the far end, which was a good twenty-five yards away, and maybe get lucky with a connecting corridor somewhere on the way. Or perhaps these swing doors might lead somewhere. I pushed them gently open to reveal a small room full of filing cabinets, with no external window and no other exit, either.

Feeling exposed and vulnerable, I moved forward as quickly and as quietly as I could, treading on the sides of my soles and then putting my weight fully on each foot – an old Ninja method that I had learned in the dojo but had never used, until now. It was surprisingly effective, or maybe my heart was thumping so hard in my chest I couldn't hear anything above the accompanying rush of blood in my ears.

There were two more pairs of doors on the way. The first opened into a locker room, the kind where you store safety equipment rather than clothing. Again, there was no window and no exit. The second pair of doors were locked, but even if they opened, I didn't expect to find anything much different inside. The main entrance was at the front of the plant, so the staff clothing and changing rooms would have been located there, along with the radiation exposure badges and portable detection equipment, not here around the back of the complex.

There must have been a workforce somewhere in the building – you don't just shut down a nuclear plant, switch off the lights and put the cat out before heading home – plus I had seen several vehicles outside. So, where were they? Not here, that was for sure. Even if all the nuclear fuel had been taken out of the reactor and stored, there would still need to be a crew onsite to keep the spent fuel covered with water in the storage pools, assuming this was an old boiling water design, the same as the reactors at Fukushima, which I suspected it was. You'd also need to maintain the pumps, the piping, the refuelling system and all the other equipment that kept the plant functioning.

Then it suddenly occurred to me; the tsunami was a decade ago, and by now any fuel should have been removed not only from the reactor but also the whole building. So how the hell was Ohno going to initiate a nuclear catastrophe without the requisite means to do so?

A sound.

Footsteps, two people at least, maybe three. I was still standing at the locked doors – the unlocked doors were behind me. I didn't want to trap myself inside one of those rooms, but I wasn't a lot better off standing in the open corridor, either. There was nowhere to hide, no handy cabinet to duck behind, no convenient manhole to drop myself into.

I inched backwards. The sound came closer, louder – two men speaking Korean in un-hushed voices that were clear enough for anyone nearby to hear. The end of my corridor was ten yards away, forming a T-junction with the corridor that they were on. Their shadows came first. I could see the familiar outline of the AK-47s they were both carrying. I wasn't too pleased to have been right about those nastily effective weapons. My options were hopelessly limited. Unless I sprinted, I'd never make it back to one of the rooms – and if I did that then there was no way they wouldn't hear me. I crouched low against the wall, ready to spring forward.

A walkie-talkie crackled. The two men stopped in their tracks, inches from the T-Junction, while one of them answered the call. I could see the front of their torsos – if they moved forward half a step I'd come into their field of view.

"Kim," he said, then was quiet for a while as he listened to the somewhat garbled instructions – garbled from where I was, that is. "*Ihae haess-eoyo,*" he said as the call finished, meaning he had understood. It was the just about my entire Korean vocabulary. He said something else in Korean to his partner and they turned and headed back the way they had come.

I breathed again.

I moved quietly forward to the corridor intersection and glanced around the corner. The two of them were about fifteen yards away, oblivious to my presence, and were chatting quite openly in their native language. They wore black combat utilities and carried pistols on their belts to go along with their assault rifles. With their gear and weaponry they may have thought they looked the part, but they were holding those AKs like a couple of untrained extras in a B movie. Good. On the other hand, all they had to do was spray rounds in my general direction and that would be the end of my part in this particular scene.

They stopped and looked through a small window into a

room," then turned and exited the corridor through a pair of swing doors. I waited for thirty seconds – they didn't come back. I stepped forward and tried the doors at the T-Junction. They opened into a short passageway that led to a flight of stairs, which I was about to take when I realized that there must have been a reason for the two players to have checked that room.

I stepped backwards, headed down the corridor and peeked through the same window, conveniently labelled in English as 'Auxiliary Feed Pipe Room 3.' There were some twenty men inside the room, all wearing uniforms emblazoned with 'Joetsu Nuclear' on their chests, all bound with ropes to the series of pipes that ran across the floor and through the ceiling. Each one of them had duct tape across their mouth. Some had blood on their faces, the tell-tale result of being pistol whipped, or worse. One or two looked in pretty bad shape. Now I knew why Ohno's associates had walked past talking so loudly. They'd wanted their voices to be heard, to be understood as the perpetrators, to be identifiable later by the poor bastards in that room as they spewed up their guts, their insides dissolving from the deadly radiation that was about to be unleashed.

The two handles of the swing doors were barred with an axe taken from a fire hydrant to my left – the shattered glass from the casing littered the floor. Why bother securing a room that no-one has any hope of escaping from? Being thorough, I supposed. I removed the axe and went in. Every eye that was still capable of seeing was on me. I placed a finger across my lips, removed the sword from its scabbard and approached the oldest one of them, guessing that he, as the most senior, would be the group leader. The sight of me with the sword frightened him, and he desperately tried to push himself away.

I knelt beside him. "It's OK," I said quietly. "I'm here to help." He still wasn't convinced. I reached forward and removed the tape from across his mouth. "Do you speak English?" I asked, not wanting to confuse him any further with my brilliant Japanese language skills.

"A little," he replied, nervously.

"What's your name?" Getting him to say who was would help to center him, to bring away from his fear, back to himself.

"Morishita. I am Morishita."

"Ok Morishita-san, like I said, I'm here to help. I'm going to cut the rope. Ok?"

He nodded. It took me a moment to position the blade between the stands of rope, but when I did it cut through quickly and efficiently. The man was soon free and massaging his aching joints.

"Morishita-san, please listen carefully. They're going to blow the plant and flood the whole area with radioactivity." I said, though I think he had already figured that out for himself. "But there shouldn't be any fuel here, right, since the shutdown? Or is there?"

The look on his face said it all.

"There is fuel here?"

"We are get ready stage for reactor stress test, next week after. Reactor is full, but shutted down, not started yet."

He wasn't wrong when he said he spoke a little English, but I got what he meant. "But you're only a small workforce. Where's everybody else?"

"New automation system is put in," he said. "No need for many worker forces. That is test. For restart approving."

"I see."

So, that was it. The plant would be viable while they tested the systems. It was public knowledge that various reactors around the country were doing something similar, as part of the government's drive to improve safety. They must have had permission to re-fuel and run the tests, and would either de-fuel later or leave the uranium in place while negotiations for a return to full operations continued.

"The back-up generators? Where are they?" I asked.

"Same place. But, inside, how to say, like box, to stop sea coming. With air pipe, like submarine."

"A snorkel, you mean."

Glad to have been understood, Morishita smiled. "Yes. snorkel," he said.

Ohno's plan was clearer to me now; disable the generators, blow the main power lines and, to be doubly sure, wreck the hydro-electric back up too. Then remove the control rods, get the reactor going and then remotely set off the charges to blow every pipe in sight. With the coolant water leaking the reactor would melt down in hours, if not minutes. As long as you'd made your getaway in time, you'd be safe enough. Except Ohno's men were still here, which meant they were still setting things up. Unless that call was the signal to leave. In which case I'd better get moving.

"What about emergency procedures?" I asked. "Who do you call in case of a terrorist attack?"

"Government and army. But we cannot call. No keitai phones, all taken, and calling government phone is in control room. They are there."

"How many?"

"Fifteen, I'm think. Maybe could be twenty. From Korea."

I corrected him. "Some of them are from Japan."

Morishita found that hard to believe. "From Japan, too?"

I nodded. Wherever they were from they had AK-47s. I had a sword, a pistol and surprise on my side, which wasn't much, but these poor souls had nothing. If I asked for their help, they'd end up being killed, or getting me killed, which I didn't fancy at all. I returned the sword to its scabbard, then took out a sharp-edged shuriken from an inside pocket and handed it to him.

"Here, cut everyone free, then get out through the back entrance, the one by the car park, and as far away from here as you can. There's a hole in the fence, you'll see it easily. Then call the police and everyone else you know, tell them what's happening. Understand?"

Morishita was fascinated by the shuriken, and more so by this strange creature in front of him. "You are Ninja?" he asked, incredulity in his voice.

"No. Yes. It doesn't matter. You need to get everybody moving. I expect you can untie everyone." I pointed to the shuriken. "But that is just in case you can't. Understood?"

"Yes, but I stay, help you."

It was a brave offer, but there was no way I would accept it. "No, thank you," I said. "Your job is to help these people."

I took the pistol from my belt and handed it to Morishita-san. "Take this. You might need it." From the way he took the weapon I guessed he was ex-military. "Do you know how to use it?" I asked, hoping I wouldn't need to use it myself.

He nodded. "JDF, ten years, before here."

Morishita had been in the Japan Defence Forces. Good. "These men are under you care now." I said, confident he would lead them to safety. "Get them back to their families and prepare for the worst."

"But who will look after for you?"

Morishita was more concerned for me than for himself. I already liked him a lot. "Don't worry about me," I said. "I have friends on their way."

"JDF friends?"

"You could say that." I turned to go.

"Wait!"

I stopped and turned around.

"Who are you?"

"I'm the test prevention officer." I said, confusing him with my wonderful sense of humour. "Peter. My name is Peter."

And with that I was gone.

#

As I climbed the stairs behind the door at the T-junction it struck me that I could have used Morishita-san's help, at least with regards to the internal plant layout. I had no idea where the stairs would lead to, but I was guessing it was the route to the main turbine and generator area. It made some sense, as the building itself was long and rectangular, very different from the cylindrical reactor building, which I had seen from the outside and had estimated to be a hundred feet tall.

I by-passed the second and third floors and gently eased open the door at the top of the staircase. I was right, it was the turbine room. It was big, too, significantly bigger than the equivalent room at the hydro plan. From my vantage point on the fourth floor I was looking down at a single turbine, fed by four large steam pipes straight from the reactor. In line with the turbine was the generator, and together the whole assembly was around thirty yards long. From my experience on exercises in the UK I'd expected a sea of pipework, with feed lines and other paraphernalia going every which way, but it wasn't that way at all – just the big reactor lines coming up through the floor and going into the top of the turbine, plus similar pipes leading back down through the floor, where there'd be a more complex network in the space below. Japanese efficiency at its best.

Which wasn't something that I could say for myself. From my position I could see most of the room, but the area below the walkway that the door opened on to was hidden from view. It meant no one could see me, but I wasn't doing anything useful either – which made me wonder what the hell I was going to do anyway. I had zero chance against a small army of armed and determined men, and even if they couldn't shoot straight it wouldn't take a great deal of effort for twenty of them to defeat a solitary Peter Walker. No, my best chance was to make a nuisance of myself, to keep them guessing, to delay any actions they were planning until the boys with their tanks and helicopters got here. And if the bad guys thought they could negotiate their way out with hostages, well, they'd be wrong about that.

I opened the door fully, crept to the other side of the walkway and carefully looked over the edge. There were four charges with remote detonators on the feed pipes directly beneath my position. I wasn't too happy to have been proven right about Ohno's plan – but there wasn't much I could do about those packages. Even if they weren't booby-trapped, de-activating each one would take too long, and I'd need a ladder to reach two of them, so that idea was a no-go.

Then suddenly and alarmingly, sirens blasted, orange lights flashed and "Turbine Start" blared over the loudspeakers.

Christ.

They'd already started the reactor. Then everything went quiet, expect for the ominous sound of the turbine starting to spin under automated control.

The control room! I had to find it. I spotted a metal staircase leading to the turbine room floor. With the noise from the spinning turbine as cover, I was down the stairs and across the concrete to the exit point at the far end of the complex in seconds. The doors opened into another corridor, running at right-angles. Thankfully right in front of me was a sign saying, 'Main Control Room,' with an arrow pointing to the left, and beneath that was a schematic of the plant layout. Finally, I knew where I was and where I needed to go. What I was going to do when I got there was something I'd figure out on the way – and I had a whole twenty yards and a couple of flights flight of stairs to do that in. Whatever it was going to be though, making a nuisance of myself wasn't going to be enough.

I headed towards the stairs, passing doors on my left marked 'Main Condenser Area.' Another pair of doors led to the 'Condenser Pump Room.' Signs at the foot of the stairs pointed downwards to 'Feedwater Area' and upwards to 'Main Control Room.' All very helpful, especially if you were on an unguided tour, like I was.

I went up the single flight of stairs that led to the main control room as softly, carefully, and as noiselessly as I could. As I climbed, I began to make out the voices of those inside, and although their words didn't carry it was clear they were speaking Japanese – or was it Korean? I couldn't tell from this distance. Pausing and keeping deathly quiet, I peered over the top step, keeping as low as possible. Ahead of me the control room doors were jammed wide open, giving me a clear view of a little over half the area, the rest of the room being hidden by the thick, radiation resistant walls.

There were fifteen men visible. Five were dressed in black with radio headsets and walkie-talkies on their belts, three of whom knew how to handle their Kalashnikovs. Two sat at the control desks, wearing the same uniforms as the men who'd been tied up downstairs – Ohno's insiders, no doubt. The rest wore suits with tell-tale bulges under their armpits. I recognised several of them from the hydro-plant, plus two more from the battle at the building site, when Naomi had saved me. God, how I wished she and her cousins were here now. I hoped they were on their way, but with more armed players somewhere beyond my field of view a small would-be army of Ninjas wouldn't be enough – we needed the real thing.

I had half an idea to close the doors and jam them solid, just as they had done to the workers downstairs. But for that I'd need an axe, plus a set of Ironman body armour to keep me alive while everyone reacted to those heavy doors creaking shut. I'd need a better idea than that.

Then I heard Ohno's commanding voice. "Bring them forward."

Two middle-aged men in what the locals called 'guardman' uniforms were pulled into view by a couple of Ohno's team, their hands tied behind their backs and their mouths taped.

The rest of his group stood back to allow Ohno to come through. Tanaka came with him, a silencer-equipped pistol in hand. The fellows with the two guards stood away, leaving the two men exposed with fear in their eyes. I didn't like the look of this.

"I must improve the security at my other nuclear plants," Ohno said, in English, presumably for the benefit of the Koreans in the room. "But, thank you for your gallantry in defending my property."

Ohno nodded to Tanaka, who fired two quick shots. Both men fell backwards, blood oozing from the holes in their chests, their hearts having instantly stopped.

Christ.

I'd let that happen. I could have stopped it, should have intervened. Instead, I'd done nothing, and two innocent men were dead.

Ohno addressed the men on the floor in Japanese. *"Your families will be well looked after, do not concern yourselves with their fates. In their eyes, in Japan's eyes, you will be heroes."*

Fuck this. It was time to start making that nuisance of myself. I stood up.

Ohno turned to address his crew, again speaking English. "It is time, make the final arrangements," he said, "and bring me the detonator device-"

Everyone was in a rough semicircle, facing Ohno, their backs to me. Only Ohno was looking in my direction. I was standing at the top of the stairs, in full view, and it must have given Ohno the surprise of his long life to see me there. Tanaka turned first – the priceless look on his face said it all. The others followed. Half of them hadn't met me yet, but those that had were as astonished as Tanaka. One of the men in black raised his weapon.

"Put down your guns," Ohno commanded, with the quiet authority of one who is always obeyed. He moved forward a step but remained within the protective circle of his men. From this range I could have shot him straight in the head with my eyes closed. I was already beginning to miss that bloody pistol. We stared at each other; my third Mexican stand-off of the week.

"Ah, that is why we have not yet heard from my men," Ohno said. "I should have known. Congratulations, Peter-san, could it be that you really are the Mamoribito?"

So, the two in the GT-R hadn't been in contact. Either the police had arrived and arrested them for possession of firearms, or the car had slipped through the trees and the poor bastards had crashed with it to the valley floor. Either way, I said nothing, mostly because I was working out what to do when the firing started.

The trouble was my options were limited. I could either dive away down the stairs or charge down the corridor and take the intersecting passage, which I was sure would lead to the reactor itself. Whichever I chose I'd want to put as much distance between myself and those angry barrels as I could. Neither way was enticing, but there weren't many other choices – especially as at this range I was a sitting duck. Correction, a standing duck. Whatever happened, though, I had an advantage, as they'd have to assume I'd disabled some of the charges. If I could keep evading their pursuit, or even if I couldn't, they'd still have to check everything. It might delay them enough to give the quick reaction force time to get here – providing they believed Naomi. At the very least it would give Morishita-san a chance to get everyone clear of the building, and then find a phone and call the QRF himself.

Maybe I could make a severe nuisance of myself, after all.

"You don't look well, Peter-san," Ohno said. "Perhaps you would prefer to join us. We can offer you more than you could possibly expect, I'm sure."

Two of the men in black moved to their left. They were professionals who clearly knew what they were doing, unlike the rest of the crew who stood perfectly still. I, on the other hand, couldn't just stand there, I had to do something, and each few seconds of conversation would add more delay, more disruption.

"I saw it all, Ohno." I said. "In the house on the mountain, in your secret room. That's why you destroyed the hydroelectric plant. It's the fail-safe back up to keep the cooling pumps running, and with them offline and the reactor in full meltdown, when you blow this place the fallout will blanket everything from here to Tokyo. Nothing can stop it. What is it, Ohno? A false flag? Making everything look Korean?"

Ohno smiled. "North Korean, Peter. As are the weapons, and the uniforms. And some of our friends here, too, along with their shared desires to end that terrible regime. It adds authenticity, don't you think? And you're wrong about my hydro-electric plant, Peter. It's no more than a distraction, a complication designed to show how Ohno, the great industrialist, is himself a victim of this tragic day. Not that anyone should have any doubts, if we consider what will soon happen to this installation."

So, Ohno had wrecked the hydro plant to shift suspicion away from himself for what was about to happen here, at Joetsu. Maybe that was the real reason why he had left me in there; not as an anti-saboteur, but as *the* saboteur who got trapped in his own game of destruction. Well, I was delighted to have not complied with that little idea of his. But it was his bigger idea I was worried about.

"If you do this, Ohno, you'll start a war."

That hit a nerve.

"Yes, I am starting a war! They deserve it! Each and every one of them, they all deserve to die! All of them!"

Ohno checked himself. He took a slow, deep breath, which I doubted anyone noticed, except for me. It was the first sign of a chink in Ohno's perfectly composed armour.

"For half my life," he continued, calmer now, "I have waited for this moment of retribution."

"By destroying your own country?" I said, keeping one eye on Ohno and every other one on his men. All it would take is for one itchy trigger finger to be scratched and I'd be in host of trouble. But I knew how hard it is to hit a moving target, and I was ready to move faster than I had ever done before. Until it came to that, though, I'd keep Ohno talking.

"What do you know of destruction?" he said. "I was there, in Hiroshima, the day that hideous bomb fell. I was just a child, but I saw my whole life, my whole world destroyed. I survived, a Hibakusha, but I never forgot that day, what it means to lose everything you have, everything you love."

I hardly knew Ohno, but from what little I did know I couldn't picture him as loving anything. Maybe I was wrong, but that didn't make him right, either.

"I lost everything I cared about. And then again, at the

hands of that madman! Everything! And now they aim their missiles at us, and we do nothing. Nothing! What has become of my country, my people? We are impotent, useless fools, just waiting. And waiting for what? For destruction to rain down on us again? For the American President to hold hands and smile with that dictator? Is that who we have become? Why is it only I who can see this? Only I who knows what must be done? Only I who can awaken Japan? Because only I can see what will happen if we do nothing. And you come here with your blue eyes and your false superiority. You should be with me, helping me, not trying to stop me!"

What did he mean, lost everything again? Was this what Naomi had been wanting to tell me back at the mountain retreat? I was missing something here, that was certain, and I wasn't happy that Naomi and her grandfather had been holding things back from me. But that would have to wait. I'd find out later, provided I could get myself out of here in one piece.

"You've forgotten something, Ohno," I said. "This is where I live, this is where my family live. And I will defend them and this beautiful country until my dying breath."

"Then we are not so different, are we?" he replied. "Take him!"

The two professionals in black needed no further invitation. I lunged to my right as bullets slammed into the wall behind me, the deafening crash of those big rounds going off in that confined space scaring the living daylights out of me. So much for keeping him talking. I'd trusted my instincts, but this wasn't going to be much of a plan.

I bolted for the intersection.

I had three seconds before they made it to the control room doors and sprayed my corridor with fire.

Two seconds.

I could feel them, sense their intentions, know their minds and their hearts, but I was still too far from the connecting corridor that led to the reactor building.

One second – the slender difference between life and death.

Time up. I was in their sights.

I made it to the corner as rounds blasted again, sending high velocity bullets buzzing past my ears down the length of the main corridor. I had five more seconds before they made it to the corridor intersection and fired again. I'd only needed three to cover the same distance, but I was faster than they could ever be, as you are when your life is in the balance and your soul is screaming at you to put as much distance between yourself and danger as you can – to survive, to endure, to live.

The doors that led to the reactor building were jammed open – as the doors in the control room had been – to allow radioactive to flow unhindered, I expected, as if a few centimetres of lead-lining would have made a difference, especially if they had blown the containment building walls.

I was through and into reactor area as gunshots thundered behind me. A voice shouted something in Korean. The firing stopped.

I sprinted around to the far side of the circular concrete shielding and immediately knew why they had stopped firing. The level I was on gave access to the middle half of the reactor vessel, which pushed up through the concrete flooring like a rose bulb in springtime, extending upwards through to the next floor and downwards below my feet. These unpleasant things tended to be huge, some thirty yards tall and six across, and when you add in the concrete casing they're enormous, and intimidating with it. I'd been on several 'guided tours' back home and had no immediate concerns about standing next to a working reactor and receiving an unintended dose of a few millisieverts, but it didn't mean I wanted to hang around either, especially considering the threatening packages that I could now see fixed on the coolant feed-pipes.

Which was why they had stooped shooting. A ricocheting bullet could impact a detonator and set off one of those charges, and although that would mean goodbye to their prey, the vultures themselves would be in physical danger from the super-heated water flashing to steam and inundating the area. A decent sized bullet hole in a pipe would have a similar effect. And if they somehow avoided that burning hell, there was the imminent core meltdown to consider. I suspected there were built-in safety systems to deal with such a massive coolant failure – although Ohno's men may have already initiated a failsafe by-pass. In fact, their whole plan depended on it.

Would that stop them risking a shot at me? I couldn't imagine a sane person would do such thing, but sanity didn't seem to be a requirement for entry in this particular club. I heard whispers, then silence, followed by the ominous sounds of thick, heavy, doors being shut. That didn't sound good, not good at all. I inched slowly around the cylindrical shielding. There was no one there.

Shit.

I walked forward and tried the doors. They were locked. I searched for another exit. There was wasn't one. The only way in or out was through the main entrance. Fuck, this was a doubly-dumb idea. I was trapped next to a nuclear reactor that was going to either melt down or blow up – most likely both.

But Peter Walker wasn't the only mis-calculating idiot in the building. They may have shut me in, but they'd left me with two sets of C4. If I could get one off its pipe, I reckoned I could set it against the doors, hot wire the remote detonator and blow my way out, if I didn't manage to blow myself up in the process. Alternatively, I could pull off the detonators on both packages, which would screw up their plans. No, it couldn't be that easy. Some of those players knew what they were doing. They'd have put anti-handling devices on each charge, which would fire the detonator before anyone could remove it. I would if I was them.

I checked the nearest package. Sure enough, I could see a little mercury vial nested between the remote circuit and the detonator charge. Given time and a bomb disposal team, they could be defeated. But there wasn't time, no team in the area, and the only defeat in the room was mine.

Then the realization hit me – I'd made a bad mistake, a simple, stupid, schoolboy mistake. If I was right, and they were going to depart before remotely setting off the explosives, then all we had to was wait for them to leave and Morishita-san could have shut down the reactor safely before any detonations had taken place.

Walker, you fucking moron.

I took off the sword from my back and set it beside me as I sat down on the cold concrete floor. There wasn't a lot else I could do. What was it with power stations trapping me in enclosed spaces – did they have something against me?

"Well, Stan, that's another nice mess you've gotten me into," I said, laughing at nothing.

Twenty-Five

I sat there for ten minutes, maybe more, staring at the monster in front of me. I'd never been a big fan of nuclear energy, much less so today. I understood the benefits and the myriad of reasons why governments loved them, but there was plenty that could go catastrophically wrong, and despite the thick shielding between me and the reactor core I had my back firmly against the outside wall, as far away as I could get.

I was going to die here, today, in this place. My tomb would be a Chernobyl-like monolith, a monument to mankind's folly, a memorial to the divisions that separate us, a temple to the lies that we tell, the pretence we give to brotherhood, a shrine to the whole, sad story of everything that had once been held in balance…

Balance!

Why hadn't I thought of it before? I went through the idea from every angle. It could work. It would have to work. And if it didn't, I wouldn't know a thing about it. In any case, I'd been here a while, and at any moment they could hit the button and remotely detonate the charges. So, what was I waiting for?

I removed the sword from its scabbard and approached the most accessible C4 package, the one on the lowest of the pipes. The familiar grey-white block was wrapped in clear plastic film and strapped to the pipe by duct tape. They'd overdone it, too – there was enough of the stuff to blow a hole in a main battle tank. Maybe they'd planned to knock a chunk out of the reactor shielding but had changed their minds. Embedded in the center was the remote detonator. As long as a signal could get through the outside building walls, the whole thing was valid. I had to assume the small mercury vial was also valid. It was set vertically, and in theory the relatively small movement of someone trying to remove the package would disturb the mercury enough to cause it to swish around and connect across the two open electrodes, completing the circuit. Simple enough in principle, deadly in practice. Except there must have been a minimum sensitivity requirement – you'd have to consider both the vibration from the coolant pipes and the possibility of an earthquake. After all, you wouldn't want anything to happen while you were still in the building, particularly if you were standing right next to the thing.

With my left hand on the package and the other on the hilt of the sword, I readied myself to cut the tape. I positioned the blade, then stopped. Releasing my hand from the package I stepped back and took off my trainers and socks. If I was going to carry that thing to the door, I wanted each step to be as true and gentle as possible. I repositioned myself and began to cut the tape. The blade was good and true, and the whole assembly was soon free.

So far so good.

Keeping my left hand in place, I bent down and ever-so-softly set the sword on the floor. I stood up, trying to ignore the icy-cold touch of the concrete on the soles of my feet, and placed my right hand on the package. Ever, ever-so-gently I lifted it away from the piping, the mercury in the glass vial visibly wobbling with every thump of my heart. I took a slow, careful step towards the door. What was a mere twenty-yard journey now seeming an eternity away. But the die was cast, there was no turning back. I took another step, then another. I went two yards, then three, then five, then ten. I was halfway there, and still alive, but unless I could steady my hands that happy state of being might not last. I stood still, slowed my breathing to control my Ki, calming my spirit and my heart.

It worked. The shaking left me, and I covered the last few yards smoothly, though equally slowly. I very, very carefully positioned the package at the base of the doors, at the center point were both halves connected. These things weren't like claymores, which exploded forward, so it didn't matter in which direction I placed it. I left it there, hoping there was enough explosive to make more than a big dent, and not so much as to damage the pipes or set off the tremblor switch on the other charge – the chances of which were about fifty-fifty, despite the protection of the reactor shielding. Worse than that, in fact way worse, considering how much C4 they'd packed.

I retraced my steps and put my socks and trainers back on. I inspected the other package still on the pipe. Removing it and setting it down on the floor at the base of the reactor shielding might provide some additional protection from the blast, but I'd pushed my luck far enough already. Shit, this was turning out to be the worst idea I'd had all day. But I was out of options. I was committed.

I picked up the sword and went as far around the cylindrical containment vessel as I could, taking up a position equidistant from the door and the other charge still on the pipe. I placed the sword on the floor, removed my last shuriken from an inside pocket, took careful aim and threw it hard at the package. I dived away as the clatter of metal upon metal echoed around the chamber.

Nothing happened.

Lying on my stomach, I inched forward around the cylinder. The shuriken was lying on the floor, the mark where it had struck the door clearly visible a couple of inches above the package. I had to try again – there was no alternative. I got up, retrieved the fallen shuriken, returned to the safe point, aimed, and threw again, diving away as I had before. Nothing happened, save for the same clatter of metal upon metal.

It was the dive, I told myself. The anticipation of the movement was throwing off my aim. I needed to stay still, calm and focused. I retrieved the shuriken and, keeping as close as I could to the protective concrete of the containment vessel, took aim once more. The required technique is more akin to throwing a dart than chucking a cricket ball, but the essential method is the same – keep your eye steady and ensure that the follow-through is directly on target. I readied myself and threw, my eyes and outstretched fingers following the spin of those five-pointed stars all the way to the package.

A direct hit.

FUCK!

I leapt behind the cylinder a micro-second before the package exploded with a gigantic, roaring blast that thundered around the chamber. I was already curled up into ball with my hands over my ears and my mouth open, but the pressure wave caught me and in that relatively small space it was incredibly, violently loud. Although the thick concrete of the containment vessel had protected me from the full force of the initial detonation, I still felt as if I'd been hit by a sledgehammer. It was the ultimate stun grenade, and I was well and truly stunned. I rolled around on the floor, disoriented, opening and closing my mouth like a fish out of water, as if that would somehow do something.

How the other charge had remained unaffected was a mystery. Maybe the tremblor was defective. I didn't know and didn't care. All I knew was that I had to move before Ohno's men came to investigate. I staggered to my feet, picked up the sword and stumbled towards the doors. The area was full of residual smoke from the detonated C4, but there was enough visibility for me to see my way. Halfway there I turned back to check on the coolant pipes. They had sustained surface damage from the blast, with some serious looking indentations, but were holding true. Then I spotted the shuriken embedded in one of the pipes, blown there by the force of the explosion. It was almost comical, but with high-pressure water still flowing through those pipes it represented a weak point. It could go at any second – the reactor needed to be shut down immediately. It did anyway, before Ohno blew the rest of the charges throughout the plant.

I kept moving. The two doors had been shoved apart at the center join, as if punched by some colossal, angry giant. The gap wasn't huge, but I was through just as a thicker and heavier blast door was lowering from its station in the ceiling. It hadn't registered with me on the way in, but it was must have been part of the automated-response system that kicked into operation once an event had been detected. That was one thing Ohno's team had overlooked. Good. With any luck a notification would be on its way to the authorities. If they hadn't believed Naomi before, they would now. I'd have to update Doggy when this was over – if other plants had the same systems then things were better than I had realized.

I put that rather fanciful notion out of my mind and dodged under the blast door. Still unsteady, I sprinted as best I could to the corner were the two corridors connected. It was then that I became aware of the flash of the yellow emergency lights and the sound of the alarm. It was quiet at first, then got louder as my hearing returned. It wasn't an ear-piercing scream either, more of a strong notification that urgent attention was required. Panic is not something to be encouraged in a nuclear power plant.

I looked around the corner towards the control room. Two of Ohno's men in black were there, weapons at the ready, nervously talking to each other in Korean. How I wished I could speak their language. If I ever get out of here, I told myself, I'd learn it. They should have been looking my way but were busy arguing about what had happened and what to do about it, and I didn't need to speak any Korean to realize their confusion.

A voice called out from inside the control just as the alarm was cancelled. The two men stayed where they were, but their focus shifted to whoever was addressing them. It was all I needed. I sprang forward and was on the one closest before he could register what was happening. With my torso behind him I stretched my left arm across his face, forcing him to arch backwards across my turning, crouching frame. I grabbed his weapon hand with my right. He instinctively pulled the trigger, which was bad news for his partner who was sent flying backwards by the bullet that smashed into his upper shoulder, though it could have a been a lot worse if the Kalashnikov had been set for automatic fire.

I kept twisting, using my sinking body weight to pull my man downwards. The back of his head hit the concrete with a solid clunk that knocked him out stone cold. I rolled out across his limp form straight on to his partner, who, despite his wound, was trying to aim his weapon. In one movement I pushed the barrel to one side and smashed the inside of my fist onto his temple, knocking him out cold, a little trick I learnt from Naomi. He didn't have the strap across his shoulder, so it was easy to retrieve his AK from his lose grip. I was still moving forward and came out of the roll in a kneeling position, weapon at my shoulder, pointing straight at the open control room door.

I saw it all, instantly. Not like I had on the mountain, where I was in the mystery of the void, but as trained observer, a battle-tested fighter who knew what to look for, how to assess the situation. There were twelve in the room, three in special-forces black, seven in suits, two in operator uniforms. The others, I assumed, had gone – including Ohno. Tanaka was still there, though. All of them were staring at me in disbelief, their ultimate bad penny.

It would have been the easiest thing to have opened fire right there and then. I could have taken out everyone in that room before they had a chance to react, but a voice inside my head told me to wait, to hold, to stand down – it wasn't the way. I hesitated, the cardinal sin in any firefight.

"Get him!" Tanaka shouted.

Somebody fired, I didn't know who and I didn't want to

hang around and find out either. I jumped sharply away towards the staircase as more bullets crashed around me. It's hard to hit a fast-moving man, but they were all firing now which made the job a lot easier. I jumped down the stairs and sprinted down the corridor that led back to the turbine area. I knew they were in pursuit, but now that I was armed they wouldn't want to rush straight into my field of fire.

I charged through the open door of the turbine room and raced to the far side of the generator. As protection against a hail of bullets it was perfect, but as a defensive position it wasn't a lot better than being inside the reactor containment building – I was acutely aware of the C4 charges still on the turbine feed pipes behind me.

I should have taken that shot.

I knelt, sighting the rifle at the door, and waited. Nobody came storming through after me. They didn't have to, though, did they? Why not blow the charges and get on with it?

"Mr. Peter?"

The voice came from the corridor, out of sight. It was quiet, barely audible, but I recognized it in an instant.

"Morishita-san?" I had to shout to make myself heard above the noise of the turbines.

Morishita came into view, manhandled there by Tanaka, who was holding a pistol to his head. They were joined by the remaining three men in black and the six in suits.

"I'm sorry," Morishita said. I read it on his lips, his voice too soft for me to hear the words.

"Put down your weapon!" commanded Tanaka.

I heard that all right. I took stock. There were ten against one in an open area with plenty of cover but nowhere to hide, a reactor heading towards full power, if not already there, plus four C4 charges on feed pipes to rapidly spinning turbines, with one more still attached to a reactor coolant pipe all waiting to be set off. For all I knew one of those reactor coolant pipes could already be leaking, and there could be more charges elsewhere that I hadn't seen – should be, in fact, on the thin outside walls. But the alarms had gone off, the reactor blast doors had closed, and if an automated message had been sent then that should be enough to get the quick rection force here. Whichever way you looked at it, Ohno's plan was crumbling around him, and my part in this was over.

"Morishita-san, are your men safe?" I shouted.

"All escaped!" he replied.

"Silence!" Tanaka shouted in Japanese, pushing the barrel harder into Morishita's temple.

"Well done!" I said.

Morishita could have escaped with his colleagues but must have come back to help. I didn't blame him – how could I? He knew the danger and chose to step right back into the fray. I wish he had listened to me, but it was too late for that now. I stood up and came out from behind the protection of the generator, the AK held above my head.

"Put it down!" Tanaka loved to shout. I did as I was told. "And the sword!"

I took the Ninja sword off my back and laid it next to the Kalashnikov.

"Move away!"

I did what I was told again, putting five feet between me and my weapons.

"More!"

I moved further away. Tanaka handed Morishita to one of the men in suits, then approached. He stopped a short distance in front of me and aimed his pistol right between my eyes.

"You are a hard man to kill, mister Mamoribito."

I should have been afraid, but I wasn't. I should have knelt to the floor begging for mercy, but I wasn't going to do that. I should have thought my life was over, that Yuko would be a widow and Miki would grow up a fatherless child. But my life wasn't over. I was going to walk out of there, run out of there, even. I knew what Tanaka could never know. I sensed what he could never sense, what he could not fathom as even being possible. It was time to let Tanaka know.

"Indeed I am," I said.

Swish.

The shuriken hit Tanaka on the wrist, causing him to simultaneously fire and drop the pistol. I was already leaping to one side but felt the rush of the bullet as it flew past my head. As I span through the air I caught sight of Naomi, dressed in Ninja black, leaping down from the second level balcony, launching more shuriken as she dropped to the floor.

I landed on my feet to see Ninja pouring in through the turbine room doors, Naomi's cousins, shadows warriors all, each one living up their vow to fight the evil that men do and keep the world in harmony and balance. They swarmed on their prey, instantly disarming each and sending them crashing to the ground. One managed to open fire, but he was far, far too late. A Ninja, the tallest and physically strongest of the group, had already pushed the muzzle upwards and away from danger. The bullet slammed into the ceiling just as its shooter slammed on to the hard concrete floor, spun there by his own unyielding grip on the weapon now being turned in his hands. It was a simple move to cartwheel your opponent – and you didn't need to have much technique if you were strong enough. The Ninja had both.

Tanaka bolted for the stairs to the upper levels. He was a stocky, powerful man, but slow. Naomi gave chase, jumped on his back, wrapped her legs around his neck and span him to the ground. His head hit the concrete flooring with a thud that would have knocked a lesser man senseless, but in Tanaka's case he was only dazed.

I picked up Tanaka's pistol. "And they call me the Mamoribito." I said as I joined Naomi.

"I'm sorry we took so long, Peter."

"Perfect timing," I said, kissing her on the forehead. "You keep saving my life."

"What else is there for me to do?"

"Quite."

We stood over Tanaka while we watched the rest of

Naomi's family clear up. There wasn't a lot else for them to do either, other than bind the limbs of their captives. It had taken twenty seconds, if that, from entry to total subjugation. I was wrong about needing the entire Japanese army, and almost felt sorry for Ohno's men – they hardly stood a chance.

"How did you get here so soon?" I asked.

"They were already at the temple, waiting for me."

Ye gods, I thought, they had made good time from Tokyo. Naomi read my mind. "They drive like you," she said.

"So I see." I quickly scanned the area. "Where's Matsumoto Sensei?"

"He stayed in Tokyo, in case things did not go well." Naomi did her own scan. "Where's Ohno?"

"Not here," I replied. "I think he's gone."

Naomi turned to Tanaka, who was now sitting up and nursing his head. "Where is he?" she demanded.

"Go to hell," Tanaka answered.

Naomi took the pistol from my grip and slammed the barrel into his groin. "You won't die, but you will no longer be able to all yourself a man."

Tanaka wasn't fazed. "You know where is."

Naomi stepped back and faced me. "He's gone to the temple."

"The temple?" I said. "You mean, your grandfather's temple?"

She nodded.

"Why would he go there?" I asked.

"I'll explain on the way. Come on."

"Wait, Naomi." I took the pistol back from her and aimed it at Tanaka's head. "Where's the remote detonator?"

"You think I will tell you?" he responded defiantly.

I didn't, so I moved my aim to the right and put a bullet in the floor beside his right knee. I aimed back at his forehead.

"Where is it, Tanaka?" I asked. He didn't reply. He knew I wasn't going to shoot him, although I wouldn't put it past myself. Perhaps this was his only card, the one where he keeps us all guessing, his last hurrah as the disposal units sweated their way through the disarming process.

"Morishita-san!" I shouted.

I turned, but he was already nearby, accompanied by one of Naomi's cousins. I recognized her from my visit to the dojo in Tokyo. She was carrying my Ninja sword.

"This is Mika," said Naomi, as if it was perfectly normal to make introductions in the middle of a battle in a nuclear power station.

"Hello Mika," I said.

Mika bowed. *"Mika desu."* She handed the sword to me in the proper way.

"Onegaishimasu." I answered, receiving it with the correct bow. Even here, formality was persevered.

Morishita was looking at me, wide-eyed. "Morishita-san, are you OK?" I asked, although he didn't seem to be any the worse for wear.

"So many Ninja!" Morishita gasped. "Like movie!"

I smiled. "Look, you need to shut down the reactor as quickly as you can. Can you do it by yourself?"

"Yes, of course. That is purpose of new system."

I understood the voice now, the one that had urged me not to fire into the control room. If I had damaged any of the equipment there, Morishita's task could have been impossible.

I spoke to Naomi's cousin. "Mika, go with him to the control room, please. But be careful, there are more of them up there, and at least one of them is still armed."

"No problem," she replied.

I completely believed her.

#

Naomi and I raced out through the main entrance to the front car park.

"That one!" She pointed to a Subaru WRX, spot-lit in the

dusk by one of the car-park lamps. It was much like the one I had inadvertently left crushed under a landslide, but newer, sleeker, faster.

"Is that yours?" I asked.

"Kenta's." Naomi flung open the passenger door. "You drive," she said, as if I needed an invitation.

I handed her the Ninja sword. "Hold this," I said, adding, "Who's Kenta?" as we strapped ourselves in.

"The one who betrayed us, betrayed Michael."

"Where is he now?"

"Banished."

That sounded ominous. "Banished?" I asked.

"Banished."

"I see."

I hit the starter button, engaged first and floored the accelerator. We hurtled out of the main gate and turned right to head back along the route I had taken.

"Go over the mountain," Naomi said. "It's quicker."

"Which way is that?"

"Left here. This one!"

I powered into a narrow road that led up the mountain. I hadn't used it on the way here, having taken the coastal route which I knew, but a quick glance at the GPS helped explain how Naomi and her cousins had gotten here so quickly. It was at least ten kilometers shorter. I switched the headlights onto full beam and focused on the road ahead.

Naomi was already trying her phone. "I can't get a signal," she said.

"Keep trying."

"Of course I will. What else would you expect?"

"Naomi," I said, smiling. "What would I do without you?"

"Be dead already."

"That's true."

We charged past a cell phone transmitter in a small clearing by the side of the road. The equipment at the base of the antenna was smoking.

"That explains it," I said. "They must have knocked it out,

to prevent emergency calls."

"They are organized, but they won't-" The rest of whatever Naomi was going to say was drowned out by the sound of five army helicopters swooping low and fast overhead.

"You got through?" I asked after they had passed.

"Yes. There is still a signal at the temple."

"I'm glad they believed you."

"I have friends in high places," she said.

"Of course you do."

The road straightened out and I gave it everything the car had. I glanced across at Naomi – for the first time since we'd met, she looked nervous.

"Don't worry," I said. "I know what I'm doing."

"Are you sure?"

"Almost."

A second glance at the GPS showed there were another eighteen or so kilometers to the temple. At this rate we'd be there in no time.

"What was it you wanted to tell me?" I asked as we scythed through a series of long S-bends. "Why did Ohno go to the temple?" I could feel Naomi looking at me, but I dared not take my eyes off the road. "Yuko and Miki are there, right? With your grandfather."

"Yes."

"He's the Ninja grandmaster, Naomi, so they are safe with him, aren't they?"

"It's not that simple, Peter."

I slammed the brakes hard as we entered a tight hairpin, flinging Naomi forward in her seat, despite the racing harness.

"You need to pull that tighter," I helpfully suggested.

Naomi tugged at the straps. "I know that."

We accelerated hard out of the hairpin, throwing her back against the seat.

"So, tell me, then."

"When we get there. I can't think like this!"

"OK," I said. She was right, too. Without the need to talk I could drive quicker.

"How much further?" I asked, unable to risk a glance at the GPS.

"Too far!"

Twenty-Six

We arrived at the temple twelve minutes later.

I drove in slowly and parked in the forecourt. An expensive black limo was there – Ohno's car. Everything was peaceful and calm. We sat there quietly observing, not rushing, giving ourselves time to adjust. Naomi unbuckled her seat belt. I did the same.

"Ohno is grandfather's brother," she said, as she returned the sword to me. "I mean, his half-brother, like you and Michael. A long time ago, before I was born, there was a bomb on a Korean plane. Ohno's wife, his daughter and grandson were all killed. Ohno wanted revenge, grandfather did not. They fought, terribly. It led to this day. It's why grandfather became a priest, and I an orphan."

I knew what she was talking about. North Korean agents had blown up a South Korean Air 707 in mid-air, on direct instructions from Kim Jong-il himself. How close had we come to war then? I didn't know. Yamaguchi Sensei's words came back to me, *'A man's family is the core of his being, his whole life, what he lives for, and what he must fight to protect, even if that costs him his life.'* Perhaps Ohno and I were not that different after all.

Then Naomi's other words hit me. I looked across at her.

"I was no more than a child. I can barely remember her face," Naomi said, reading my mind, sadness in her eyes. "But my mother is always here, in my heart. I hear her voice, too, when the night is quiet, and the moon is bright."

It was quiet now, and the moon bathed the mountain with its cool, impartial light.

Ye gods, the absurdity of it all.

If Ohno had achieved his purpose then thousands, if not millions, would have died. And what for? To satisfy his personal thirst for revenge? To replace a stable but controlling system with an inadequate and flawed democracy. No, of course not. I'd heard it all before, not like this, but I'd been at the sharp end of these fake ideas, these false representations of what was merely the desire to dominate, to control, to exploit and to destroy that lurks in the darkest reaches of the human psyche.

"Always two," I said. "That's what your grandfather told me. Good and evil, right and wrong, Yin and Yang. Always two. When was he going to tell me? When were you going to tell me?"

"When the time was right, as it is now. Grandfather blames himself, but he swore that he will not harm Ohno, his own brother. He cannot, too many people were hurt. Please try to understand."

"So, he got me to do the fighting for him. Is that what you're saying?"

Naomi touched my hand. "You are the Mamoribito," she said. "You fight for all of us."

I let that sink in for a moment. "Come on," I said, and opened the car door. "It's time to put an end to all of this."

We got out of the car and walked towards the temple. As we passed Ohno's limo I saw a device on the passenger seat. It was the remote detonator; I was sure of that. Why had he brought it here? It was too far from the Joetsu plant to have any effect. Naomi had seen it too. She shrugged, another of Ohno's actions she hadn't been expecting. The man was hard to predict.

We went in through the temple entrance, bowing as we did so. We should have taken off our shoes, but today was the day when the smaller protocols could be overlooked. It was deadly quiet inside that beautiful old structure. Incense burned, and the two warrior-god statues guarding the shrine glared down at us, a reminder of our calling, of who we were and why we had come to be there.

Ohno emerged from the shadows, carrying Taiyo.

"I have been waiting for you, Peter."

"Let my family go, Ohno."

"When all is done, I will consider it."

"Where is grandfather?" Naomi demanded.

Ohno gave one of those forced smiles that are devoid of any humour. "Hiding, like the coward he is."

"Don't say that!" Naomi stepped forward.

I grabbed her arm to hold her back. "He's nearby, Naomi, and so is my family. Go and find them, please."

"No! I will stay with you, and fight Ohno Oji." Naomi had used the honorific term for uncle. Family ties run deep, even when they were stained with blood.

"Naomi," I said. "Please. Do this for me. It will be OK, I promise."

She didn't like that. I could have used her help, too, but I needed to be sure Yuko and Miki were safe.

"Yes, Naomi-chan," Ohno said. "Go and find them. Join them. I won't be long."

Naomi looked at me, as if to ask if this was this what I wanted.

"There's a small building, up the mountain. They're in there."

"How do you know?" she asked.

"You know how I know."

Naomi kissed me on the cheek. "Be careful," she said, before bowing as she exited the temple.

Ohno circled around me. I moved in the other direction. We circled around each other, like a pair of wolves, swords held forward, the tips aimed at each other's hearts in *seikan no kamae*.

"So, Peter-san. The final battle."

"It doesn't have to be this way, Ohno," I said. "You can

stop this, just put down the sword."

"Do you really think I would give myself up to you?"

I didn't expect Ohno to give up anything. I could, though. It would have been an easy thing to follow Naomi, to leave Ohno where he was. I knew he wouldn't leave this place, his spiritual home. He had come to die here, whereas I had everything to live for a hundred yards away. I could walk away and wait outside for the police, the army and whoever else was on their way.

And yet I was still there.

"You've failed, Ohno." I heard myself speaking, felt the movement of muscles, the vibrations of the larynx, the sound of the words – was it really me doing the talking? "Everything you've worked for, all your planning, all your scheming, it's all gone, floating away with the wind."

"Then I have nothing left to lose."

Ohno darted forward, sweeping his sword diagonally downwards. I stepped backwards and avoided the blade, leaving it to slice through empty space. Ohno had moved quickly for an old man, but I had also moved fast, faster than he had expected.

"Very good, Peter, very good indeed," he said as we returned to our positions and continued circling each other. "But you see," he continued, "I have prepared for this day, this moment, for my entire life. And you, you hardly know who you are. You cannot defeat me, Peter-san. Everything you know, I already know. Everything you do, I have already done. I am stronger and better than you in every way."

Ohno was the brother of a Ninja Grand Master, so I knew he was dangerous. But there was something within me that gave me a stronger faith, a deeper belief that I wouldn't be defeated, not like this, not today. Ohno attacked again, this time sweeping his blade horizontally. I evaded once more, again leaving empty space where there had been solid, frail flesh an instant before. Sensing his anger rising I moved backwards, further out of his reach.

"You've forgotten one thing, Ohno," I said.

"And what is that?"

"I am the Mamoribito."

Ohno lunged forward, blindly swinging his sword, so deeply consumed with his own fury that I could feel his every intention, anticipate his every move, avoid every attack, parry each thrust. Time slowed, as if the gap between reality and imagination had been replaced by an all knowing, all seeing version of Peter Walker that was no longer himself, something beyond his mere physical being, an entity of oneness, of unity, of completeness.

I was entering the void.

I watched impassionate as Ohno lashed out again and again at Peter, who skilfully avoided each thrust, each swing, each movement. I saw why Ohno was the way he was, what had made him become this way, his hopes gone, his world destroyed, why he had lashed out at life just as he was lashing out at Peter. I was Ohno, he was me. Yin and Yang. Neither could exist without the other. We were two sides of the same fight, the ongoing struggle to transcend the veil, to move through the barrier – opposites, but equals. Yet my understanding was lacking. Something was hidden, a new purpose was unfolding, but I didn't know yet what it was.

Ohno's sword, Taiyo, the sword of the Mamoribito, missed Peter once again but crashed into an oil lamp, sending flaming liquid spiralling across the floor. Peter slipped on burning oil, his head smashing against a heavy, solid wooden pillar. Momentarily dazed, he dropped the sword in his hand and fell to one knee. Ohno, recovering his breath, stood above Peter and raised Taiyo over his head, preparing to strike. Peter was losing, had lost.

I shouldn't have left him there. The physical form is incomplete without the spirit. Had we stayed together we could have survived, could have won the battle. But now Peter was about to die. I was about to die. I searched for Naomi. She had released Yuko, Miki and her grandfather, who were descending the slope from the small wooden hut that Ohno had locked them in. Naomi was already running back towards the temple, was almost there.

"Hurry. Peter needs you," I told her.

Naomi sprinted faster. I saw what she saw, felt what she felt. She didn't break pace at the temple entrance and charged straight in, as lionesses do when their loved ones are in danger, launching herself at Ohno with a furious roar. In one movement Ohno turned, avoided Naomi's lunge and brought his blade down across her back, cutting into the soft tissue of her torso as if it were butter. Naomi groaned in agony as she collapsed to the floor next to Peter.

"No!" Someone shouted.

It was me, returning from the void.

I was still on my knees. Ohno raised Taiyo once more and brought the sword slicing downward. I clapped my hands together and caught the blade inches above my unguarded head – an almost impossible technique that only those at the highest level could perform. I stood up and kicked the astonished Ohno hard in the chest, sending him crashing backwards onto a warrior god statue, spearing his right shoulder on the lance that the deity carried to defend against evil spirits. He grimaced with the pain, too stoic to cry out.

I turned to Naomi. She was lying on the floor, blood pooling from the cut on her back, her hands shaking, her breath fast, her life essence flooding out of her. I put down Taiyo and knelt next to her.

"Peter," she gasped. "I'm so sorry."

Naomi thought she had failed me, but it was I who had failed her. The Mamoribito was supposed to protect the ones he loves, not have them sacrifice themselves for him.

"Hang on in there," I said, as if it needed saying.

Around us, fire was spreading across the dry tatami matting and had already reached the thinner wooden pillars that supported the shrine. Unless there was a fire extinguisher nearby, there would be no stopping it.

"You must move her!" It was Yamaguchi Sensei. True to form, he had entered the temple without me noticing. "Take her out, quickly, before the fire takes hold."

It was too late. The fire, driven by the mountain breeze, had already taken hold of the old, dry wood.

"Go!" he urged.

"What about you, Sensei?" I asked.

"My place is here."

I gently picked up Naomi and started towards the temple entrance. Behind me I heard Ohno address his brother.

"Takashi, you should leave."

"I don't think so, my brother," Yamaguchi Sensei replied.

"You old fool."

"We are both old fools. But our task is finished. The Mamoribito has come. We can rest now."

What did they mean? I turned around. The speed with which the fire was spreading was frightening.

"Go, Peter!" Sensei shouted. "And never forget who you truly are!"

I could do nothing more. I carried Naomi outside. Yuko and Miki were standing there in the temple forecourt, both in distress, both unharmed. Naomi went limp in my arms as she lost consciousness.

"Peter. Thank God." Yuko whispered as held me from behind, her face buried between my shoulders.

"Daddy," said Miki, embracing my legs.

An army helicopter arrived overhead, its powerful floodlights illuminating the entire area. One of Naomi's cousins was at the door, guiding the crew. The wash from the rotor blades fanned the fire, nearly sending the four of us spiralling with the downdraft. I held firm. The pilot pulled back to find another place to land, but it was too late, the temple was already engulfed.

It was over.

Epilogue

Tokyo City hospital was a big enough place to lose yourself in, but the floor guide was helpful, and I found the room easily enough. The police officer on duty checked my newly acquired ID and waved me though. Naomi was on the bed, bandages around her torso, looking as wonderful as ever, surrounded by flowers and cards from well-wishers.

"Hey you," I said.

She motioned for me to sit next to her. "Quick," she urged, "We're on TV."

I sat on the bed next to her as she turned up the volume with the remote. It was NHK news. Naomi changed to the English sub-channel. The voice was clear, sharp and articulate; "Authorities in Japan have dismissed reports of any North Korean involvement in last week's foiled terrorist attack on the Joetsu nuclear power plant near Niigata on the Sea of Japan coast. Government spokesperson, Shohei Ikeda, said that there was no evidence whatsoever to support this conjecture, which he described as the work of conspiracy theorists trying to increase tension and promote disharmony across Asia. The North Korean spokesman, Kim YoungSun, said for once the regime found itself in total agreement with the Japanese government. Ikeda promised a full inquiry into the incident. In related news, the President of Ohno Industries, Takashi Ohno, has been admitted to hospital suffering from a stroke, no doubt brought on by stress related to the event. We'll keep you informed of any developments in his condition."

Naomi switched off the TV. "See," she said. "We're famous."

"Not really," I replied. "But it's interesting to see that Ohno has had a stroke. I expect they're still trying to figure out exactly what they should say, especially when he won't recover, and no one can find him in any hospital, either. Anyway, let's see where they go with that." I was carrying a smart-looking bag from a famous Ginza chocolate shop. "In the meantime, for you."

"Are you trying to get me fat?"

"As if."

Naomi tried to sit up. I could see that it hurt. "You shouldn't move," I said, adjusting her pillows.

"I cannot just lie here all day."

"Yes you can."

"No, I cannot." Naomi pulled the perfectly wrapped chocolate box from the exquisitely designed bag and ripped off the expensive paper that I had obviously spent way too much time and money selecting. She chose the biggest, most lavish chocolate and then offered me the box, saying, "Wanna get fat, too?"

"Yes please," I picked the darkest one.

"Are your family OK?"

"They're fine, thank you. But Miki will need time, I think. What about you?"

"Doctors said I need three months for a full recovery. I told them I'd somersault out of the window in three days."

"Physician, heal thyself," I said, although I suspected she'd need a few more days than that.

Naomi had a quizzical look on her face. "Another thing for me to google?" she said.

I nodded.

"OK." Naomi grabbed another chocolate. "Did you recover the swords?"

"With Uncle Yamaguchi's help, from the embers," I said,

although it hadn't been quite as straightforward as it sounded. "He'll have them cleaned and restored, get them back to pristine condition."

"Good. And you, Peter. What have you been doing?"

As if she wasn't already aware. "Well, I spent all day yesterday with the Japanese secret service. They're trying to recruit me, and you too, I expect. But I think you already know that, don't you."

Naomi nodded, smiling, waiting.

"While I was there, I met a lady called Naoko Watanabe."

Naomi broke out into a Cheshire cat grin.

"Your aunt. Whom you've lived with since the day you lost your parents."

Naomi nodded.

"Your friend in high places," I added.

"She is. Except nobody believed her warnings about Ohno. They do now."

"Indeed they do. Are there any more surprises on their way, Naomi? Is your boyfriend the Prime Minister, perhaps?"

She laughed at that, but I was being more serious than she realized.

"We are few, Peter," she said, becoming serious herself. "But we are here, and with the Mamoribito to guide us we will do all we can to keep peace and bring balance to the world. And don't worry, when I get out of this bloody place, I will tell you everything I know."

"I've heard that one before," I said, although I knew that even then I would have a thousand unanswered questions – not least of which was why Ohno hadn't set off the detonators with the remote, and why Naomi's grandfather had stayed with his brother until the end. All that would have to wait, although I had my suspicions that the false-flag was itself a false-flag.

"I'm sorry about your grandfather, Naomi," I said.

She kept her smile, but sadness filled her eyes. "It's ok," she said, although it clearly wasn't. "Uncle Matsumoto will take his place."

There was so much more to say, so much more to know; but there was somewhere else I needed to be.

"Look I can't stay," I said. "There's something I have to do, and I'd better not be late. I'm sorry."

"You just got here!" Naomi smiled showed she didn't mean it. "It's Ok. I already know," she said. "Cousin Mika told me."

"You and your cousins." I kissed Naomi gently on the forehead and got up to leave. "I'll come back and see you in a couple of days."

As I went out of the door Naomi said, "We were a good team, you and I, weren't we, Peter?"

I turned around.

"We are a good team, Naomi. We are."

#

I stood across the street from the 7/11 where I'd borrowed the Subaru five days earlier. I'd arrived there ten minutes before the appointed time, as was my preference, and despite the slight drizzle I was happy to stand and wait.

The owner of that Subaru arrived on foot. I could feel the envy in his heart when he saw Kenta's Impreza WRX parked outside. No, not envy, that wasn't it. More of an unfulfilled wish, undoubtedly delayed by an unhelpful insurance firm that didn't know who to blame.

Well, I knew.

The Subaru owner took a long look at the car before entering the store to collect the small package that the slip in his letterbox had said was waiting for him. I knew it was there because I had sent it, along with the box and the note inside, kindly written for me in Japanese by cousin Mika. The instruction on the package was clear – it had to be opened there and then.

I stepped back into the shadows as the man read the note. He ran outside, clutching his newly acquired keys in one hand, the note in the other, a huge, grateful smile across his face.

"*Arigato!*" he shouted to the street. *"Arigato Gozaimashita!"*

"You're welcome." I said softly, as he got into the car.

I tapped a message to Yuko on my phone.

On my Way.

She wrote back.

OK. Ki o tsukete, ne.

She didn't need to worry. I'd be careful, of course I would. I turned and headed down the narrow street towards Ueno station, the first step of the journey on my newly found path.

The path of The Mamoribito.

About the Author

Kevin A. Reynolds has lived in Japan for over 30 years, where he spends much of his time teaching leadership and business communication skills at Japanese corporations.

In his spare time, he writes novels and screenplays. *Mamoribito* started as a screenplay and is his first novel.

Also by Kevin A. Reynolds
The Girl Who Fell Through Time

Printed in Great Britain
by Amazon